How (not) to Find a Boyfriend

Boyfriend

Allyson Valentine

Philomel Books

An Imprint of Penguin Group (USA) Inc.

*n*ora Fulbright is the most talented new cheerleader on the Riverbend High cheerleading
squad. Never mind that she used to be a friendless overachiever with a penchant for chess—this year, Nora
is determined to leave all of that behind and transform from
brainiac social larva to full-blown butterfly, even if it means
dumbing herself down.

But when Adam moves to town and steals Nora's heart
with his ultra-smarts and incredibly cute dimple, Nora has a
problem. How can she prove to him that she's not really the
airhead she's made herself out to be?

Nora devises a seemingly simple plan to wow Adam with
her intellect. Yet soon after setting things in motion, Nora
quickly loses control of her strategy and struggles to keep
her image in check. Will she be able to prove that she can be
both a butterfly and a nerd?

Filled with quick wit, pitch-perfect humor, and delight-
fully frustrating romance, Allyson Valentine's debut novel
will leave readers cheering.

Despite having an excellent tan, a perfect ponytail, and an
awesome Herkie jump, ALLYSON VALENTINE did not
make the Central Junior High School cheerleading squad in
her hometown of Cos Cob, Connecticut. She somehow sur-
vived this setback, going on to earn an MFA in Writing for
Children and Young Adults from Vermont College of Fine
Arts and write books. Allyson lives in Issaquah, Washington,
where she is cheered on by her husband and two teenage
boys. This is her first novel.

You can visit Allyson Valentine at
allysonvalentine.com

One

AS WE SIT AT THE TOP OF THE bleachers waiting for cheer practice to resume, Krista smears sunblock on her arms and I entertain her with a politically incorrect version of the team fight song that I just made up. She covers her mouth to contain a laugh, and nods to the scene below us. Like seals in a nature video, a bunch of cheerleaders are stretched out on the bleacher seats sunning themselves.

"Not everyone would appreciate your sense of humor," she whispers.

Point well-taken. I look beyond the bleachers to the football field, tucking a white bra strap under the wider purple strap of my cheer jersey. Out on the field, a guy with a handlebar mustache, wearing nothing but shaggy cutoff shorts and a reflective vest, is touching up some of the white lines in preparation for Saturday's opening game. He promised it would take no more than five minutes, but that was fifteen minutes ago.

"You know, that guy would move a whole lot faster if the bathing beauties didn't have their shirts tucked up to their boobs," I say.

As if on cue, the guy stops working to swipe sweat off his forehead, then pauses, twisting the tips of his mustache as he takes in the view.

Over on the far side of the red rubber track that circles the field, the rest of the cheerleaders sit in the shade of the trailer where popcorn and pretzels will be sold during football games. Someone had the foresight to bring nail polish to practice, and now there's a whole mani-pedi convention going on. I stand, reach my arms over my head and stretch to the left and then the right. Then, facing away from the field, I set my forearms on the metal rail that keeps fans from toppling out of the stadium. It's warm and feels good against my skin. In the distance, the football players are jogging down Newport Way. When the line repair guy showed up, Coach Avery sent the team off for a run. In their pads and white practice jerseys they look like a trail of bulked-up albino ants on their way to a picnic.

Krista joins me at the railing. "I saw Jake looking at you this morning."

I can't help but smile. "Seriously? I didn't notice."

Krista bumps me with her hip. "Liar."

She's right. I did notice him looking at me. Staring, actually. Jake Londgren, number sixty-six. Junior. According to stories I've heard from Krista's boyfriend, Dex, Jake's number correlates directly to his intelligence quotient. His popularity quotient, on the other hand, is pure genius. Stud fullback. Hot body. Excellent hair. On the ice cream scale? Jake is Theo's Coconut Kiss—my favorite.

Jake Londgren. Last year he never would have given me a second glance—if he even noticed me at all.

I'm trying to pick Jake out of the lineup when out of nowhere a butterfly with checkered wings lands on the railing between me and Krista. I pull out my phone and snap a picture for my bug-obsessed little brother, Joshie. Krista offers her outstretched finger as a perch, which the butterfly politely refuses. "It's really pretty," she says.

It really is. I'm amazed that not so long ago this beautiful thing was in its larval state—practically a worm. After that, it hung out being kind of invisible for a while. And look at it now! The more I think about it, me and this butterfly have a lot in common.

Stage one: Egg. Okay, I was never an egg in the conventional sense, but close enough.

Stage two: Larva. That was me, totally larval all through elementary and middle school. Picture that kid who raises her hand and goes "Oooh! Ooooh!" when the teacher asks a question, or who simply blurts out the answer. I wasn't just a teacher's pet—I was their teacup Chihuahua. Other kids treated me like a worm, and wormlike existence is lonely.

Stage three: Pupa. Last year we moved two school districts over so Joshie could go to an all-day gifted kindergarten, and I entered my pupal stage as a ninth grader here at Riverbend High School—coincidentally my father's alma mater. New school, new Nora. I'd figured out there's a difference between being smart and being a smarty-pants. I kept my answers and test scores to myself. I joined the JV gymnastics team. I found a best friend. Nora Fulbright, brainiac nerd, was mostly invisible, and I never revealed my life as a larva to anyone, not even to Krista. Who'd want to be friends with a former worm?

Stage four: Butterfly. I swapped out my glasses for contacts. Lost the braces. Sprouted some semblance of breasts. Krista joined me at cheer tryouts last spring, and here we are, the only sophomores on Riverbend's varsity cheer squad. Cheer camp in July was amazing. We've been practicing all of August. And when school starts tomorrow and I walk through those big double doors with a bag of cheer gear slung over my shoulder, I will have fully evolved.

Nora Fulbright has wings! Now I just need to learn how to use them.

I absently flap my arms.

"What are you doing?" Krista asks.

"What? Oh. Um, airing out my armpits?"

"Excellent idea." Krista joins me, waving her arms up and down. A welcome breeze riffles the leaves of the maple trees that line the far edge of the football field, and the butterfly lazily opens, then closes its wings, and finally flies away. It flutters toward the school, heading for the faded remnants of a huge black-and-white chessboard painted ages ago onto the flat roof of the gym. Last year during freshman orientation, where Krista and I first met, our tour guide explained that chess geeks used to skip class and sneak to the roof to play matches with giant chess pieces. I suspect when my dad was a student here he led the chess-geek charge. I can picture him up there, sliding his bishop into position, kicking over some poor girl's queen.

"What's the matter?" asks Krista.

"What?"

"You just made a weird face."

"It's nothing." I jerk my gaze and my thoughts away from the chessboard, away from Dad. I think again about my butterfly metaphor. Last year I thought all cheerleaders were created equal—a rabble of sixteen perfect butterflies. I wanted to be one so badly. But as the summer has worn on, I've realized that not all cheerleaders are the same species. The girls doing their nails are like the stiff Cabbage White butterfly pinned to a sheet of foam board in Joshie's collection—they're practically moths. Chelsey and her friends, the bathing beauties, they're Monarchs. Beautiful, striking, impossible to miss in a crowd. As for me and Krista, we have yet to be given our taxonomic identification.

I've figured this much out—it's not enough to just simply have wings. You have to have the right wings.

"Jeez, look at that. She's still reading her book." Krista nods toward the blandest butterfly on the squad, a junior named Vanessa. She's *always* absorbed in a book, which Chelsey, Queen Monarch, blames for Vanessa's tendency to routinely botch up routines.

"You need to decide whether you're a cheerleader or a bookworm," Chelsey chided this morning when Vanessa missed her cue and stomped when she should have jumped. "And I know it's only going to get worse when school starts, and instead of practicing for cheer, you'll be busy doing homework for all your smarty-pants AB classes."

"AP," Becca, Chelsey's sidekick, corrected her.

"Whatever!" Chelsey tossed up her hands.

It remains a mystery why Vanessa is even on the squad.

I tug at my ponytail and straighten the bow clipped to the back of my head. Chelsey's rant has got me thinking. Stressing. Freaking out. I'm signed up for AP biology and AP French. What would Chelsey say about that?

Krista drops the tube of sunscreen into her gear bag and pulls out a packet of Skittles. "Want some?" I nod and she pours us each a handful.

"I'll swap you my green ones for your orange ones," I offer, holding out my hand.

"What is it with you and the swapping? Don't be so picky. They all taste the same."

"No, they don't. And it's good to be picky. That way you get exactly what you want."

"Or you wind up with nothing." Lightning fast, she snatches the Skittles from my open hand and tosses them into her own mouth.

"Hey!"

"See? You could wind up with nothing." Skittles clack against her teeth as she talks. In response to my look of abject disappointment, she finally grins, reaches into the candy bag, and plucks out a single orange Skittle, which she places into my hand like it's the key to the kingdom.

"Thanks a lot, pal." I pop the lone Skittle into my mouth.

We point our chins to the sky and soak in some sunshine. Me and Krista, "the Salami Twins," as Chelsey calls us. I think she means Siamese, not salami, because neither of us resembles anything in the processed meat family. We *are* practically joined at the hip; however, that's where the twin analogy stops working. Krista and I look nothing alike except for the fact that we're both crazy short, we both have shoulder-length hair and we are both genetically predisposed to have excellent eyebrows. But according to the lab-coated lady at the Clinique counter at Nordstrom, Krista is an autumn and I'm a summer—we can't even wear the same lip gloss. Thankfully, I'm a season that Jake Londgren clearly approves of.

This year, with my new wings, I am on a popularity-quotient-building regimen. In scientific observations of my own older brother, Phil, who is admittedly awesome despite the fact that he never actually evolved beyond the larval stage, I have witnessed what high school is like when one is lacking the popularity gene. For this girl it's time for a little genetic engineering. This is the year that Nora Fulbright, brainiac nerd, completes her metamorphosis. Having Jake as my first-ever boyfriend could be an excellent catalyst.

Krista faces the field again and leans back against the railing. "I can't believe there are only three days till the opening game. Are you as nervous as I am?"

Nervous? I run through my mental thesaurus. *Panicky. Edgy. Jumpy. Anxious. Nervous* will do. "Yeah, definitely."

Krista groans and starts chewing a cuticle like she hasn't eaten in a week. I picture myself jumping when everyone else squats. Shouting an extra "O" into "V-I-C-T-O-R-Y." Falling off the top of the pyramid and sending my burgeoning popularity quotient right into the gutter. We need to get back to work!

Down on the field, the repairman has stopped to guzzle an energy drink. I scramble down the bleachers and nudge Chelsey, who sits up like she's been stung by a bee.

"The guys will be back soon," I say. "And you said you wanted to practice something special before they get here."

Chelsey jumps to her feet. "Oh my gosh! Thanks, Nora." She rubs sleep from the corners of her eyes and lifts a megaphone to her mouth. It's purple with gold writing that says "Chelsey" on one side and "Captain" on the other. She waves an arm over her head.

"Hey! Line-maker Man!" she chirps. "Are you almost done?" Chelsey could do voice-overs for a cartoon bluebird.

The guy flashes a wide grin. "Don't you worry your pretty little head. I'll be finished up real soon."

"Pretty little head"? It's precisely the kind of comment that would cause my mother to march down onto the field and park a quick knee in his groin. Chelsey on the other hand tucks a loose strand of strawberry blond hair behind her ear and giggles.

"It would be really sweet if you could finish up fast. We still have a lot of work to do. You want us to be great at Saturday's opener, don't you?" She lowers the megaphone and pushes out her lower lip in an affected pout.

Every day I become more convinced that watching Chelsey in action is like taking an AP Popularity Quotient Enhancement course—build your PQ in just one semester!

"You got it!" Line-maker Man picks up the pace, and within minutes he's packing up his gear.

Down on the field, all sixteen of us stand in a circle and Chelsey warms us up, calling out movements rapid-fire: "High V! Low V! T-Motion! Punch! Right L! Left L! Right Diagonal! Left Diagonal! K-Motion! Touchdown!" We do pike jumps, straddle jumps, and Chelsey's favorite, the Herkie jump. It's her favorite because it's named after Lawrence Herkimer, the father of cheerleading. If there were a Church of Herkimer, Chelsey would be a nun. A very hot, very popular nun.

Finally, she opens the loose-leaf binder where she keeps copies of all the chants and cheers. She's made up most of them herself, and they're good—really good. In fact, everyone credits Chelsey and her cheers for leading the cheer squad to take first place in the county-wide cheer competition last spring. I'm convinced the part of her brain that would otherwise be used to form complex thoughts has instead become a dedicated cheer-writing center.

She snaps open the binder's metal rings and lifts out the top sheet. "When the guys get back," she says, "we're going to do the short version of the Form One dance and end with the pyramid stunt like we did earlier, but we're not going to mark it up to music like we usually do."

Chelsey becomes excited in a

six-year-old-who-just-got-cotton-candy kind of way. "Instead," she says, bouncing on her toes, "we're going to call out this preseason, get-stoked, we-love-you cheer that I wrote!"

Chelsey reads the cheer aloud. Jazmine, a Monarch and a six-foot-tall defector from the girls' basketball team pumps a fist into the air. "Let's do it! The guys will love it."

Everyone agrees, and Chelsey rushes us into formation because the guys could be back any minute.

We do a couple of runs through the movements with Chelsey clapping and counting off eight beats like usual, then we add the words. We get through it twice before we hear an approaching stampede and the guys file onto the field. They drop onto the grass or benches, dump their helmets and guzzle from water bottles. A staggering cloud of sweaty boy odor drifts our way.

Chelsey nods and we line up behind her, fists on our hips. "Coach Avery?" she calls out. "We have a special cheer to welcome you and the boys back for the best season ever."

We prance out to the middle of the field and I can practically feel my adrenal gland kick into gear as the limbic region of my brain snaps into primal fight-or-flight mode. This is it—our first performance! I had no idea that performing cheers in front of an audience would be so different from simply practicing them unwatched, and as we begin to move through the cheer, I realize I like it. I *love* it. I *do* have wings! Competing at gymnastics meets was nothing compared to this. We shout and sweep through the movements:

Welcome back, boys!
Hope your summer was good
And you're ready to rock
Like Cutthroats should

'Cause Cutthroats dominate!
Cutthroats rule!
Cutthroats topple every other school
Some fish flounder and some fish sink
Some go belly up or they just plain stink
Today we're gonna tell you how fishies thrive—
They beat the other teams
They eat 'em alive
Summertime is over
So get ready for fun
The Trouts are gonna fight until we're number one
Go, Cutthroats!
Fight, Cutthroats!
Win, CUTTHROATS!

The cheer ends as I drop into a basket of arms. They toss me, and I bound into a front handspring, landing in a split about five feet from the football team, my arms in a high V over my head. I can barely breathe. Thank god for eight years of gymnastics lessons. And that I remembered to shave my pits this morning.

Geoff, the team mascot, who'll wear the giant Cutthroat trout suit at our games, hoots and pumps a fist into the air. "Go, Cutthroats!" he shouts. The football players, on the other hand, look like they've been hit with a freeze ray. Mid-sip of water. Mid-stretch. Mid-crotch scratch. Nobody moves. Then Jake jumps off the bench, makes a sort of great ape grunt, and the guys go wild. I sense my PQ making a leap of meteoric proportion.

The cheer girls clap and jump up and down. Krista throws her arms around me. "You were terrific!"

"We were all terrific," I say.

Coach Avery claps, too. "Nice job, girls. Love that tumbling run, Nora! That was a dynamite welcome back—let's hope we can live up to it."

He turns to face the players. "All right, fellas. Take ten, then we'll do some pursuit drills and run some gorillas before we finish up."

Chelsey motions for us to huddle. "Boyfriend break. Then we'll do one more run through of Saturday's set list and call it a day." She looks at me with a broad, perfect smile. "Excellent tumbling run, Nora! You rock!"

Krista nudges my foot with hers. Wow. I rock! We clap and break the huddle. Most of the girls bound over to the football players where Chelsey is instantly swarmed by eager guys. Swarmed! And she already has a boyfriend! Vanessa drifts over to the bleachers and picks up her book. The combination of cheering, stunting and tumbling has left me parched.

I tap Krista's shoulder. "I think I left my water bottle up in the bleachers."

She hooks her arm through mine. "Let's go."

We reach the top of the bleachers and I drain my water bottle.

"He's watching you again." Krista speaks without moving her lips.

I follow her gaze and Jake grins, beats his chest Tarzan style, then turns to talk to the guy beside him.

"Do you like him?" she asks.

"He has an outstanding exterior."

"Mmm-hmmm," murmurs Krista. "But do you *like* him, because he clearly has his eye on you."

"Well, I don't really know him that well—"

Krista laughs. "Oh, cut the crap, Nora. You know all you

need to know about him. He's the hottest thing on two legs and he's dumb as a post. But Dex says he's a lot of fun. And he seems sweet. Face it—there isn't a girl at Riverbend High who wouldn't give up a full bra size to get to hang with him."

She's right.

"I know you're smarter than him," Krista says. "But brains aren't everything."

I stare out at the field. Krista knows I'm smart—she wouldn't have made it through algebra I without me helping her in the library after school last year. What she doesn't know is just how important academics are in the Fulbright household, where brains are, in fact, everything. She's eaten dinner at my house a few times, but thankfully it was always when either Mom or my stepdad, Bill, was out so she's been spared mealtime brain fest.

I picture Jake at our dinner table. My mother, the women's studies professor, regaling him with her latest research on the effect of large-breasted female anime characters on the male teen brain, and Jake guffawing at the mention of the word *breast*. I envision Bill, the calculus teacher, requiring Jake to solve a math problem before he'll pass him the salt. I can just see Joshie challenging Jake to identify by domain, kingdom, phylum, class, order, family, genus and species one of the residents of his bug tank. And if my older brother, Phil, happened to be home on break from Harvard that day? Forget about it.

Dating Jake would send my popularity quotient to the moon—but could it work?

Krista keeps going. "We could all go out together. You and Jake, Me and Dex. Go talk to him."

Krista takes my hand and pulls me down the bleachers. She gives me a little shove when we hit the field and I practically fall into Jake's arms, which are massive.

"Hey! Nora, right? Looking good out there!" He places a playful punch on my upper arm, which will likely require ice when I get home. "So I don't remember seeing you around school last year. Are you new?"

"Sort of."

"Hang on." Jake grabs a set of poms off the bleachers. He sweeps a shock of summer-ized light-brown hair out of his eyes. His off-kilter smile is achingly cute. In a high, girly voice he does a little impromptu cheer, swinging his hips, waggling his butt, sweeping the pom-poms back and forth across his extra-wide chest. I can't help laughing.

"Nora, Nora, she's so hot. Shouts out cheers—"

He stops. Looks at the sky, down at the ground. "Shouts out cheers—"

He knits his brows together and stares off into the bleachers.

I look at Krista, who beams encouragement.

"Shouts out cheers with all she's got?" I offer.

"Yeah! Yeah, that's it! Nora, Nora, she's so hot. Shouts out cheers with all she's got!" He gives me a little punch on the other arm. At least the bruises will match. "Excellent rhyme!" he says. "Right on time! Slime!"

The hottest guy at school, with the highest PQ imaginable, and direct lineage to Ogg the Caveman. Maybe cavemen aren't so bad once you get to know them?

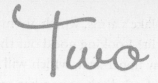

Two

IT'S CLOSE TO ONE O'CLOCK when Chelsey calls it quits. We overhear her flinging Vanessa another load of crap as we leave the field. Chelsey reminds Vanessa that the first game is three days away and that she had better spend all her free time working on the dance steps that she messed up today. If you want to get Chelsey angry, mess up a cheer.

"How did Vanessa even make the squad?" I ask. "She was as lame at tryouts as she is now?"

Krista is as clueless as I am. Meanwhile, Chelsey makes another crack about Vanessa's smarty-pants classes. How does she even know the details of Vanessa's schedule? Maybe she has the inside scoop about all of our schedules? Oh god. What if she finds out about mine?

I can just see Chelsey in her cheer uniform and fluffy slippers, a pair of cat's-eye reading glasses perched on the bridge of her nose as she pores over a stack of cheerleader schedules.

"Becca? Check. Gillian? Check. Jazmine? Check. Nora—" She peers at my schedule over the top of her glasses. "So many As and Ps! Such a smarty-pants!"

Chelsey absolutely cannot see my schedule. But really, what can I do? As we head toward the school I have the brainstorm equivalent of a mental tsunami. I know what needs to be done. "Hey, Krista. I need to get something fixed on my schedule. Can you give me a few minutes?"

"Sure. I'll wait for you in the courtyard."

I jog down the freshly scrubbed hallways to Ms. Ostweiler's guidance office. Her door is wide-open and I find her sitting at her desk working at the computer. A small boxy window fan makes a steady whir but offers little relief from the heat.

"Come in if you can stand it," she says. "The AC isn't working. Again. I swear it's always way too hot or way too cold in here." She gestures toward the two chairs across from her desk. One is a poofy spill-your-guts-out chair, the other is hard backed and nothing but business.

"Have a seat," she says.

I go for nothing but business.

"So what brings you here today, Nora?"

I take a deep breath. Ms. Ostweiler's office smells like graham crackers and apple juice. "I need to make some adjustments to my schedule."

I glance around the room. Books about educational theory and psychology, and assorted college preparation guides fill the bookshelves that line her walls. A table at the back of her small office is littered with fidget toys and little plastic figurines of nurses, farmers and tiny bathroom fixtures.

"Okay, let's see what we have here." Ms. Ostweiler brings my schedule up on her computer screen and turns it so that we can both see it:

Period 1—Precalculus
Period 2—US History
Period 3—Honors English
Period 4—AP French
Period 5—PE
Period 6—AP Biology

"This schedule looks pretty perfect for you. What were you hoping to change?"

"Well, I think I'll have a better semester if I switch out the AP classes and just take regular French, regular biology and algebra two instead of precalculus. I mean, that's what most sophomores take, right?"

Ms. Ostweiler slowly brings her hand to her chin and strokes it like she has an invisible beard. She looks at me like I'm a puzzle with a piece missing. "You're not like most sophomores, Nora. Is there something else going on that you want to tell me about?"

How lame would it be to tell her that I want to be a Monarch butterfly, not a Cabbage White? How embarrassing would it be to admit that I want to make my PQ soar, and that if Chelsey's reaction to Vanessa's schedule is any indication, those As and Ps are going to get in my way? I scratch the back of my neck.

"No, there's nothing going on. It's just that I'm on varsity cheer this year and I'm worried about having the time it'll take to ace those classes. I mean, an A in biology is probably better than a C in the AP class, right?"

Ms. Ostweiler wobbles her head from side to side as she considers. I jump in to keep her from thinking about it too much. "I know most people take regular biology, *then* they take the AP class. So I would really be setting myself up for a more successful experience by taking the regular class first, right?"

She shakes her head. "But you tested out of the regular biology class. And haven't you already done the summer reading in preparation for the AP class?"

"Well, yeah, but the reading I did will help me in the regular class, too."

We go back and forth.

"The school *does* encourage students to choose their own classes," she says, wavering. And in the end, I win. Those pesky As and Ps are gone, and I leave her office with a copy of my new and improved schedule:

Period 1—Biology
Period 2—French
Period 3—PE
Period 4—English
Period 5—Math
Period 6—US History

From Mrs. Ostweiler's office I swing by the car and toss in my gear bag along with the plain white envelope containing my new schedule, then head to the courtyard to find Krista.

"How did it go?" asks Krista. "That took a while."

I give her two thumbs-up. "All good. Molly Moon's for double dips?"

"You know it!"

This is it! The last day of summer break.

"Too bad we can't take your car," says Krista as we walk toward the bus stop. We have the date circled on our calendars five months and twelve days from now when we I can legally drive with passengers who are not members of my family. What good is it to be a sophomore with a car if I can't take my friends places with me? Of course, with my August birthday, technically I should be a junior, but my parents opted to start me a year late. Anything to gain an academic edge, and they figured my edges would be sharper as one of the oldest kids in the class instead of the youngest. We walk a couple of blocks to the bus stop. The bus is a hassle, but it's the only way into Seattle. Krista and I have the date circled on our calendars— five months and twelve days from now— when I can legally drive with passengers who are not members of my family. Whatever. Still, when I'm allowed to drive with a friend in the car and we don't need to hassle with the bus? Krista and I will go into Seattle for double dips every single day.

Molly Moon's is packed. Krista goes for Salted Caramel and Vivace Coffee with sprinkles. For me, it's Theo's Coconut Kiss all the way. We finish the day on a high note at Pike Place Market, with a side trip to the Nordstrom, where we give ourselves makeovers, dabbing on a little of this and a little of that from about thirty different cosmetics counters until we are stunning. And then? Summer is officially over.

I pull into the driveway and park behind Mom's Prius. At six o'clock it's still warm out, and the sun hasn't even begun to think about taking a break.

"Nora!" Joshie, my biggest fan, flies across the front yard and wraps himself around my lower torso as I climb from the car. Our dachshund, Copernicus, yips and jumps, pawing at my kneecap. I hug Joshie, scratch Copernicus.

"Do a cheer for us!" Joshie begs. Not one to disappoint my fans, I grab the pom-poms out of my gear bag and do an impromptu cheer.

> *Joshie! Joshie! He's the best!*
> *Cutest brother in the West!*
> *He's fun, he's smart, he's super cool.*
> *He doesn't bark! He doesn't drool!*
> *Ya-aay, Joshie!*

Joshie laughs and takes a turn shaking my pom-poms. He

follows me to the mailbox, where I sift through the mail. There are things for Mom from NARAL, Planned Parenthood and the university. There's a martial arts magazine for my stepdad, Bill. Some science magazines for Phil, even though he's lived in Boston since he started school there last September. Shuffled into the mix is a cheesy postcard featuring historic Boston landmarks. I turn it over and find a message scrawled by Phil:

Happy first day of school. Word to the wise re: AP bio—skip breakfast on pig dissection day.

XOXOXOX Phil

Crap with a snout! What will Phil say when he finds out I'm skipping AP bio altogether?

It's too late to worry about that now. Instead, I check the mailbox to make sure I really got it all. I'd thought there might be something for me from Dad. It's been weeks since my birthday, and though we're not exactly in regular communication, not even a little bit, he usually still sends a card with some cash. It looks like he forgot me this year. I slam shut the mailbox door.

"Anything for me?" Joshie asks. I hand him the latest issue of Phil's *Scientific American*.

"But, Joshie, that's not all there is for you." I pull my phone out of my purse. "I got something cool for you at cheer practice today." I show him the picture of the butterfly.

"A Checkerspot! *Euphydryas editha*—they're one of my favorites."

The truth? Everything that creeps or crawls is one of

Joshie's favorites.

"Look at what I found today." He rolls down the cuff of his sock so that I may admire his caterpillars. He used to bring them inside in his pockets, but Mom found him out. He is nothing if not resourceful.

I feign amazement at his bugs. "Make sure you dump all those things out before you put your socks in the wash, okay?" I dread the day that my underwear and Joshie's socks comingle in the washing machine.

"I'm going to put them straight into my tank," he says. "Want to play soccer with me and Copernicus?"

"Not right now." I tousle his hair. "I want to start getting my stuff together for tomorrow. And I think it's probably almost dinnertime."

Inside the house I set my gear bag by the front door and wander to the kitchen, where streamers and balloons hang from the light fixture above the table. "What's in the oven? It smells great."

Mom is at the sink, washing artichokes. "It's just some chicken."

I drop the mail on the counter. "What's with the festive décor?"

"Nora!" Mom turns from the sink, stricken. "It's the twenty-sixth of August."

She dumps the artichokes into pan of water on the stove and cranks the heat.

August 26th—how could I have forgotten? Some families whoop it up on Saint Patrick's Day, or maybe Cinco de Mayo. For us, party time is August 26th, when we toss it up for Susan Anthony, Elizabeth Cady Stanton and the rest of the gang who worked their feminist butts off to pass the Nineteenth Amendment.

"I find it a bit ironic that of all the rooms in the house you choose to decorate the kitchen," I say. "I mean, sure it was about the right to vote, but wasn't it also about getting women *out* of the kitchen?"

Mom tapes a fallen streamer back into place. "Even suffragettes had to eat. Maybe next year I'll decorate my office."

She gives me a peck on the cheek and picks up the mail.

"How was practice?" She removes the reading glasses from the top of her head, settles them into place, and begins rifling through the mail.

"It was great. Look what we got today." I unzip my gear bag and pull out the new uniforms that Chelsey handed out after practice.

"Pretty fancy. But don't you already have a uniform?"

"Yup. These are special uniforms just for homecoming." They're totally glitzy, like something a figure skater would wear—but they're also insanely cute. "They were donated by an über-rich alumnus who's some kind of cheerleading freak."

"It seems like a little much," she says.

Everything that has to do with cheerleading seems like a little much to her. "So—" she says. "Still enjoying cheering on the boys?" Hard emphasis on the word *boys*.

"Yes, I'm still enjoying cheering on the boys. You know, cheering is a varsity sport, Mother. It's hugely athletic, and Chelsey thinks we have a really good shot at winning the county-wide championship again this spring."

As she glances at each piece of mail she sorts it into one of two piles, keep and recycle. "Gymnastics is a varsity sport too, Nora. And with all those years of lessons I paid for you'd be the star of the team."

She's probably right. I was definitely a force to be reckoned with on the JV squad, and the coach had more than once assured me that my gymnastics future was bright—possibly with a college scholarship looming. Every time we have this conversation I can't help wandering down the path I've been down a zillion times before—was the switch to cheer ridiculous? But I turn back when I remember how it felt out on that field today, the applause from the football team, the kudos from the other cheerleaders.

"You're not being fair," I say. "It's because of all the gymnastics that I get to be the flier in my stunt group. And as far as metaphoric celestial bodies go? Flier is pretty stellar."

Mom slaps a couple more pieces of mail into their appropriate piles. "I'm not saying that you're not good at cheer, it's just—" She pauses and examines the last remaining envelope in her hand. A plain white envelope. "What's this?" She turns it over in her hand.

Oh, crap. Crap, crap and crap to the hundredth power.

"That's mine!" I lunge for the envelope, but Mom has already removed the printout of the schedule I revised this afternoon with Ms. Ostweiler.

Outside, Joshie laughs and Copernicus barks as the soccer ball thuds against the side of the house. Usually Mom would be out there in a flash reminding him that the house is not a soccer goal. But Mom is not going anywhere.

"Nora, what the *hell* is this?" She flicks the paper with her finger.

"It's my schedule of classes."

On the stove, the artichoke pot is starting to leak steam. Mom marches to the refrigerator and thumps a piece of paper held in place by a magnetic banana.

"*This* is your schedule of classes."

I correct her. "That is my *old* schedule. I revised it today."

"You dumbed it down! Standard biology? Regular French? Algebra Two? What were you thinking?" She holds her hand up like she's stopping traffic. "Wait. I'm sorry, I implied that you *were* thinking. Clearly you were not. At least not about your future."

She doesn't give me a chance to respond.

"You are fully capable of an accelerated schedule, young lady. Your brother Phil took all AP classes as a sophomore. Even after skipping the eighth grade."

"My brother Phil did nothing but schoolwork and as a result he was a friendless nerd."

Mom's jaw snaps open and stays there. "He was not friendless. He had Louis. And Zeebo."

I roll my eyes. "Please. And some people have leprosy and herpes—that doesn't send them sailing up the rungs of the high school social ladder. Louis and Zeebo were social outcasts just like Phil. I mean, I love him and all, but seriously, Mom."

"Seriously?" Mom's voice goes up an octave. "Need I remind you that your brother, the 'social outcast,' is pulling a four-point-oh GPA at Harvard?" She doesn't stop. "And need I remind you that if you want to pursue a career in the sciences you'll go further faster if you get AP biology and precalculus out of the way as a sophomore?"

It's an effort to unclench my teeth. "Need I remind *you* that Phil never went to a single dance? He didn't play any sports. He was a social pariah."

Mom folds her arms over her chest. "Oh, for god's sake, Nora."

"What? I want more out of high school than just good grades. I want people to know my name. I want people who matter to invite me to join them at their lunch table."

Mom blinks. "'People who matter'? And you don't think you'll get invited to have lunch with them if you're taking AP classes? If that's the case, are they really the kind of people you want to spend time with?"

God! She sounds just like a mother. "Look. You're not in high school," I tell her. "You don't see what I see. There are just certain things you need to do if you want to be—"

I stop, knowing full well how the *P* word will go over with Mom.

"If you want to be what?"

I dodge. "Last year I figured out how to at least not be in social exile like I was in middle school. This year, I want more. I want to be—" Oh, to hell with it. "I want to be popular."

Mom drops her head into her hands. It's like I've just told her I aspire to being a porn star. "Oh, for crying out loud. Is that really what this cheerleading thing is all about? About being one of the 'popular girls'?"

What can I say to repair the damage I've done to her feminist sensibility? "What about making choices, Mother? Choosing for oneself? Isn't that sort of the feminist ideal? I *chose* not to take AP classes. And I'm not a cheerleader simply because there were no other options open to me. I *chose* it. It's fun. It's athletic."

I can't keep the corner of my mouth from lifting into a glimmer of a smile at the memory of how it felt to be out there today in front of the guys. "I kind of like being right out there in front of a crowd."

On the stove the artichokes hit full tilt and steam spews out the sides of the pot. Mom races over to turn down the heat. She comes back and touches the revised schedule like it might be contaminated. "I really don't get it. What does bimbo-izing your schedule have to do with being a cheer-leader or with popularity? You do realize you're perpetuat-ing the 'dumb cheerleader' stereotype, don't you? Right or wrong, cheerleaders have a reputation for being a little dim."

I pause. As much as I hate being known as a mega-brain, I don't really want to be thought of as dim, either. Still, am I not basing my actions on observation? And isn't that what a successful scientist would do? Chelsey has a popularity quotient that's off the charts. So does Jake. Neither of them would be in an AP biology class unless we were dissecting them. If dumbing down my schedule will make me more likely to fit in with people like Chelsey and Jake, then that's what I want to do. But that line of logic will fall flat here at Mensa headquarters and I know it.

I give Mom the same argument I gave Ms. Ostweiler, re-minding her that this is my first year doing cheer—the year I figure it all out. I can take more rigorous courses next year.

The timer goes off. Mom opens the oven door and a cloud of heat fogs her glasses. She turns and points in my general direction. "We are not done with this conversation, young lady. Go call your brother in for dinner."

Dinner may be mere minutes away, but I'm starving. I grab an apple from the bowl on the kitchen table and am almost to the front door when she calls out after me. "I hate to see any woman waste her potential."

She doesn't get it. I am brimming with potential. If I play things right I might even be captain of the cheer squad when I'm a senior. By then I'll have established my popularity. I can probably take any courses I like. As, Ps—whatever. Chelsey, who's a senior, will have graduated—well, hopefully—and I will be Nora Fulbright, newly crowned queen of the Mon-arch butterflies.

I peek out the long, thin window beside the front door before opening it, just to make sure I'm not about to get clocked in the head by a soccer ball. There's Joshie, chasing the ball. Copernicus is literally running circles around him. Joshie catches up with the ball and kicks it hard in the direction he just came from—which would be right where my car is parked, only from where I'm standing I'm spared the sight of the ball smacking into my driver's side door. I charge outside to give Joshie crap, and as I do the ball comes flying back, nailing me just above my ear.

"Ouch!" My hand flies to my head. I spin toward whoever it is that just beaned me, expecting to see one of Joshie's little booger-eating friends standing there with a lead foot and a guilty face. But that is not who I see. Not at all.

"Oh jeez! Sorry! I'm so sorry!"

My heart drop-kicks itself against my ribs. My hand falls from my head to my chest. I blink, considering that I may actually have been knocked out and am seeing things, because the creature coming toward me is not one of the local pack of snotivores. Not even close. This creature, this guy, this six-foot-something guy in khaki shorts and a Molly Moon's T-shirt, of all things, is stunning. A Molly Moon's T-shirt! Kismet! His hair, coffee-bean brown, looks like it was curly once, but has loosened into a maelstrom of waves. And his end-of-summer skin is the color of a marshmallow toasted to perfection. He is hot. About sixteen million units on the Scoville heat scale hot. And on the ice cream scale? He's not merely Theo's Coconut Kiss like Jake—he's Theo's Coconut Kiss with hot fudge, whipped cream and fresh strawberries.

I wobble. He hurries over. "Here. Let me help you." He puts his arm around my shoulder, eases me onto the grass and crouches beside me.

26

My hero.

"I'm so sorry. You kind of appeared out of nowhere," he says.

"A vision." I offer. He laughs.

"Did you kill her?" Joshie runs over for a closer look.

Hero Guy's eyes crinkle and his lips break into a grin. A lone dimple blossoms on his left cheek. It is a dimple that one should require a license to operate. "I think she's going to make it," he says. Then, with sublime tenderness he touches the spot where the ball connected with my head. I stare dumbly back at him, and not because I've just been clocked in the head. No. I stare at him because he is undeniably stare worthy.

He cradles the back of my head with his hand and, with the other hand, pulls a key chain with a small flashlight from his pocket and shines it in my right eye, then my left. I don't feel a thing except for the tingling pressure of his hand on my head. I could be paralyzed for all I know.

"I don't think it's a concussion," he says. "I think you're going to be fine, but you should take it easy for a while." He helps me sit up taller. My ponytail has gone all cockeyed from the soccer hit so I reach back, pull off the hair band and run my fingers through my hair. I am so glad that Krista and I had the foresight to give ourselves makeovers at Nordstrom.

He is still looking at my eyes. And I am looking at his. His eyes! They're that intense greenie-brown kind that seem to change color depending on what the owner of the eyeballs is wearing. Or maybe depending on his mood. Yes! Mood eyes. And the current mood indication is decidedly happy.

I start to get up when he offers his hand and gently pulls me back to standing. His fingers are long and lean. Piano-playing fingers? Cheek-stroking fingers? Hand-holding fingers? He grabs what's left of my apple off the lawn, wipes it on his shorts and holds it out to me.

"I'm Adam," he says. "Adam Hood."

His skin is smooth, with a hint of pink at the tip of his nose from the sun. Adam—the original man. I picture him in nothing but a fig leaf, and my voice wavers. "Nora Fulbright." I take the apple. "It's nice to meet you, Adam. I'd tempt you with a bite of my apple but I'd hate to get you into any trouble."

He laughs. Oh! That dimple! "That's good! I haven't heard that one before."

Me neither. Sometimes I surprise myself.

Again, he looks into my eyes and I look right back into his and it's like an invisible beam is pulling us toward each other. Closer. Closer.

"I'm Joshua Joseph Templeton." Joshie suddenly inserts himself between us, latches on to Adam's hand and shakes it hard. "I'm six and seven-eighths years old. Would you like to see my insects?" I catch my breath as Joshie rolls down his sock, flicking away a couple of caterpillars that couldn't handle the soccer. "They're from the family *Nymphalidae*."

"Caterpillars," I translate.

"They're very nice." Adam gets down on one knee and listens, rapt, to Joshie's more-than-you'd-ever-care-to-know description about his squiggly sock friends. As Adam listens, he nods and asks questions. From time to time he glances up at me and smiles. I smile back. His left front tooth overlaps the right one ever so slightly. God, I want to touch his hair. I hope he lives near here and isn't just someone's cousin or something. Does he have a girlfriend?

A question zaps my brain—what about Jake Londgren?

A response zaps back. Jake who?

The bug lecture ends and Joshie rolls Adam the soccer ball. "Kick it as hard as you can," Joshie demands. Copernicus hovers nearby, huffing ninety breaths a second.

Adam looks at me as if to ask permission. I hesitate. Back in the kitchen Mom has got to be wondering where we are—

"Sure. Go for it."

Adam obliges, and the ball veers off his foot at a crazy angle, bouncing over the waist-high fence that runs around the edge of our lawn into the neighbor's yard. Joshie whoops and takes off after it.

Adam winces. "Soccer isn't exactly my strong suit."

"Don't worry," I confide. "It's not Joshie's either."

"Whew." Adam wipes imaginary sweat off his brow. "So you're . . ." He pauses. "The babysitter?"

I laugh. "No. Josh is my little brother. Well, half brother. I was just coming out to call him in for dinner."

"Ah." Adam slips his hands into his front pockets and rocks from his toes to his heels in a pair of well-worn sports sandals. "So, we're practically neighbors. I live over that way, on Dogwood."

Ah! Not a visiting cousin. He turns and points toward town. He's as cute from the back as he is from the front. He has great calves. I don't think I've ever noticed someone's calves before. "We moved in last week and I was just going for a walk to try and figure out where I am," he says.

"It can be very confusing," I say. "But I can help." I mark an X in the grass with my toe. "You are here."

His eyes light up. "Cool! I go out for a walk and I find treasure."

Am I the treasure? The bliss of the moment is shattered by Mom's banshee wail. "Nora! Joshie! Dinner is on the table!"

I wince. "Sorry. Apparently dinner is going to leap off

the table and run away if we don't get right in there. Joshie? Come on. It's time for dinner."

"Coming." Joshie tosses the ball over the fence and then scrambles after it.

"Um. Before you go. Do you go to Riverbend?" Adam asks.

"Yeah. I'm a sophomore."

"Sweet. Me, too. Maybe we'll have some classes together."

"That would be nice." Oh please oh please oh please. Joshie grabs my hand. "Say thank you to Adam for playing with you," I remind him.

"Thanks! Here's a present." Joshie reaches into his sock and offers Adam a bug.

Adam cradles the caterpillar in his hand. "Is it going to turn into a butterfly? I love butterflies."

Joshie considers. "Someday."

I turn to Adam. "It was really nice to meet you. See you around?"

"If I'm lucky." That smile! It's Ebola infectious.

Joshie and I walk hand in hand to the front stoop. I turn and stare after Adam.

"You like him," Joshie says, startling me.

"What? I don't even know him." My attempt at incredulity fails.

Joshie squeezes my hand. "Don't worry, Nora. He likes you back." The dog yips twice. "Copernicus thinks so, too."

They run to the kitchen and I follow slowly behind, hoping that Copernicus is as smart as he seems.

We've just started eating when Bill comes home, a whistle and a stopwatch hanging from a bright orange cord around his neck. He kisses Joshie's cheek, squeezes Mom's shoulders and asks me how practice went today.

"Fine." I dart a glance in Mom's direction. Thankfully, she has declared a temporary truce. She passes me my artichoke, and because it is August 26th, she reads a quick passage from Henrik Ibsen's play, *A Doll's House*. I know why she chose it. The main character, who I happen to be named after, finally figures out that life is about more than perpetrating the common mythology that women are meant to serve men.

Mom clears her throat to indicate that her point has been made. I rub my forehead so she won't catch my eye roll. Dinner proceeds as usual.

Fade in. Dinner at the Fulbright household.

JOSHIE. Can I have the salt?

MOM. *May* I *please* have the salt.

JOSHIE. Okay, okay. *May* I please have the salt?

BILL. That depends. What's the cubed root of sixty-four?

Fade out.

I absently dip artichoke leaves in melted butter and set them on my plate uneaten.

Adam. He just moved here, so he probably doesn't have a girlfriend.

Adam. Does he play any sports?

Adam. Is he into cheerleaders? I prick my finger on an artichoke leaf, but smile. Isn't every guy into cheerleaders?

Later, in my room, I pull yet another shirt from my closet, try it on, then toss it into the growing pile on my bed as I try to get just the right outfit together for tomorrow. It will, after all, be the first day of my sophomore year. The first day that I show up at school with a sport bag full of cheer gear slung over my shoulder. My first day with wings. I'm working on a complex series of angled mirrors to look at myself from behind when a freshly bathed Joshie lopes into my room wearing shortie pajamas and carrying a box wrapped in brown paper. Copernicus rushes in behind him.

"I forgot to tell you. The UPS man brought this for you today." Joshie sets the box on my bed and runs his finger along the return address. "Massachusetts Institute of Technology. It's from your dad."

Dad. Professor of statistics and logic. Smartest guy on the planet. Marital defector who left us for a dream job teaching at MIT. It was Mom's choice not to follow him—but it was his choice to go anyway.

"Aren't you gonna open it?" Joshie pulls at the wrapping.

"Hey! Wait for me." We tear the thing open. As rocky as my relationship is with Dad, a gift is a gift. Inside the cardboard box is another box, wrapped in the business section of the *Boston Globe*. A card is taped to the top. I start to untape the newspaper.

"Always read the card first." Joshie reprimands me with a finger shake.

I oblige him and read the card aloud:

Dear Nora,

I'm sorry to be a little bit late with your gift this year. Sixteen years old. Quite an accomplishment. I had lunch on campus last week with your brother and his girlfriend. It's so nice to have him in the same town. Maybe you'll think about studying here on the East Coast, too? Phil tells me that you are driving his old Honda. Beats walking to school in that *dismal Seattle weather, I suppose.*

I was going through boxes that have remained unpacked since I came out here—can you believe it has been eight years? And I came upon this—do you remember it, my little Judit Polgár? Perhaps one day you'll go back to it?

Love, Dad

And at the end is a quote:

The game of Chess is not merely an idle amusement. Several very valuable qualities of the mind, useful in the course of human life, are to be acquired or strengthened by it, so as to become habits, ready on all occasions. For life is a kind of chess, in which we have often points to gain, and competitors or adversaries to contend with, and in which there is a vast variety of good and ill events, that are, in some degree, the effects of prudence or the want of it.

—Benjamin Franklin

"It's time for you to go to sleep," I snap at Joshie and I flop onto my bed.

"But you didn't open your present."

"I don't want to open my present."

"Are you mad because Phil got a girlfriend before you got a boyfriend?"

"No." Well, maybe a little bit.

"Who's Judit Polgár?" Joshie asks.

"She's just a girl who's really good at playing chess."

While other fathers tucked their little girls in at night with once-upon-a-time stories about princesses and mermaids, Dad sat at the edge of my bed and told the story of the little Hungarian girl who took the title of international grandmaster at the age of fifteen. "You could be just like her," he would assure me. It's funny to think that, once upon a time, I'd hoped he was right.

Joshie picks up the gift and shakes it. "You should open it."

"I don't need to. I know what it is." I flop over onto my stomach and drop my chin onto my folded arms.

"Then can I open it?"

There will be no rest until Joshie sees what's in the box. "Go ahead."

Joshie shreds the packaging. He gasps.

I close my eyes tight and picture the pieces that I played with so many times. They're probably still covered with my sticky little-kid fingerprints. "It's an American Revolutionary War chess set, right?"

Joshie reads aloud the description on the side of the box, confirming my guess.

I open my eyes and stare out the window. At eight o'clock the sun has dropped behind the trees. "My dad got that set from his parents when he graduated from high school. It's the one he used when he taught me to play back when I was even younger than you are. Then, we played with it all the time."

All the time.

All the time.

Joshie sprawls onto the bed beside me. "Let's play now."

"No."

He maneuvers around so that his cheek is pushed up against mine. "Are you sure?"

I am so sure. Copernicus sits at the foot of the bed and whimpers. Somewhere in my brain there is a Pandora's box of chess knowledge and I would just as soon leave it locked. "No! Out!" I hop off the bed, fling open my bedroom door and usher Joshie and Copernicus into the hallway.

Joshie bursts into tears and runs to find Mom. I shut the door a little harder than I'd intended. The board sits on my bedside table; Joshie has placed the pieces in all the wrong positions. I set them up correctly, unable to stop myself, pausing to examine the Benjamin Franklin bishop with the chipped base from where I hurled it against the wall the day Dad told me he was leaving.

The last thing I would have asked for is a chess set. Especially not this one.

Three

I KEPT MYSELF UP WAY TOO Late imagining I was on one of those bachelorette television shows with a panel of guys that included Adam, Jake and Phil's friend, Zeebo. The girls in the audience shook pom-poms screaming, "Jake!" and "Jake, I love you!" and "Jake, I want to have your baby."

I sat in a tall director's chair wearing my special home-coming cheer uniform and a pair of Jimmy Choos, with an offstage fan providing a perpetual wind-swept look. Adam gazed at me with pleading eyes. Zeebo played a chess app on his phone.

"Who is the lucky bachelor going to be?" the announcer guy asked.

I bit my lower lip. "I choose—"

"Jake!" two hundred audience members screamed in unison.

"Adam," I declared.

Jake's head hung in despair. Zeebo picked at something on his chin. Adam, meanwhile, leapt off his chair and ran to me, sweeping me into his arms, twirling. My Jimmy Choos flew off into the audience . . .

It's amazing I got any sleep at all.

In the shower, I lather, rinse, repeat and consider my options. If Krista is right, I could almost certainly go out with Jake. Me, Nora Fulbright, dating the hottest guy at school. But when I think about Jake, I don't get the feeling I get when I think about Adam. And it's only intensified with an entire night of obsessing about him.

The hot water raining down on my head helps me think. Adam is the new guy at school. He just might top every girl's hottie list. He may even be a hotter commodity than Jake. I replay for the millionth time our parting words:

"See you around?"

"If I'm lucky."

I'll bet he's an excellent kisser.

Post-shower, I finally settle on a sundress, dangly earrings and strappy sandals. It's an outfit that says, "I'm fun, not too into myself, and I was never a larval nerd in my previous life." I grab a protein bar and a banana, and glance at the clock. I'll be plenty early, which is good, because Krista will be waiting for me in the commons for a first-day latte. And I want to scope for Adam. Being new to the school he'd probably be glad for someone to show him around.

Adam. He was so easy to talk to. My goal for today? To reveal to Adam that I am perky, self-assured, and I have a totally normal relationship with books and calculators.

I toss my gear into the backseat of the Honda and rub a couple of soccer ball–shaped dust marks off the passenger door. I brush some pollen from the windshield and shine the driver's side mirror. I pick at a little remaining glue on the back window from where I scraped off the incriminating MIT and Harvard stickers. For my first day driving to school I want my car to look perfect.

Halfway to school I spot a guy up ahead in khaki shorts and a pink button-down shirt, long-sleeved, untucked. Instead of a backpack he's carrying one of those over-the-shoulder courier bags. He's wearing a familiar pair of sports sandals.

Adam.

My heart chases itself in circles inside my chest. I glance in the rearview mirror and wipe a mascara freckle off my eyelid, tuck my hair behind my ear. Untuck it. I can't believe there are still five months and eleven days until I'm sixteen-and-a-half and can offer him a ride! But I can at least pull over and say hi. As I get close, I press down on the clutch to disengage it as I ease on the brakes. But instead of the brake I accidentally push the gas pedal to the floor, gunning the engine. Adam jumps, then jerks around. He looks terrified.

I consider racing away, but pull forward and roll down the passenger-side window instead.

Adam peers in and his look of concern breaks into a smile, dimple and all. "It's you! I should have recognized the car."

His hair is still damp and his eyes have that just-woken-up look—sleepy, but fresh, and bright. He rests his hand in the open window frame. His nails are clean and trimmed. A leather cord with a single bright-blue bead is tied around his left wrist.

"Sorry about the noisy approach," I say through a pained smile.

I look at him standing there looking at me, the pink of his shirt accentuating his summer-kissed skin, and I think, how bad would it be if I got caught giving him a ride? I mean, the worst-case scenario for first-time offenders is that you're stuck with all the ridiculous passenger-and-nighttime-driving restrictions until you're eighteen instead of them ending when you're sixteen and a half.

Wait. Who am I kidding? That would totally suck. My dream of daily excursions to Molly Moon's would be put on hold for way too long. I might not even like ice cream anymore by the time I'm eighteen. No. There is no way I can give him a ride.

But I think about how he twirled me in his arms on the bachelorette TV show, my Jimmy Choos soaring into the crowd—

"Want a ride?"

"Sure!" He climbs in and drops his bag on the floor at his feet. "Thanks for stopping. I'm glad I didn't ride my bike today."

"No problem." So he rides a bike. That would explain the awesome calves. I need a bicycle—pronto.

Adam settles in and turns to face me. "Wow! Pickup soccer games, insect lectures, rides to school—pretty friendly neighborhood."

I remind myself to breathe. I glance in the rearview mirror to make sure there isn't a cop behind me. They can probably sense from three blocks away when a teenager has picked up a passenger illegally. "Friendly," I finally say, grinning like a crazy person. Oh my god, really, Nora? Is that the best you can do? Lack of sleep, a night of obsessing and a sudden fear of men in blue uniforms have shorted my brain.

Adam laughs. "Friendlier than my old neighborhood, that's for sure."

Breathe, Nora. Breathe! I can't believe how uptight I am. I shouldn't have picked him up. I really shouldn't have. I try to relax, grateful for the time alone with him and for the obvious entrée. "So where did you move here from?"

"Denver," he says.

"Hmmm," I say. "Never heard of it." I mean it as a joke, of course. Like who has not heard of Denver?

Adam cocks his head. His left eye twitches ever so slightly. He twiddles with the bead on his bracelet. "You're kidding, right?"

I force a laugh. "Of course!" If my goal is to keep from being pegged as a super-intellect, I'm doing a fantastic job. And I'm rapidly losing confidence. We need some noise in the car that is not me making a fool of myself, so I turn on the radio, which is, as always, tuned to KUOW, Seattle's NPR station—nerd news. Krista is forever giving me crap about it. She calls my cell and leaves me voice mails pretending she's the assorted public radio personalities I've forced her to listen to. Just yesterday she was Sylvia Poggioli, NPR's senior European correspondent. "This is Sylvia Poggioli calling to say that Nora needs to get a life and listen to a normal radio station."

I quickly reach over and press a random preset, choosing one that must have been keyed in by the guy who changed my oil. Mind-numbing techno-bop wails from the speakers. I smile at Adam and bob my head in time with music. "My mom must have borrowed my car," I say, explaining away the NPR.

"No problem. I actually really like public radio." Adam raises his voice to be heard over the music. "I'm kind of a news junkie."

Seriously? "Oh! Okay." I reach for the button to switch it back ,but Adam blocks my hand with his. Our fingers touch. My breath stutters. We both freeze.

"You were nice enough to offer me a ride," he finally says, slowly pulling his hand away. "I insist we listen to your station."

The music etches itself into my cranium. And it's almost impossible to watch the road with my eyes constantly darting to Adam. He taps his feet on the freshly vacuumed floor mats. He runs his fingers along the seam of the seat cover that hides the hole Phil's AP chemistry project ate into the upholstery.

He's totally at ease, and his easiness calms me down a bit. I can do this. I can have a normal conversation with him.

"Nice car," he says. "Is it yours?"

"It is now. It's kind of a hand-me-down from my brother. He bought it off Craigslist when he turned sixteen."

He considers. "Not your brother Joshie, I take it?"

It's a joke, I know. And an invitation to tell him about my other brother—the one old enough to own a car. But I can't respond. I can't even breathe, because at that moment we pull up to a red light where a police officer, not ten feet away from my car, is holding up his hand like Superman stopping an oncoming train. Apparently the traffic light is not working and he is here to help everyone cross the street without getting killed. By someone like me. Stay cool, Nora. Stay cool.

"Um, I was just kidding," says Adam when I don't respond. "About Joshie."

"What? Oh. Yeah, totally." My laugh is strained.

The police officer waves a herd of high schoolers across the street. He blows a whistle and motions for a couple of guys from the football team to hurry up. He glances at me and nods. I smile and try to look taller. Or cuter. Or something. Do I look old enough to have a passenger? Do I even look old enough to drive? A bus pulls up behind me.

"We were talking about your car," says Adam. "You said you got it from your brother. I made a lame joke about the car not having been a hand-me-down from Joshie. So your brother must be away at school or something?"

I consider my reply. My mother would be quick to gush, "Premed at Harvard," assuming all the world is as impressed by Phil's brain as she is. The last thing I want is to seem pretentious.

I hesitate. "Yeah. My brother Phil is away at school."

Adam nods. "I can't wait to have my own car. But I don't have any sibs, so there are no hand-me-downs coming my way."

I glance in my rearview mirror. A second bus has pulled behind the first one. The cop waves a couple of kids on bicycles across the street. If I got arrested here there would be at least sixty witnesses. Sixty-one counting Adam.

"A new car is the carrot my folks are dangling in front of my nose," Adam continues. "If I get a four-point-oh for the year they'll buy me a car. It's kind of ridiculous."

Ridiculous? Could it be that as smart as he seems, a 4.0 is a ridiculous prospect? I am *so* glad I changed my schedule around! We're way more likely to be in classes together. God, this is a long traffic light!

"I know what you mean." I say, trying to sound as if I understand what it would be like for a 4.0 to be a ridiculous goal. "If I had needed a four-point-oh to get this car I would still be riding the bus."

Adam, who looks confused, is even cute with his eyebrows all scrunched up. "Ah, I see what you mean," he finally says. "No, getting a four-point-oh is easy—they know I'll pull off the grades. What's ridiculous is that they're making me wait all the way until June to get a car even though I'll turn sixteen in January." His eyes dart from me, to the road, to me. "Um. The policeman is waving for you to keep driving." Behind me the bus driver blares his horn.

I lift my foot off the clutch too fast and stall out. Crap! Could this get any worse? The music is actually causing my brain to turn into a hamburger. I start the car and pull away. Thankfully the cop does not come running after me. I line up to pull into the school parking lot, turn the radio volume down a couple of notches and make a final stab at salvaging the conversation.

"So, what brought you here from Colorado?" I ask.

Adam has rolled down the car window. His elbow is half in and half out of the car. "My mom's an oncologist. She got a job heading up a research division over at Fred Hutchinson. Dad's a shrink. He's worked out a pretty sweet deal Skype-ing with his old patients while he builds up a new clientele here."

Brains × Brains = Brains^2. We were made for each other, but now I've gone and made him think I'm a total dimwit who could never get a 4.0, who doesn't know where Denver is and who has terrible taste in music. I have completely and utterly blown this. As we enter the parking lot, I don't say a word. He looks at me for a response and takes my silence as confusion.

"An oncologist is a cancer doctor," he says. "A shrink—"

"I know what a shrink is!" I bark at him, releasing my inner pit bull. "He's a head shrinker. A psychiatrist. I get it."

Adam examines his thumbnail. I death-grip the steering wheel as I cruise past a line of parked cars looking for a spot. Did I really just shout at him? I click off the radio. "Look, I'm sorry. It's been kind of a tough morning."

Our eyes meet. He smiles. I wince. "It's no big deal," he says. "The first day of school can be a little bit—"

His gaze shifts to the front of the car and his eyes grow wide. "Watch out!" He clutches the dashboard as a guy cross-ing on foot from the bus lane leaps to get out of the way of my car. It's Stuart Shangrove—the guy who announces the home football games. I hit the brakes. Stuart scowls and gives me the finger. I roll down my window. "Sorry!"

I fold my arms over the steering wheel and set my fore-head down. All I want is to start over. To tell Adam all about the extra-credit report I did when I was in eighth grade on the state of the mining industry in Colorado and the resulting impacts on the Denver economy. I want to tell him that my iPhone is loaded with podcasts of my NPR favorites. I want to share that I've had one B in my entire life, and it was when we did square dancing in phys ed.

I lift my head, blow out a big breath and pull into a parking spot. I turn off the car and can't even look him in the eye.

"Hey, are you okay?" Adam asks. "You know sometimes head injuries take a while to present symptoms. I could walk you to the school nurse." He's searching for a lump or a bruise on the spot above my ear where the soccer ball whacked my head yesterday.

If only I could blame this car ride on a brain injury! "No. Thanks anyway. I'll be—"

BAM BAM. BAM BAM BAM. BAM BAM BAM. Adam and I share a terrified glance. What the hell? Someone is pounding on the roof of my car.

"Nora!" Jake pokes his face, his neck—every portion of his massive upper torso that will fit, through my car window. He grins and reaches in to give my horn a couple of short blasts. "Too bad you didn't kill Shangrove back there. I hate that dude. He always mispronounces my name. You heading in?"

"Um." I look at Adam. It's like Jake doesn't even see him sitting there. Adam grabs his bag off the floor and slips it over his chest. A flicker of a forced smile crosses his lips. "Well, thanks for the ride. I'll see you later." He glances at Jake and can't get out of the car fast enough. He's gone before I can say good-bye.

As Jake and I make our way across the parking lot, I watch Adam, way ahead of us, as he enters the school. How did I manage to mess up what started so perfectly yesterday? The bigger question—how do I fix it?

The morning passes by in a blur. Jake and I get stopped by so many of his admirers on the way into the school that I miss meeting Krista for a latte, and barely make it to biology on time. Regular biology, it turns out, is like the coloring-book version of what I know I would be getting in the AP class. In French, the teacher might as well be speaking in tongues, because I am so wrapped up in the botched car ride that I hardly hear a word he says. Then, in PE, I take a volleyball square on the chin. Do they ever stop torturing kids with volleyball?

Finally, the bell rings for first lunch, where I know I'll catch up with Krista. I get in the food line, drop a yogurt and an apple onto a tray, plus a chocolate chip cookie to lift my spirits. Now, where to sit? I don't see Krista yet, or any of the gymnastics girls we usually sat with last year. I scan for Adam, not sure whether I want to see him or not, but he's nowhere to be seen.

"Nora!" From all the way over at one of the rectangular tables by the window, Chelsey waves for me to join her. Chelsey, Queen Monarch, waves for *me* to join her. She's with Becca, Jazmine and a couple of seniors from the football team. I wave back, noticing that heads at random tables turn toward Chelsey, then me. Is it my imagination or are there cameras flashing? My crushed spirits start to lift. Nora Fulbright is becoming visible.

Chelsey introduces me to the table. "Nora is the one I was telling you about. She's the most athletic flier we've ever had!" she gushes. She pats my back. I focus on peeling the top off my yogurt to keep from grinning like an idiot. Chelsey has been telling people about me. Bragging about me. Me!

Krista waves from across the room and makes her way to the table. There's another round of introductions. Krista, it turns out, already knows some of the guys through Dex. "You must have given the maître d' a huge tip to get seated at this table," she whispers as she slips into the seat beside me.

Gillian shows up. Instead of eating, she pulls a hairbrush out of her bag and starts doing Becca's hair. Jazmine tosses onto the table a copy of European *Vogue* her mom brought back from a business trip, and pretty soon the entire table, even the guys—well, especially the guys—are ogling the hot trends that the models are, and mostly are not, wearing.

Krista dumps the contents of a brown paper lunch sack on the table and tears open a little pouch of gummy bunny rabbits. "Where were you this morning?" she asks. "I waited as long as I could."

Everyone else is totally absorbed in the magazine. I scooch closer to Krista, stirring my yogurt, speaking in a low voice. "Oh, Krista. It was awful."

"What happened?" Krista asks.

I'm about to begin my tale of woe when a new wave of people rushes into the commons. And rushing in with them like he's being carried by a wave?

Adam.

"Oh my god!" I shift in my seat so that my back is to the entrance and hide my face with my hand.

"What's wrong?" asks Krista.

"See the guy who just came in? The one in the pink shirt?"

She shifts in her seat. I grab her arm. "Don't stare!"

She gives me a don't-be-pathetic look. "Give me some credit."

She looks over at the CUTTHROATS RULE! poster on the far wall, her gaze lingering on the crowd as she turns back to face me.

"Do you mean the guy talking to the Teapot?"

I risk a quick glance. Adam is in the burger line chatting with the girl Krista and I call the Teapot because of the part she played in last year's school production of *Beauty and the Beast*. Appropriately, she is both short and stout.

"I don't think I've seen him before," she says. "Is *he* what happened this morning?"

Between spoonfuls of yogurt I tell Krista about Adam playing soccer with Joshie, and me stopping the ball with my head. I tell her about how good it felt talking to him—giddy, but at the same time totally comfortable. I tell her about my sleepless night of obsessive wondering. Will Adam be my boyfriend? Will we have kids one day? What'll I do if he turns senile at ninety and I have to choose whether or not to have him institutionalized?

"Jeez, Nora, get out of your head!"

"I know, I know, and then this morning, I made a total fool of myself."

"How?"

"Well, I gave him a ride to school—"

Oops.

"You what!?" Krista snaps. "You are such a loser giving that guy a ride. You don't even know him. He could be a rapist. Or worse, you could lose your license! Over a guy! And why would you, Miss Picky, choose a guy like that when you could have Jake Londgren?" She presses the inside of her wrist to my forehead. "You, my friend, are sick."

Is that what it is? *Did* that soccer ball do something to my brain?

Krista shakes her head. "Forget this Allen guy—"

"Adam."

"Whatever. Forget about him and focus on Jake. Dex thinks you guys would be great together."

A burst of laughter erupts at the table as Jazmine and Gillian purse their lips making their cheeks go gaunt like a particularly emaciated model wearing a dress that appears to be made of cutlery. Krista nudges me, encouraging me to look casually to the left. Adam, his tray heaped with a burger, fries and some apple slices, has just sat down at a table that is empty except for himself and the Teapot.

"Who knows? Maybe your hottie has already found a girl-friend," Krista says.

"Stop it. I'm sure they just had a class together or some-thing. I mean, he's new, and you know how over-the-top friendly she is."

Adam and the Teapot? Well, she does have a killer South-ern accent. And she is the very embodiment of school spirit, wearing purple, gold or both pretty much every day. It was the Teapot who first gave me the idea to try out for cheer last May when I saw her pass by a tryout poster, clutch her heart and exclaim dramatically to one of her fellow thespians, "I would give anything to be a cheerleader."

But Adam and the Teapot?

Krista kicks my foot. "Look who's here."

Jake has just entered the commons. There is an audible screech of chairs as girls turn to watch him saunter toward us.

"See? Now *that's* who you should set your sights on," says Krista. She starts to get up.

I grab her wrist. "Where are you going?"

"I'm making a place for Jake to sit."

"No!" I pull her back into her seat. Meanwhile, Jake picks up a chair from the table where Adam and the Teapot have been joined by a guy in a loud striped polo shirt who's shaped much like a pear.

Jake is big, too, but he defies fruitlike description. He's wearing one of those black, stretchy nylon sports shirts and his muscles pop as he hoists the chair over his head and struts across the room. A girl at the next table sighs.

"Always extra chairs at the loser table," says Jake with a guffaw.

The "loser" table? I happen to know from last year's science class that the Teapot is no slouch in the brains department. Adam is a 4.0 shoe-in. And while I don't know anything about the guy in the striped shirt, he certainly looks smart. At least, he looks like a guy my brother Phil would have hung out with. In short—I would fit right in at the "loser" table.

Jake sets the chair down near me and Krista, spinning it so that he sits in it backward, resting his bulky forearms on the back of the chair as he leans in. "So how's the first day going?"

Krista launches into an animated story about her English class. Jake listens, but his eyes dart from Krista to me.

And my eyes? They're fixed on the loser table.

Four

MY DAYS AS A LARVA MAY BE behind me, but after English, I walk into math class and struggle against my inner nerd to avoid taking the empty seat front and center. Instead, I slide into a chair all the way at the back of the classroom. A steady line of people file in and I calculate the chance that Adam will be among them: zero. Sure, this is the math that most sophomores take, but with his head-of-a-research-division mother, psychiatrist father and his breezy lock on a 4.0, he is almost certainly in the advanced algebraic functions class, or precalculus—right where I should be.

I pull a fresh notebook and a mechanical pencil out of my book bag as the teacher, Mr. Bolger, rushes in and sets a pile of books and papers on his desk. He's got a total Mister Rogers thing going on: grandpa pants and a cable-knit cardigan with a shirt and tie. The only things missing are canvas sneakers and a couple of puppets.

The seats are about half filled when Jake enters like he's walking onto a stage. He stops at the doorway and scans the crowd. He sees me and his face breaks into a smile. Krista is right—he's stunning. He heads in my direction and I wish that I wanted him. I wish that my heart would get all *ker-thumpity,* but it doesn't miss a beat.

"Hey, Jake!" a football player in the second row holds out his hand for a fist bump as Jake passes by.

"Dude!" Jake pops him one in the knuckles.

"Hi, Jake." A girl with pink hair rolls her fingers at him. Jake winks and flashes a grin.

"Yo, Jakey!" Nathaniel, the kid who played the Teapot's son in *Beauty and the Beast* gives Jake a thumbs-up. Little Nate is either twelve years old or has a serious pituitary issue. Jake struts past, appearing to neither see nor hear him. Little Nate slowly lowers his hand. Rejection stinks.

"Nora!" Jake arrives at the last row and slides into the seat beside mine, shoving it a few inches closer to my chair as he drops into it. His teeth shine milk-white. He leans so close that I can feel the heat radiating off his body. "Saturday. You stoked or what?" he says.

It takes me a moment to get there. Saturday? Saturday! The opening game—just two days away. I am three parts stoked and one part terrified. "I can't wait," I say. "Are you guys going to clean their clocks?"

I can see from the look on his face that the idiom I tossed him went way wide. I translate: "Do you think we're going to win?"

Jake pretends to excavate wax out of his ear. Nice. "Did I really just hear you ask if we're going to win?" He barks out a laugh and raises his voice. "We're gonna kick their butts, and I'm going to show those losers what Jake Londgren looks like when he means business." Jake pumps his fist. "Yes!"

The Jake fans in the room clap and hoot. More people filter in. Elsa and Simone, some of the Cabbage White butterflies from the cheer squad, stop by to say hi to me, but mostly to Jake.

"See you at practice, Nora." Elsa waggles her fingers and they take seats a couple of rows up.

At the front of the classroom Mr. Bolger counts heads. He shuts the door and calls names off the roster. He's only gotten to *Carrigan, Heather* when the door flies open and a guy rushes in out of breath.

Hood, Adam.

"Sorry. I'm still trying to find my way around," he tells Mr. Bolger.

What is he doing here? And why do I care—at least he's here! His cheeks are flushed from the race to arrive on time. He drops into an empty chair right in the front row. He bends forward to rifle through the book bag he's dropped onto the floor beside his chair, and as he bends, his shirt hitches up revealing the tiniest sliver of skin at his waist.

Kerthumpity!

Mr. Bolger sets down the roster. "Tell you what. I'll finish roll at the end of class in case any more stragglers come in. For now, let's get started. We've got a lot to cover." He goes through about fifteen minutes of first-day stuff: where we can find an online copy of the book so we don't need to bring it back and forth from home; what he'll do if he catches someone using electronics in class; how we can access his website for assignments and to correct our work.

Jake leans in and whispers, "Dude! The answers are online! Sweet!"

Mr. Bolger passes out copies of a course syllabus and goes through it with us. He talks about some of the specifics we'll be covering this year. There's little that I haven't seen before. On one hand, it's nuts for me to be here because I'll be bored out of my mind. On the other hand, with any luck Mr. Bolger will call on me to answer some seemingly gnarly problems, and when I rattle off their solutions, Adam will get that I'm not the half wit I seemed to be by the end of the ride to school.

"And now, for a little review," says Mr. Bolger, and he

starts tossing out questions to see how we rate on his smart-o-meter. I avoid raising my hand. That line between smart and smarty-pants is such a fine one. Here I am a mere three rows away from two other cheerleaders, and there are a handful of other football players in the room—the air is thick with popularity potential. Do I want to be that girl who reaches her hand toward the sky like she wants to pinch it? The girl who knows all the answers? What would Chelsey do?

Who am I kidding? She wouldn't know the answer so it would not be an issue.

Mr. Bolger scans the classroom. "The sum of the three angles in a triangle always equals . . . ?" His eyebrows are like little gray haystacks. "Come on. Somebody must know this."

Surely someone other than me knows the answer. I glance over at Jake, who is doodling a picture of the Heisman Trophy, which I can only make out because he has also written in large block letters, JAKE LONDGREN WINS THE HIES-MAN TROFY!

"Anyone?" says Mr. Bolger.

Adam shifts in his seat and Mr. Bolger is on him like a square in need of a root. "Mr. Hood. Can you help me out here?"

Adam taps the eraser of his pencil on the desk a couple of times. "Sure," he says. "One-hundred-eighty degrees."

"Thank you." Mr. Bolger heaves an exasperated sigh.

Jake nudges me and nods toward Adam. "Loser."

I want to leap to his defense. He is not a loser! He is *so* not a loser! In fact, it won't be long before that "loser" and I leave this classroom each day arm in arm, commiserating about radical functions. I can picture us, sitting out in the court-yard at lunchtime investigating the relationship between the graphs of functions and their symbolic representation. I can imagine Adam rushing to my house clutching a piece of graph paper, his hair wild and unkempt from having tugged on it while struggling to solve a complex problem—"Nora! Nora, check it out! I've graphed a system of linear inequalities in two variables."

I would reward him with a system of linear kisses, in two variables.

Mr. Bolger continues asking questions even Joshie could muddle through, waiting for a volunteer, then picking some hapless student when no one responds.

A basketball player raises his hand. "I don't really see how any of this stuff will help me get a job as a physical therapist."

There is a murmur of assent.

Mr. Bolger offers the usual explanation—that basic mathematics courses are building blocks for future mathematics classes. We've got to get through the boring stuff to get to the interesting stuff. Why doesn't he tell everyone some of the coolest things about math? The stuff my dad kept me and Phil riveted with during car trips. How trigonometry tables were created more than two thousand years ago to chart astronomical events. How Christopher Columbus used his copy of the mathematically charged Regiomontanus's *Ephemerides Astronomicae* to save his starving crew when he accurately predicted a lunar eclipse, thus convincing the indigenous Jamaicans that they'd better fork over some food for his crew, or else.

I don't realize how far I have zoned out until Jake nudges me. I jerk to attention, knocking my pad and pencil on the floor. As I pick them up, I bang my head on the desk. Mr. Bolger is looking at me. The other cheerleaders are looking at me.

Adam is looking at me.

Mr. Bolger folds his arms over his chest. "Surely you can answer that simple geometry refresher for us, Miss—"

I swallow.

"Fulbright," I croak. "Nora Fulbright."

"Miss Fulbright? It's one of the most basic principles."

"I'm sorry. I don't—I wasn't—"

"For crying out loud," snaps Mr. Bolger. He slaps his open hand on his desk. "Would you people please pay attention? Or if you truly did not know the answer to that question, Miss Fulbright, I suggest you rethink whether you ought to perhaps be in a different class." He waves an open hand at Little Nate. "Can you please help out Miss Fulbright?"

Little Nate clears his throat, "The square of the hypotenuse of a right triangle is equal to the sum of the squares of the other two sides."

Oh triangular crap! Really? All Mr. Bolger was after was the Pythagorean theorem? I could recite it in my sleep. For Phil's ninth birthday he insisted on a cake in the shape of a right triangle with $c^2 = a^2 + b^2$ drizzled on top in blue icing. He let me have the piece with the equation. Even Mom, whose strength is neither math nor hard science, can recite the Scarecrow's famously incorrect version from *The Wizard of Oz*, "The sum of the square roots of any two sides of an isosceles triangle is equal to the square root of the remaining side. Oh, joy! Rapture. I've got a brain!"

Oh, joy. Rapture. I have, once again, demonstrated to Adam that I've got a football field of empty space where there ought to be a brain.

The bell rings. I can't even look up.

"Hang on." Mr. Bolger hurries to his desk and grabs the roster. "I need to check who's here before I can let you go."

He rattles off the names, rapid-fire. Then asks, "Is there

anyone here whose name I didn't call?"

Two hands shoot into the air. Mine and Jake's. He tells us to stay for a minute, dismissing everyone else. I lift my eyes and meet Adam's as he stands and hoists his book bag over his shoulder. I'm standing beside Jake, who is flanked by Elsa and Simone. Elsa's hands are folded over Jake's bicep and Simone giggles like a chipmunk. Through the miles of desks between us, and the wall of people racing to leave the classroom, Adam smiles. Then, his eyes dart to Jake, and he leaves.

As Mr. Bolger approaches, Elsa and Simone beat a hasty retreat.

"And you are?" Mr. Bolger asks, eyeing Jake.

"Jake Londgren." Jake says it with an implied "Duh?" at the end. Like who doesn't know who Jake Londgren is?

Mr. Bolger scans his roster again. "Are you sure you're supposed to be in algebra two?"

"Hang on." Jake pulls a crumpled schedule out of his front pants pocket and scans it. He laughs. "No wonder nothing made any sense."

Shaking his head, Mr. Bolger checks his roster a final time. "Miss Fulbright, I don't see you on here either."

"I just changed my schedule last minute. I was supposed to be in . . ." I hesitate. "I was supposed to be in a different class."

"Mmm-hmm," murmurs Mr. Bolger. "And as I said earlier, perhaps you *should* be in a different class."

"Try algebra one, it's not so bad," offers Jake. "I should know, I've taken it twice."

Jake and I reach the hallway and Adam is nowhere to be seen. "Where are you headed?" Jake asks.

"US History."

"Piece of cake," he says. "All you need to know is that we beat the British, we voted to pay the slaves minimum wage, and that pretty much brings us up to today."

"Thanks, Jake. That'll really give me an edge in class."

"Dude! No problem!"

Jake takes off for wood shop. I finish up with history. And finally, *brrriiing!* It's the last bell of the day, and I'm shuffling stuff between my locker and my book bag when Chelsey happens by.

"Oh my gosh!" she says. "Was this just the best day ever?" She closes her eyes, leans back against the lockers and inhales deeply through her nose. "Ahhh. Don't you just love this place? It's so good to be back."

I follow her lead, pulling in a deep breath. All I smell are industrial cleanser and an overpowering mix of personal care products. Is it good to be back? In my mind I draw a line graph of the day. It is marked by euphoric peaks—I ate lunch with the Monarchs!—and dismal valleys—don't get me started. But throughout it all, there was Adam. We breathed the same air. Our feet walked down the same hallways. There could be little Adam atoms nestling into my being at this very moment. "Yeah," I say. "It's good to be back."

As we head to cheer practice, the halls are nearly empty. It's eerily quiet except for the buzz coming from a few classrooms where after-school clubs are having welcome-back meetings.

"How are your classes so far?" I ask Chelsey.

She groans and fishes for a book from her hot-pink book bag. She holds up a copy of *Hamlet,* one of my favorite plays of all time. "Did you know that this story has absolutely nothing to do with ham?" she says.

I laugh, then stop when I realize she's serious.

"And I'm not only supposed to read this thing, I'm expected to write a paper about it! Isn't that what college is for?"

I mumble condolences. Apparently *Hamlet* is senior phenomenon everywhere, because Phil went to the high school I would have attended if we hadn't moved, and he did a *Hamlet* paper senior year, too. As we make our way down the hall, Chelsey babbles on about her boyfriend, about his car, and about the way she plans to wear her hair for the homecoming dance, which is over a month away. As we walk, I glance into the classrooms on either side of the hallway. The yearbook committee pores over a stack of yearbooks from days gone by. Mitchell, a guy with red hair and invisible eyebrows, who was in my English class last year, snaps pictures of his committee friends looking at pictures. How totally meta.

Next door, the French club smears chunks of baguette with gooey cheese while conversing in fractured French. A Warren Miller movie plays a few doors down. Who but the ski club would watch a movie while wearing ski goggles?

We're about to go through the double glass doors that lead to the commons when I spot Adam in one of the math classrooms. He's talking to Little Nate and the pear-shaped, striped-shirt guy from lunch.

I pull Chelsey to the wall. "What club is that?"

Chelsey cocks her head. "I'll find out." She walks through the open doorway and asks in a chipper voice, "Hey, you— chubby guy with the unflattering striped shirt—what club is this?"

"Chess club," says Chubby Stripes, completely unfazed by the personal assessment that only Chelsey could get away with.

"Thanks!" Chelsey flips her ponytail and waves good-bye.

I slip from my hiding place and follow her through the double doors.

"Chess is, like, the national sport in Nerdville," she says, "Don't you think?"

As a former resident of Nerdville I can attest to the correctness of her assumption.

"Why did you want to know what club that was, anyway?" asks Chelsey. "You're not thinking of joining it, are you? That would be such a Vanessa thing to do." She rolls her eyes.

I slide my book bag higher on my shoulder and force a laugh. "Of course not. I would never join chess club."

Seriously. Never.

As we walk down the corridor toward the locker room, we pass the student activities bulletin board where the chess club has a flyer inviting new members. It's right beside the glass-enclosed trophy case, which I can still remember peering into when I was just seven years old.

"Look at that, Nora." Dad had pointed into the case at the plaque titled RIVERBEND HIGH SCHOOL STATE CHESS CHAMPIONS. There were seventeen brass nameplates, with the oldest dating all the way back to 1976. I followed his finger to the third name from the left, his name, and felt like royalty. I can't help noticing that the plaque is still there as I quicken my pace and hurry past it.

Chelsey hooks her arm through mine. We squeeze through the door into the locker room, still joined at the elbow, and I cannot believe that I, Nora Fulbright, am on a walking-arm-in-arm basis with Chelsey Oppenheimer, who could write the book on how to be popular. Well, the board book version anyway. I should be overjoyed—I'm practically her protégé. But I can't help wondering how Chelsey would feel about her protégé's choice in guys?

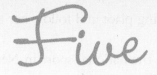
Five

DAY TWO OF SCHOOL WE WEAR our cheer uniforms and the guys wear their jerseys in an effort to drum up some last-minute school spirit before tomorrow's opening game. I arrive at the commons and find Krista waiting with a pair of tall lattes. I slip into a chair and she slides a drink my way.

"Extra hot, nonfat with a sprinkle of cinnamon," she says.

"Thanks!" That Krista. What would I do without her?

I quickly scan the area—no sign of Adam. I wrap my hands around the cup to warm them. "Is it just me or is it freezing in here?" In my sleeveless top and butt-skimming skirt I am rapidly turning into a cheersicle.

Krista has a cute purple cardigan draped over her shoulders. "I know, it's awful. I heard someone say the AC is messed up. Again." She sips her latte through a thin red straw, a technique she claims keeps her teeth white and shiny, then she leans way in. "By the way, every single person with testicles was checking you out when you came in."

I smile. "Guys can't resist a girl in a uniform."

She clears her throat and glances at my chest. "Or a girl who's recently been crowned Queen of the Nipple Kingdom."

"What?" I follow her eyes. With the arctic chill in the air it looks like I shoved a couple of jelly beans in my shirt. I cross my arms over my chest. "Oh my god! I should have worn a padded bra. Give me that sweater!"

Krista laughs and dodges my grab. "No way. But I'd be

happy to lend you the muskrat. It's in my locker."

I groan. The muskrat—a heinous pelt of a sweater that Krista's mother insists she keep in her locker all year long—just in case.

"I guess I'd rather be warm and rodential than look like this."

"Excellent point. Or should I say 'points'?" Krista laughs her ass off. "Sorry," she says. "Look, I have PE first period and can leave early. Give me your combo and I'll stick the sweater in your locker."

The first bell rings and I head to bio with my arms crossed firmly over my chest. Between periods I race to my locker and find the muskrat in all its fuzzy glory. It's a longish, brownish wraparound with horrific faux-fur trim and a belt. All I need are buckteeth and a tail to complete the outfit. But the sweater is not all Krista has left for me. The inside of my locker door is dominated by a huge heart drawn in red Sharpie. Inside the heart are the words *Jake + Nora*. Crap! Anyone passing by will see it. I slam shut the locker door and head to French.

The morning is much like yesterday was and like I suspect the rest of the year with my current load of classes.

Give me a B!
Give me an O!
Give me an R-E-D!

Thankfully, the day picks up at lunchtime when Chelsey stops me before I even make it to the commons. She's wearing a little jacket that looks like it was custom-made to go with our uniform.

"Nora? Why are you wearing that—that 'thing'? You're

supposed to be wearing your cheer uniform."

I untie the sweater and pull it open. "I *am* wearing my cheer uniform, but I was freezing."

"Whatever," she says. "Ugly sweaters aside, me and some of the other girls are heading to Flying Fish for lunch. Want to come?"

"Sure!" I find Krista in the lunch line and we meet the Monarchs out in the front circle. It's plenty warm outside—much warmer than inside, so I peel off the muskrat and we all climb into Becca's mother's SUV. We have not even walked halfway across the Flying Fish parking lot when I make an astonishing discovery. My cheer uniform is like a superhero suit. It's like I slipped into a phone booth, put on my uniform and came out a different person. Nora Fulbright—Super Cheer Girl!

Everyone we pass in the parking lot wishes us luck in the game tomorrow. The restaurant is packed with people who have first lunch, and as I make my way to the restroom at least a dozen guys smile and say hi. Guys I've never spoken to before. I take a quick glance down at my chest. All clear. It's definitely the uniform that's getting me the attention. At Chelsey's suggestion we do an impromptu cheer and the owner gives us a free round of soda. We are so hot!

I know what Mom would say about all the attention we're getting—that a woman should not, for any reason, allow herself to be placed upon a pedestal. She'd quote her own superhero, Gloria Steinem: "A pedestal is as much a prison as any small, confined space."

But I must say, life on a cheerleading pedestal is a pretty cushy prison.

By the time I stroll into Mr. Bolger's class, even in this ridiculous sweater, my confidence, which was so rattled

62

yesterday, is fully restored. I do a quick scan for Adam, who is not yet here. I slide into the seat beside the one he sat in yesterday. Mr. Bolger stops me. "Same seats as yesterday, please."

Sigh. It would be a lot easier to have some face time with Adam if we sat next to each other. I make my way to the back of the class.

"Hey, Nora!" The football player who gave Jake a fist bump yesterday is holding his hand out for a high five. I slap his hand and wink. My god. When did I learn to wink?

"Nora!" Elsa waves from across the room. "You were so awesome at practice yesterday! You nailed that new tumbling pass!"

I wave back. "Thanks!"

Where is Adam? He should be here, watching me being popular.

"Yo, Nora!" Little Nate gives me a double thumbs-up. He cracks a grin. Wow. I didn't know they even made front teeth that big. I think about how Jake blew Little Nate off yesterday.

"Yo," I say, and give him a smile before I slide into my chair.

The bell rings and the front row has an empty chair where Adam should be. I didn't see him at lunch, but then again, I ate at Flying Fish. He's probably just late again—still a little confused about the geography of Riverbend High.

Mr. Bolger shuts the door and calls names off his roster.

Could Adam be out sick? Of course I didn't pass him this morning on my way to school because, lamely, I drove a different route. I worried that he would see me and wonder why I didn't stop and offer him a ride. After how much it freaked me out yesterday, my days of toting around illegal passengers, even Adam, are over.

God, what if he was walking down the street wondering where I was, not paying attention, and *wham!* he got taken out by a school bus. I picture the scene at the hospital. Adam, in a coma. His entire body in traction. I stand beside his bed in a black cheer uniform. My face, stained with tears, is buried in my hands. My nose is pink from crying. Adam's parents, Dr. Mom and Dr. Dad, hold each other, weeping. They're faced with the awful decision about whether to take their precious only child off life support before he earned that 4.0.

I pick up a pair of black and silver pom-poms and do a mournful dirge of a cheer, raising my pom-poms in a slow, shuddering circle around my head, taking great care not to knock into any of Adam's wires or tubes:

> *Heal those bones*
> *You gotta*
> *Heal those bones (I do a little sob/torn gasp here,*
> *but soldier on)*
> *Shout one out for Adam through my megaphone*
> *(fist pumps) Go. Adam. Rock. Adam.*
> *Heeeeaaaaallllllllll (Herkie jump), Adam!*

Adam's eyelids flutter open! His face breaks into a weak smile. There is a chorus line of nurses in white dresses, clapping. Clapping. Clapping.

"Miss Fulbright!"

Mr. Bolger is two feet away from me, clapping.

I stiffen in my chair. Once again the entire class stares at me. Thankfully, Adam is not among them. Mr. Bolger leans in and speaks in a firm voice. "I realize that some of the math might be over your head, Miss Fulbright, but I trust that responding with the word *here* during roll call is not too much to ask of you."

My temples pulse as my body pumps all available blood into my face. I raise a tentative hand. "Here."

Mr. Bolger shakes his head as he returns to the front of the room where he grabs a pile of worksheets and hands them out. Anyone who has had any algebra *ever* could solve these problems. I'm racing through them when I'm distracted by the girls in front of me, whispering excitedly. The guy in front of them turns in his seat and speaks in a hushed voice. "I was at the next table over. I saw the whole thing. She totally almost died."

Who almost died? When? Where?

"Excuse me?" Mr. Bolger is at his desk fiddling with a Rubik's Cube. He pushes himself up to standing. "Mr. . . ." He scans his roster. "Mr. Hennif, is there something you need to get off your chest so the rest of the class can stay focused on their work?"

"Oh." The guy who "saw the whole thing" turns back in his seat so he's facing the right way. "We were just talking about, you know, the thing that happened in the lunchroom."

Mr. Bolger clasps his hands at his waist. "No, Mr. Hennif, I don't know what happened in the lunchroom. Perhaps you would care to enlighten me?"

The guy shifts uncomfortably. "What? You mean you want me to tell you? Here? Out loud?"

"Yes. Tell your story to the class so that you will stop hissing to the ladies behind you and we can all stay focused on our work."

The guy starts to talk, and Mr. Bolger stops him, insisting that he stand for his oration. For a Mister Rogers lookalike, this guy is brutal! But Mr. Hennif obliges. He rises to his feet, shoves his hands into his front pockets, and tells his story.

"So, me and my friends were eating lunch in the cafeteria when all of a sudden, like, one table away, this guy jumps behind this girl and wraps his hands around her chest. My friend was, like, 'Dude, check it out, that guy is humping her from behind.' So we all check it out, but pretty soon we figure out that he's actually doing that choking thing to her."

"He was choking her?" asks Mr. Bolger.

"No, *she* was choking. He was doing the Heimlich maneuver," chimes in a girl a couple of rows up. "I was there, too. It was amazing! Her face had gone this kind of pasty color, and he had his hands like this on her chest." She places her own folded hands below her sternum and turns so everyone can see. "After three or four squeezes, something came flying out of her mouth."

"A chunk of hot dog," says the Hennif guy. "It landed right near my chair." He reaches into the front pouch of his backpack and holds up the trophy. Mr. Bolger looks like he's going to puke.

"He saved her life," gushes one of the girls in front of me.

"He's a hero," adds the girl beside her.

"Who?" I ask.

They point to Adam's empty chair. "The guy that sat there yesterday."

I bolt to attention. Adam? Saved someone's life? Of all the days to grab lunch at Flying Fish! I should have been there to watch. Or to cheer. Or to hand him a sponge or clamps or something.

"Yeah, that was him," confirms someone else. "And then he took the girl to the nurse's office."

Mr. Bolger presses his pale lips together and nods. "Well.

That's some story. Our Mr. Hood deserves quite a bit of credit. And now, can we please finish our worksheet without further comment?"

People adjust in their seats. Pencils scratch on paper.

So, Adam did not get hit by a bus or even a car on his way to school. He's probably still at the nurse's office with the girl. That lucky girl, who had his arms wrapped all the way around her. Who was she?

At the end of the day I'm fumbling with the dial on my locker when I look up and, in the throng of people squeezing through the hallway, I see him. Adam. He's alone, reading a book as he walks, magically managing to avoid a collision with walls or people. Today he's traded in the khaki shorts for Madras plaid, with the sleeves of his white button-down shirt rolled down against the chill of the malfunctioning AC. Absorbed in his book, he is completely oblivious to the fact that everyone he passes stops to stare. People point and whisper. In two days he has gone from being the anonymous new guy, to being pegged a loser by Jake and a citizen of Nerdville by Chelsey, to being a Riverbend High living legend. In history, it's all anyone talked about:

—My friend said he's already been through medical school and only came here because his parents wanted him to have a 'normal' high school experience.

—I heard that girl was technically dead for, like, seven minutes and he brought her back to life.

—Someone told me that back where he used to live he pulled a whole class of kindergartners out of a burning school bus. Man. That guy could have any girl he wants.

He probably could. And I want him to want me. He's about to walk right past me when—

"Adam. Hi." I wave shyly.

He lowers the book, and when he sees me, his face lights up. In the cartoon version of him, little stars would sparkle at the edges of his eyes. "Hey! I haven't seen you around today," he says. "How's it going?"

He noticed that he hasn't seen me! "I'm good. Really good. Um, I want to apologize again for the awful ride to school yesterday. The whole day was kind of out of whack. I just wasn't myself. I stalled out at the light. Then I almost killed Stuart Shangrove—"

As I talk, Adam watches me like he is bird watcher and I am a new, rare breed. And like a bird, I seem to be chirping incessantly, trying to explain away yesterday's insanity and make room for a new start. I am mid-babble when he reaches toward me and puts a finger so close to my lips I that feel warmth radiating from his skin. I am suspended in a breathless Sistine Chapel moment, when God and Adam reach out their fingers and almost touch, almost touch, almost touch.

And like the Adam reaching out for God on that legendary ceiling, this Adam, my Adam, never quite touches me. Instead, ever so slowly, he withdraws his hand. "Shhh," he says, almost in a whisper. "It's all good. You were having a bad day. We all have those sometimes."

He smiles and I am teetering on the top of a mountain, on the head of a pin.

The girl next to me slams shut her locker and I am jolted back to the moment. Adam pushes an unruly wave of hair behind his ear. He swallows. "You might think it's nuts, but I do worry that the soccer ball affected you more than you think it did. I still feel awful about that." A pushed breath escapes his lips, followed by a laugh. "But really, it was pretty funny when Joshie thought you might be dead."

I laugh with him and, laughing, I relax. Words, at last, come easily, like they did that first day. "It was pretty impressive that you knew how to blind me with your flashlight and confirm that I was concussion free."

"It's what they do in the movies," he says with a shrug.

"Well, apparently helping girls in life-threatening situations is a specialty of yours," I say. "I've heard all kinds of rumors since lunch about the amazing Dr. Hood and his extraordinary life-saving exploits. I wish I could have been there to see it."

Adam cringes. His shoulders fold in. "And *I* wish people weren't making such a big deal about it. I only did what anyone else would have done."

I look at him askance. "Anyone else who happened to be savvy to the fact that she was choking. And who happened to know first aid."

"My parents are both doctors," he says, as if I needed a reminder. "They had me practicing the Heimlich maneuver on my first teddy bear. And who knows, she might have coughed it up on her own if I hadn't stepped in."

"You're being pretty modest," I say, reaching up to give his shoulder a playful poke. It is only then, when I see my own furry sleeve, that I realize I am still dressed like a rodent.

Behind Adam, a group of girls slows down. One of them dabs on lip gloss. Another takes a picture with her phone. No kidding, he could have anyone he wants. He may even currently top the hottie list of every girl in school. But Nora Fulbright, Monarch-in-Training, is about to flaps her wings and soar above the crowd.

I smile at him coyly. "So, I was just getting my stuff together to go to practice."

"Practice?" he asks.

Slowly, striving for sultry or sexy or somewhere in between, I untie the wooly brown belt and the sweater falls open. I let it slide off one shoulder, revealing purple, gold and the exuberant jumping trout embroidered above my left boob. I shake my arm out of the sleeve, then reach around and free up the other arm. I stand facing him, the sweater dangling from my fingertips like it's a silk bathrobe. I turn, fling open my locker door and go up on tiptoes to slide the muskrat onto the locker shelf. When I turn back, Adam's eyes are wide.

I smile. It's a cocky smile. Adam Hood, meet Super Cheer Girl! Riverbend High School's most talented flier.

With me standing in my cheer uniform in front of my open locker, this is supposed to be the moment when he's wowed by my short skirt, my tanned legs, my perky demeanor. The moment when he falls into a testosterone-induced coma—Nora is a cheerleader! But instead, he pulls the book he's holding, a book about chess openings, close to his chest like he's protecting his heart.

Something is not right. It feels like an icy gust has come in and snuffed out the spark that was glowing here just minutes ago when he pressed a finger almost to my lips.

"Is everything okay?" I ask. I take a step closer, he takes a half step back.

"Yeah, of course," he says matter-of-factly. "Everything is fine."

Everything is not fine. I can feel it. I can see it as the muscles in Adam's jaw tense.

"Um, I noticed you weren't in algebra," I say, searching for some common ground, for a way to breathe life back into our conversation. "I thought maybe you were . . ." Spit it out, Nora. In the hospital. In traction. Waking up from a near-death experience. "You know, sick, or something. Then

I heard what happened at lunch. But don't worry, all we did was a review worksheet and I grabbed an extra so you could do it at home. It's right here."

I reach for my book bag. Adam stops me.

"No—thanks anyway, but I don't need it. I, um, switched to a different class."

My one class with him and he switched out? My arms dangle lifeless by my sides. "Why?"

He shakes his head so that a lone shock of hair falls across his face. I want to reach up and brush it away. But more, I want to give it a sharp tug and demand that he tell me what the hell just happened that made him turn to Jack Frost.

"Well, Mr. Bolger seems like a good guy," he says, "but it really wasn't the right place for me. The review questions were ridiculously easy, but still, almost no one knew the answers."

If I only had a brain. I look down at my feet.

"Oh, wow. I'm sorry." Adam's expression is pained. "I mean, I know math isn't everyone's strong suit."

Wait a minute. Is that what this is about? The sudden chill? Does he see the cheer uniform and instead of seeing me as a giant bucket of awesome he assumes that I'm perhaps even dumber than I seemed in Bolger's class? That because I'm a cheerleader I'm not smart? Not smart enough for him?

"Woohoo! Adam! There you are!"

Crap with a spout! The Teapot waves from all the way down at the other end of the hall. Her chestnut-colored Shirley Temple curls, pulled back in barrettes on either side of her face, bob as she ambles toward us. She's got on what appears to be a purple mechanic's jumpsuit with gold epaulettes and matching gold sneakers. "All the world loves a hero!" she sings out.

Adam stiffens.

I glance from the Teapot and her friends back to Adam. "Is that who was choking?" I ask, unable to keep the terseness out of my voice.

Adam's head barely moves as he nods. He looks—embarrassed? A thought makes my breath catch. Is he embarrassed to be seen talking to Nora, the dumb cheerleader?

The Teapot makes her way through the thinning crowd with Little Nate and Tallulah, the girl who played Beauty in last year's play. Again, perfect casting. Tallulah is stunning, with thick, black Rapunzel-like hair that cascades over one shoulder as she sashays along between Little Nate and the Teapot. It is rumored that one day last year she came to school wearing nothing but her hair and a well-placed belt. And she is not just beautiful, she is supposedly very smart. And while she is not popular in a Chelsey or a Jake way, everyone knows who she is.

They stop when they reach us. At the sight of my uniform, the Teapot inhales like she has entered into a field of poppies. "Y'all look so darn cute!" Her smile is warm and genuine. She appears to have recovered nicely from her near-death experience.

"I heard about what happened at lunch," I say. "Lucky for you Adam was there."

The Teapot beams at him. "You're telling me! If he hadn't been there to save Tallulah, I would be short one best friend." She nods toward Tallulah, who has sidled in between me and Adam and is looking at him like he's made of cheesecake.

Wait. What?

Tallulah touches the back of her hand to her forehead and speaks in voice that is low, smoky and smooth. "I just don't know where I would be if you hadn't been there to save my life." She places one long, silver fingernail on Adam's shoulder and runs it down the length of his arm. "We're on our way to drama club. You should come. We're doing improv today and you just never know where things will go." She licks her lips like she took the AP How to Get a Guy class and got a perfect score on the final exam.

"It's tons of fun," quips Little Nate. The Teapot wraps an arm around my shoulder, and the warmth of her bulk reminds me that, without Krista's sweater, I'm freezing. "If y'all ever have a Friday free you should come," she tells me. "You'd be great!" She leans in and whispers, "No offense but y'all might want to try a padded bra."

I clamp my arms across my chest.

Adam twiddles the blue bead on the leather cord around his wrist. "Thanks for the invite. I'm not much of an actor. And anyway, I need to get home. I have a lot of work to do." His eyes drift toward mine but stop somewhere around my cheekbones. "And, um, have a good cheer practice."

Tallulah watches him go. "He's really something," she says to the Teapot and Little Nate, because I seem to have become invisible.

He really is something. He is something smart and kind and lifesaving and funny and beautiful. He is also something that has just confused the crap out of me. Now to figure out how to convince him that I am something, too. Something way more than just a dimwitted cheerleader.

But do I even stand a chance against Tallulah?

They leave and I turn back to my wide-open locker where Krista's giant heart screams a reminder that maybe she's right. Maybe I should just go for Jake. He's funny. He's hot. And as far as I can tell, Jake does *not* think he's too smart for me.

Six

PRACTICE GOES EXTRA LONG Because Vanessa completely muffs up the dance routine we're planning to do at halftime and Chelsey is relentless, making her do the same moves over and over again. I'm frustrated by the repetition. I'm frustrated by what just happened with Adam. Frustrated by the mere existence of Tallulah and her magnificent hair. Her magnificent brain. Her magnificent luck and timing when it comes to hot dogs and hot guys.

Vanessa slams her pom-poms onto the gymnasium floor in a huff. "Look, I'll just sit out halftime," she offers.

But Chelsey maintains that it'll be impossible to pull off the routine with an odd number of girls. In exasperation Elsa offers to sit it out, too, because then we would be an even number again, but the math confuses Chelsey, and in the end we are all stuck going through the routine again and again until Vanessa has it down. For now.

It's much later than I wish it was when I finally pull into the driveway. Joshie and Copernicus greet me at the front stoop.

"That guy was biking by and he stopped to play soccer with me again," Joshie reports.

My breath catches. "Adam?"

Joshie nods like he's trying to shake something loose. "He's nice. You should marry him."

"First I'd need to go out with him."

Joshie shrugs. Copernicus scratches. Apparently he has no four-legged wisdom to share today. Joshie switches gears. "Want to play with me?"

I'm wiped out, but maybe a little soccer wouldn't be such a bad idea. Maybe a certain bedimpled guy would happen by twice in one day and I'd have a chance to redeem myself here, where I'd have the home-field advantage.

"Okay." I look around the yard, the centerpiece of which is a little blow-up pool littered with Popsicle sticks and dog hair. "Where's the soccer ball?"

Copernicus yips and jumps at the mention of the word *ball*.

"No. Not soccer. Come on." Joshie grabs my hand and pulls me inside, where he's got the chessboard set up on the living room coffee table. All the pieces are in their correct squares.

I tug my hand away. "I am not playing chess with you. I don't even remember how to play," I lie. I don't think you can really forget how to play chess. At least not the basics. Not when you played as much as I did.

"I know how to play," Joshie claims.

"You do not."

"Do too. I read that book your dad sent you. And I looked things up on the computer. Did you know that in medieval times you couldn't be a knight unless you knew how to play chess?"

"I have virtually no interest in becoming a knight, Joshie. None. And I don't want to play chess. And you know what else? *You* don't want to play chess. Trust me. It can turn you into a total nerd."

Joshie's hands ball into fists at his side. "Phil plays a lot of chess. He isn't a nerd."

I laugh. "What? He's the biggest nerd ever!" Okay, he's a lovable nerd, but still—"

Joshie stomps his foot. "You can't laugh at my big brother!" His lower lip trembles. Copernicus growls.

I forgot. In addition to being Mr. Bug, Joshie is the president of the Phil Fulbright Fan Club. "Don't cry. Please?" I try to hug him and he backs away, bawling.

"Nora? What are you doing to your brother?" Mom calls from her office.

"Nothing!" I lower my voice. "Look, I'll play with you for a little while if you stop crying, okay?"

"Okay." Joshie sniffs, hiccups and runs to the chessboard. "I'm white. White always goes first." He delivers a tutorial on which pieces do what. I take him out in six moves. More tears. Clearly that is not the outcome he was looking for. We play again and I let him win. And again.

"Okay, that's it," I say finally. "I'm tired of being beaten."

Joshie, who's been kneeling on the carpet while I took the seat on the couch, glows. "See? I'm pretty good! I'm going to go show Pratik."

Joshie takes off for his friend's house and I am left with a sad, hollow feeling inside. It's got nothing to do with Joshie. It's all about chess. And Dad. And Adam and Tallulah.

Adam. What is he doing right now? I cross the living room and look out the front window on the off chance that he's returned and is outside staring longingly at my bedroom window. He's not.

I flop back into the sofa.

Adam.

Tallulah has that mane of hair, plump lips, curves in places where I don't even have places. He turned down her offer to go to drama club, but I don't know if that was about her or about drama club. It was pretty clear from the way she looked at him that she is not going to give up. And she's not the only one. Even some of the Cabbage Whites were talking about him at practice:

—I heard that this really cute guy at first lunch saved a girl who was having a heart attack.
—No, not a heart attack. She was choking. My friend said that he had to perform an emergency tracheotomy.
—I heard there was blood everywhere.

Upon hearing them, Krista pushed her headband into place, rolled her eyes and nudged me with her elbow. "So he's a hero. Big deal. Stick with Jake."

Now I jump when Mom reaches over the back of the sofa and gives my shoulder a little squeeze. "Thinking about the first big game tomorrow?" she asks.

"Um, yeah."

"Nervous?"

I groan as I sit up. "Probably not as nervous as I should be. But I've still got all night to obsess."

"You'll be fine. Remember how nervous you got before the PSATs? All that vomit, and still, you got a twenty-four hundred. It's Joshie I'm worried about. He's so excited to watch you cheer that I don't know if he'll even be able to sleep."

She scans the kid-free, dog-free living room. "Speaking of Joshie . . . ?"

"He went to Pratik's."

Mom heads to the kitchen without a single snide comment about "cheering on the boys." Maybe she's finally gotten over it? I sink into the sofa cushions and fall asleep until

Mom wakes me up for dinner. With the long nap, and then a pile of chocolate ice cream for dessert (grocery store brand, but any port in a storm), by the time I crawl into bed my brain is on full alert.

What if Vanessa messes up and I fall off the pyramid?

What if everyone at school is there, watching?

What if no one is?

At seven o'clock in the morning I'm still in bed when I get the first text from Krista:

Today's the day! Nervous!!!!!!!!!!!!! What if I puke?

Five minutes later:

My hair looks like crap!!!!!!!!!

And then:

Ack! Bethany used my eye glitter for an art project! Bring yours to the game!!!!!

I shower and get ready to go. Krista texts some more, and when texting isn't enough, she calls. Her voice has as many exclamation points as her texts do.

"Oh my god, Nora! I think I just forgot all the cheers!"

Somehow I talk Krista down, despite the fact that I'm as nervous as she is. I force myself to take a couple of deep breaths. I know the cheers. My hair looks fine. So does my eye glitter.

Still, I'm nervous. It isn't the act of messing up that worries me so much. It's about who will *see* me mess up.

Will he be there?

I hope so.

I hope not.

Krista texts a final time:

!!! Mom and Dad are ready to go. C U there in 15!!!

I take a last look in the bathroom mirror and adjust my hair bow. I tuck eye glitter for Krista into my purse. Here we go! It's finally the day I've worked toward since last spring when I first saw the poster that caused the Teapot to drool:

> *Cheer for the team!*
> *Cheer for the school!*
> *Tryouts Friday—*
> *Cheerleaders Rule!!!*

I enter the kitchen expecting to see everyone packed and ready to go, but no. Mom, in jeans and a Harvard sweatshirt, is frying a breakfast hot dog for Joshie. Joshie feeds mustard and crackers to Copernicus beneath the kitchen table. Bill, still in his morning-run attire, sips iced tea and fills out Su-doku squares with a permanent marker. His eyes lift as I enter the room. "Well, look at you!"

Joshie gasps. "You look as pretty as a butterfly!" He scrambles from under the table, and before I can stop him he hugs me, dotting my top with round, mustard-yellow fin-gerprints.

"Joshie! Look at what you did!" I push him away, but I push a little too hard and he trips over Copernicus, who has trotted through a dollop of mustard, and emerges from be-neath the table to see what all the fuss is about. Joshie erupts in a swell of tears. Copernicus jumps up on me, smearing yel-low paw prints on my kneecaps.

"Nora!" shouts Mom. "Do not push your brother!" As she lunges to help Joshie she knocks the pan off the stove and Joshie's hot dog bounces across the floor. Bang! Copernicus is on it. Joshie's wail hits a crescendo, "MY HOT DOG!" as I tear off my top and run to the sink.

"Are you okay?" Mom, on her knees, hugs Joshie.

"Bad boy!" Bill chases the dog.

"Yip! Yip! Yip!" Copernicus runs in circles around the table, cheering his own ingenuity—not only did he get a free meal, he got an awesome game of chase. Bill follows Copernicus out the back door.

"What about me?" I shout, standing there in my sports bra and pleated skirt, wringing out my soggy top. "I'm supposed to be at the school in fifteen minutes. I told you guys we needed to leave at nine thirty!"

Mom snarls, "Well, *somebody* shoved her little brother. You need to calm down!"

I shake out the top. It's clean, but soaking wet. "That's because *somebody's* little brother got mustard all over her! And I didn't mean for him to fall."

"She didn't mean for me to fall." Joshie gulps like he'd be more comfortable breathing through gills.

I slip the dripping top over my head. My eyes well up. I wipe them and come away with wet, glitter-smeared pinkies. I stamp the kitchen floor hard. "Crap! I wanted to look perfect for the first game."

Mom looks like someone whose team has just lost the big game one thousand to nothing. "Looking perfect is what matters most in the world, isn't it, Nora? Got to look our best for the boys?"

I knew she wasn't over it! I am actively crying. "Why don't you just say what you mean? You think I'm stupid! You're embarrassed by me!"

She hoists Joshie off the floor. A smear of mustard, like war paint, is splashed across her cheek. Joshie flies to my side but keeps his hands to himself.

"I'm sorry," says Mom, "but I will never understand how a young woman with your talents could choose to use her hard-earned gymnastics skills cheering on a bunch of testosterone-charged boys rather than competing on the gymnastics team. Do you remember when you were in middle school? You were dying to go to a high school with a gymnastics team."

I remember. In middle school there was no gymnastics team. All the cool girls played volleyball. Sure, I competed in meets at the gym where I took lessons, but at school? Unless I chose to celebrate each perfect test score with a standing front somersault there was no way for anyone at school to know that Nora Fulbright, Girl Genius, was also an athlete.

Mom doesn't quit. "We moved so that you could go to Riverbend, where they have an excellent team—"

"What?" I shriek. "We moved so that Junior Einstein here could get into the right kindergarten!"

Josh looks from Mom to me. "I liked my kindergarten."

Mom tosses up her hands. "Whatever. The point is that you go to a school with a powerhouse gymnastics team. You did great on the JV squad last year, but do you go on and follow your dream? No. Instead it's become all about shaking those silly pom-poms and waggling your butt in a skimpy outfit—"

Joshie reaches for my hand. "You look pretty in your shrimpy outfit."

Mom gazes at the ceiling, holds out her open hands and beseeches the spirits of dead feminists everywhere: "Where did I go wrong?"

Her words are like a wrecking ball to my abdomen. "Never mind!" I yell. "I'll drive myself to the game. If you can stand to watch me shake my silly pom-poms and waggle my butt, you know where I'll be."

I hoist the gear bag over my shoulder and storm out to the car, leaving a trail of dripped water behind me. Mom thinks cheering is stupid. Adam thinks cheer*leaders* are stupid. Stupidly, I care way too much about what everyone else thinks. Maybe I should have just stuck with gymnastics.

Krista is the first to see me as I walk into the locker room. "You're here! I was so worried something had happened and I would have to go out there without you." She pauses. "You look awful."

"Thanks." I hand her the eye glitter and catch a glimpse of myself in the mirror. My bow is cockeyed from pulling my shirt off and on. My eyes are rimmed pink. Thank god for waterproof mascara.

Krista studies me in the mirror as she dabs some glitter onto her eyelid and smoothes it out. "Your top is all wet."

"I had a fight with my mom."

She laughs. "What? A water balloon fight?"

She gets me laughing, too, and the knot in my stomach loosens a tiny bit. I begin to feel like I am actually here, in the locker room the day of our first game, where the pregame buzz is like a triple-shot mocha—totally caffeinated. Vanessa, alone at the far end of the locker room, tries unsuccessfully to nail her side-hurdler jump. Over by some lockers, Jazmine and Becca practice a thigh stand. Gillian climbs onto a bench and channels Taylor Swift, singing into her hairbrush about painful love. The air smells like a test site for the Body Shop.

"Has anyone seen—?" Chelsey's usual chirp is more of a squawk as she rounds a corner and spots me. She plants her fists on her hips. "There you are! You're late! And your uniform is all wet!"

"She had a water balloon fight with her mom." Krista drapes an arm around my damp shoulders.

Chelsey rolls her eyes. "Before our first game? Seriously? You should have worn a raincoat or something." She heaves a big breath in and out. "Okay, well at least you're here. I was getting worried." Chelsey's smile transforms her back into Cheerful Chelsey. "Okay. Everyone, get it together. We have about a half hour to run through some warm-ups. Let's go!"

There are whoops and cheers as we grab our poms and our megaphones and head out to the field, where the bleachers are filling up. The warm morning promises to turn into a hot day, and the air is thick with the smells of popcorn and freshly mown grass. Up in the stands, the band blasts out a boppy version of Paul Simon's "Call Me Al."

I steal a quick glance into the crowd. Joshie, Mom and Bill must have raced right over after I left because they have grabbed seats right in the front row of the parent section. Mom has washed the war paint off her face. Beside her, Bill claps to the beat of the music. Joshie hangs over the railing, "Nora! Nora!" I blow him a kiss. I avoid Mom's gaze. I will show her that I am excellent at what I do, and that I'll get way more recognition for my gymnastics moves here than I ever would at a meet where only a handful of people would attend.

We set our megaphones and water bottles beside our pedestals and do some stretches. The band hits their final note and Joshie calls from the stands, "Nora, do some flippy things!" I grab Krista and we move to the edge of the field to warm up with tumbling runs. The growing crowd cheers us on. This is the stuff that makes my body sing. Back when I was eight and Dad left, Mom put us into chess camp— naturally. Phil thrived, but Mom moved me into gymnastics camp after I spent the first three days of chess camp crying.

I remember how coordinated I felt mastering a cartwheel. I can still feel the instructor's hand on the small of my back when she spotted me for a back handspring. Then there was the day I screwed up enough courage to try one on my own. It was a little bit like flying.

I sneak a glance at Mom. She's got Joshie by the hand and is heading for the bathrooms. There are definitely parts of gymnastics that I miss. The intense control of keeping it together on the balance beam. The incredible charge of flying around on the uneven bars. The satisfaction of nailing a landing off the horse. But would I be happier on the varsity gymnastics team than I am here?

Krista and I count to three and push off into standing aerial cartwheels. Chelsey claps. "I wish I could do that!"

"You could," Krista says. "With practice. Lots and lots of practice."

The band kicks into a frenzied version of "Louie, Louie." We dance, free-form, shaking our poms. For the record, I do not waggle my butt. People pour into the bleachers, picking up our energy, dancing as they walk. Scanning the bleachers, I spot Ms. Ostweiler. Nearby, in the aisle, there's a woman my mom's age in a retro cheer uniform shaking a set of faded pom-poms. I point her out to Krista and we dub her the Ultimate Fan.

There's no sign of the Teapot. I'm stunned. I figured she came to every game. And it looks like it's going to be an Adam-free morning, too. On one hand, hooray! I can relax. On the other hand? I really do want him to come to a game and see me in action. I want to show off for him and have him see that I'm great at what I do. I'm a varsity athlete! Maybe if he came to a game he would see that it actually takes coordination and brains to keep synched up during our cheers.

That cheerleaders are more than pleated skirts and hair bows. What we do takes dedication and hard work. Not to mention intelligence.

The music stops and the crowd grows quiet. Stuart Shangrove, the guy I almost killed the first day of school, booms in a warbly echo over the loudspeaker, "Ladies and Gentlemen-*men-men*! Join me in welcoming our very own Cutthroats-*oats-oats*!"

The crowd jumps to its feet as the football players stampede onto the field. Geoff leads the way in his Cutthroat trout costume, scales glittering in the morning sun, sweeping his arms like he's doing the breaststroke across the football field. Chelsey climbs onto her pedestal and the rest of us climb onto ours. The football players jog around the field as Chelsey leads us in our first cheer. "Cutthroats! Fight song! Are you ready?"

We clap one pom onto our hip, shoot the other into the air and respond, "Hip, hip!"

The crowd sings along. Chelsey leads us in a clap, pause, double-clap rhythm. The pedestal gives me an extra couple of feet of height, and as we sing and clap, I make eye contact with the entire crowd. I am not in math class puzzling out a problem. I am not in the kitchen arguing with Mom. I am not obsessing about Adam. I am here. I am so very here.

And then, *whap!* I am not, because I spot Adam, making his way up the bleachers.

Everywhere, girls turn and wave as he passes by.

Keep breathing. Keep singing. Keep the beat. Clap, pause, double-clap.

The Teapot, in a purple dress and a yellow cowboy hat wrapped with purple streamers, walks up the stairs behind him. They stop to search for a place to sit. Adam, in faded jeans and a pale orange T-shirt, points up into the bleachers. I look to where he's pointing.

Tallulah. She stands and waves to Adam and the Teapot, then motions to the seats she has saved for them. She is the only person in the crowd wearing a black cocktail dress. Her hair is wrapped on top of her head like a 1950s diva and she's got on a pair of cat's-eye sunglasses. From the side, she looks like a Barbie doll with a slight boob reduction—just enough to keep things from seeming impossible.

Adam lifts his hand to block the sun. I can't take my eyes off his arms. Having spent the past month around football players, I'm used to guys who lift chunks of metal for fun and have upper arms I can't get my fingers around. Adam's arms are strong in a longer, leaner way. What would it feel like to have them wrapped around me?

But he's sitting with Tallulah. And if he were not with her, there are plenty of other girls who want him.

We're on the second-to-last verse of the fight song. Adam and the Teapot have squeezed into their seats where he is sandwiched between the Teapot and Tallulah. He looks out at the field, he scans the line of cheerleaders and he stops when he gets to me. He stops, and he smiles. He smiles! I swear I can see his dimple from here. He turns to say something to the Teapot and I study his profile, which is perfect. His hair is a little messy today. A little rumpled. A little dying to have me run my fingers through it. Tickle the back of his neck with my fingertips—

"Ouch!"

Chelsey, on the pedestal beside me, jabs me lightning quick in the side and resumes clapping. "You're off beat!" she barks through a stiff smile.

The band plays. The crowd sings. I cannot find the beat! I

turn to catch it from Chelsey, but I turn a little too far.

Thankfully, the music hides the sound of five hundred people gasping as I fall off the pedestal and onto my face. The song comes to a close as my skirt flops up in the back, and I flash the entire crowd with my purple spanks.

There you have it, Adam. It takes brains *and* coordination to be a cheerleader, and I have neither.

For a stunned moment that seems to last several lifetimes I lie there. I just lie there, willing myself to disappear. But I need to get up. I need to get up and smile and get on with it, right? If you fall down, get back up, right? But how?

"Oh my god, Nora, are you okay?" Krista is right there to offer a hand.

I force back tears and push myself to sitting, brushing little flecks of rubber track off my legs. I can't bear to look into the crowd. I can't bear to see the look of disbelief on Adam's face, or the look of satisfaction on Tallulah's.

Krista is not the only one who races to my side. Chelsey is right there, too. Pink ears. Pinched mouth. Her arms hang rigor-mortis-like at her sides. "I am so embarrassed!" she huffs. "This is not a practice, Nora. This is real life! Even Vanessa got it right. Get it together or get lost!" She stomps over to Becca for consolation.

Krista shakes her head as she crouches beside me. "You okay?"

"I guess so."

"I should thank you," she says.

"For what?"

She grins. "I'm not nervous anymore. Come on. Let's cheer."

I steel myself and, with Krista's help, I manage to stand. I'm mortified when the crowd claps like they do when an injured football player is led to the bench.

Out on the field, the football team lines up. We lead the crowd shouting the word *GO* until it hits a crescendo as the ball is kicked, and the Cutthroats and the Eagles begin battling it out on the field. Yards are gained and lost. Balls are fumbled and recovered. There are even a couple of touchdowns. And throughout it all, we cheer our hearts out, our chants changing to match the action:

Block that pass! You gotta block that pass! You gotta . . .
Hit 'em again! Hit 'em again! Harder, harder. Hit 'em
again Hit 'em again! . . .
Pluck those birds! Let's pluck those birds! Let's . . .

It is while I am shouting about defeathering the Eagles that I notice something; when I risk making eye contact with the crowd, only Joshie sees me. Mom is fixed on the game. So is Ms. Ostweiler. The Ultimate Fan. I dare to look a few rows up—Adam, the Teapot and Tallulah are all glued to the action on the field.

We might as well be invisible, because clearly the crowd is not actually here to see us. They're here to watch a football game. Suddenly, I feel a little bit like an ornament. Nice to have around, but not essential. With gymnastics I'd nail a routine and my points would add to the team total, helping us win a meet. Here, are we even helping the guys win the game? They don't even look at us. Could it be that Mom has it right, after all? Did I make a totally lame choice giving up gymnastics?

Then, halftime rolls around and *bam!* I bust right out of my stressatorium. Seriously—what was I thinking? This is definitely where I should be. Suddenly, all eyes are on us, and our mid-field formation goes off without a hitch. The bases are right where they need to be as I fall into their arms. I ace my tumbling run and the crowd goes crazy. The football guys cheer *us* on for a change. I am not much of a lip reader, but from here I can see the word *wow* as it leaves Adam's lips and is followed by an impressed grin.

Perhaps I have redeemed myself. Aside from skinned knees and a bruised ego, I think I'm okay. I wish I could say the same for the football team. When the game is over, the mighty Cutthroats have been filleted, losing thirty-six to thirteen. Small clusters of people move past us as the crowd slowly files out of the stands. I turn at the sound of my name from over by the stairs.

"Nora! Bye-bye, Nora!" Joshie gives me a shoulder-dislocating wave. Bill holds two thumbs up.

"See you at home, honey!" Mom's smile is earnest. She shouts to be heard over the din. "You were terrific! You really were!"

Could there be room on Mom's feminist agenda for cheerleaders after all?

I hear shouting and turn to where the football team is slumped on the sidelines. Coach Avery, his face mottled red, yells at them. I thought they saved that kind of thing for the locker room. Jake sees me and looks away, head hung. From what I can tell he played really well. They all did. But the other team played better.

By the bleachers, Chelsey is draped in Becca's arms. "We should have won. It was our first game!" They are both sobbing. Sobbing!

"We (*gasp*) worked (*sob*) so hard." Chelsey is inconsolable. Someone needs to tell her about waterproof mascara.

Are cheerleaders supposed to be apoplectic when we lose

a game? We never talked about this in practice. I suddenly feel guilty for feeling great. The cheering, the stunting, the crowd—I loved it all, even when we weren't the center of everyone's attention. Still, perhaps I should dredge up tears to avoid committing cheerleading treason. I glance around to see what the other Monarchs are doing. Gillian, fully engaged in hair therapy, gives Jazmine an impromptu updo. They are hair involved, but undeniably morose. Most of the Cabbage Whites pack away their megaphones and poms. They are bummed but not devastated. Vanessa, over by the entrance gate, is getting cheer tips from the Ultimate Fan.

Am I a Monarch or a Cabbage White?

Krista gets right in my face. She motions with her eyeballs toward the Monarchs. "Jeez, who died? It's just a freaking football game. Sometimes you win, sometimes you lose. We could still go on to have a twelve and one record."

Excellent point.

"I thought we were *cheer*leaders," she goes on. "Shouldn't we be cheerful?"

I ponder for a moment. "How about this." I make sure no one is looking, then jump to attention and make up goofy, flailing arm movements as I cheer to Krista:

> *Hey, hey, dry those tears*
> *We'll get tougher*
> *Have no fears!*
> *Cutthroats don't give up and cry*
> *They swim back home—*

I search for a word and Krista helps me out,

> *They swim back home and multiply!*

Krista and I laugh until—

"Hey! You two!"

Crap with a touchdown stance! Chelsey is right there. She mops her cheeks with the back of her hand. She's going to freak about inappropriate behavior, I know it.

"That was perfect!" she says, sniffing. "Do it again!"

Seriously?

Krista joins me as we improvise movements. A couple of the Cabbage Whites line up and we do it again, louder. Chelsey laughs. She adds a verse. I add another one.

"Hey." Chelsey points at me like she's just identified me in a police lineup. "You could be a cheer writer!" She throws an arm around my shoulder. "That was awesome!"

I grin like an idiot.

With all the excitement I suddenly realize I'm not even thinking about Adam. Until I think about Adam. A lot of people are still in the bleachers. I allow myself a moment to seek him out, and spot him surrounded by at least a half-dozen girls. One of them hands him a Sharpie and he signs her T-shirt. He signs another girl's forehead.

It takes a minute, but I finally find Tallulah, who is with a bunch of drama people over by the band. The Teapot is there, too, gesticulating wildly as she speaks, but Tallulah is not paying attention to the Teapot. Her arms are crossed hard across her chest. Her lips are drawn tight. And behind her sunglasses I can tell that her eyes are locked on to the same thing that is at the center of my attention. The center, it seems, of every girl's attention.

Adam.

Seven

BY THE END OF THE FIRST FUll week of school the monotony of my classes makes me want to scream. The work is far too easy, and the lack of motivation on the part of many of my classmates is palpable. Like the guy in math who always shows up fifteen minutes late, with narrow bloodshot eyes, a dopey grin and an unquenchable hunger for M&M's. But at least he shares. Or the girl in biology who spends the entire class texting, until she gets caught. Then she zones out to music, which leaks from her earbuds, seeps into my head and makes me relive that awful morning when I drove to school with Adam.

On the upside, I am a regular at the Monarch lunch table.

Yaaaaaaaaay (straddle jump)
Nora! (Wide V stance)

But as Gillian messes with my hair, and Chelsey poses for pictures with passersby, and Jake regales me with stories about past moments of football glory, I can't help watching the action over at the loser table, which has become anything but. Concentric rings of people orbit the table, some of them sitting, some standing. Tallulah, eating food cut into very small pieces, is always within flirting distance of Adam. The Teapot occasionally belts out a country-western tune, or an aria. Only once all week, yesterday, did I manage to actually have a moment alone with Adam.

Fade in. Thursday, in the pizza line.

NORA, *nodding toward the packed lunch table where the Teapot, with Little Nate on her lap, is pretending to be a ventriloquist.* Hey! So you, uh, seem to have made lots of friends.

ADAM, *winces.* It's a little embarrassing. I'm not big on crowds.

NORA. You toughed out the crowd and came to the first football game. It was really nice to see you there.

ADAM, *eyes brightening.* You were amazing, by the way. God! Where did you learn to do those cool flips and things?

NORA, *insert coy laughter.* I started gymnastics lessons when I was practically prenatal.

ADAM, *visibly concerned.* I worried about you when you fell. It's crazy to make people, I mean, you know, cheer-leaders, stand on those pedestals. Someone could really get hurt.

NORA. I hoped no one had noticed. But it's nice to know there was a medic in the crowd in case I needed one. (*Uncomfortable pause. The guy doling out slices announces that they've run out of Hawaiian.*)

NORA. So, Joshie said you stopped by last Friday. I'm sorry I missed you.

ADAM, *looking at his feet.* I wasn't sure when you'd get back from practice.

(*Adam looks up. His gaze settles on Nora's eyes. His breath smells like mint tea. Someone bumps him from behind causing his hand to brush her arm. Is it her imagination, or does he allow it to linger?*)

ADAM. I'm sorry we don't have any classes together.

NORA, *gulping for air, stepping closer, gazing up at him like he is wearing a halo of light, or holding a scepter of fire, or some other godlike cinematic device.* I know what you mean.

ADAM, *searching her face.* Maybe—

JAKE, *playfully punching the recently healed bruise on Nora's upper arm.* Nora! Grab me a slice of pepperoni, would you? Actually, make it two. (*turns to Adam*) Dude! Nice job saving the chick with the hair. Where the hell did you learn how to do an emergency appendectomy?

ADAM, *stiffening.* I, uh, I think I'll get a burger instead. Fade out.

So that was yesterday, and today, Friday, after an entire lunch period of covertly watching Tallulah fawn over Adam, I finally crack. Maybe they're a thing, maybe they're not. But I don't stand a chance with Adam unless I have more Adam time in my life. More time to demonstrate my penchant for intelligent conversation and witty reprisals. And I think I know how to do it. If my plan works, he will observe first-hand that cheerleaders, this cheerleader in particular, are not the dimwits he thinks they are.

The bell rings. People scatter for their classes. The halls are eerily quiet, which makes the echo of my sneakers pounding on the gray polished-concrete floors seem even louder. I arrive at the attendance office out of breath and take a moment to steady myself before going in. The guy sitting behind the desk straightens in his chair and snaps shut the book he's reading.

"Hey, how's it going Nora?"

I nod. "Hi, Mitchell. How's yearbook committee going?"

"Pretty awesome," he says. Then, Mitchell looks at his hand as he polishes the nail of his ring finger with his thumb. "And it's Mitch, not Mitchell."

"Sorry." I was certain that last year in English class he went by Mitchell.

"Hey, that's okay. You'd have no way of knowing that I changed it over the summer when I was working as a lifeguard over at the Waverly Beach Park."

The way he punctuates his delivery of the word *lifeguard* makes it clear that this information is meant to impress me, but I am not here to be impressed by Mitchell, cum Mitch. "I can see why you changed it," I say. "I imagine that the extra syllable could have been a real impediment in life-and-death situations."

I don't give him time to mull this over. "I need to speak with Ms. Turner. Is she here?"

Mitch pushes his lank red hair behind his ears. "She goes home early on Fridays. She leaves it to me to keep this whole operation running smoothly." He leans back in his chair and folds his arms across his chest. "So, uh, congratulations on making cheer. I'll be doing the cheerleader shots for the yearbook. You know how it is. People love pix of the cheer squad." By "people" I am quite certain he is referring to people named Mitch.

"Great. That's just great. So, anyhow, if Ms. Turner isn't around, maybe you could help me. I need to find out some-one's schedule."

Mitch leans forward. His chair squeaks. "We don't just hand out student schedules."

I lower myself into the chair in front of his desk. I smile and try to look at him as though I am really seeing him for the first time. "Wow. You got a terrific tan sitting in that lifeguard chair." The truth, of course, is that he is a sun-spanked shade of pink. Skin like that does not tan. Ever. "Did you have to save many lives?"

While there were not, in fact, any human crises to contend with, Mitch recounts in painful detail a rescue involving a duck and a chunk of Laffy Taffy.

"And now you work here," I say. "You must really like jobs where you get to help people. Well, and animals."

Mitch, who is wearing far too tight a T-shirt for a guy with his meager build, puffs his chest. "Yeah, I guess I kind of do."

I produce an audible sigh of relief. "I'm so glad, because I know you can help me out."

Mitch shifts uncomfortably in his seat. I give him my best cheer smile. "There's a new student in school. His name is Adam Hood. And I need to know his schedule. I don't need a printout or anything. Just a quick peek will be fine."

"Why do you need it?"

I laugh, and flip my ponytail the way I've seen Chelsey flip hers when she's talking to the football guys. "Well, you know that we cheerleaders are sort of goodwill ambassadors here at Riverbend. Apparently this Adam guy just moved here, and I'm supposed to show up at his classroom door and do a little welcome cheer." I wrinkle my nose as I have seen Chelsey do when she is pretending not to like something, but actually, she loves it.

Mitch narrows his eyes. "I've never seen anyone do a welcome cheer."

"It's a new policy."

Mitch shakes his head. "It's totally against the rules to give out a schedule. And isn't Adam Hood the guy who sewed that girl's finger back on with nothing but a sharpened paper clip and a piece of dental floss? I don't think he needs any special help making friends."

I lean forward, and may my mother and all the dead suffragettes forgive me, I press my upper arms against the sides of my post-pupal boobs to create the illusion of cleavage. "Are you sure?"

Mitch's eyes drift south. "No—Wait! I mean yes. I'm sure."

Crap. There's got to be a way to get him to fork over Adam's schedule. What have I got that he might want? I glance over at the book he was reading—Isabel Allende's *House of the Spirits*—mandatory reading in tenth-grade English here at Riverbend. Bingo! I tap the book. "How about a little swap?"

Mitch furrows the place where eyebrows would be. "What do you mean?"

"Well, I know you struggled a little in English class last year. If you show me Adam's schedule I would be happy to, oh, I don't know, maybe give you tips on some of your English homework?"

Mitchell shakes his head. "I can't be bought. I have a responsibility here."

I'm losing patience. "Come on. There must be something you'd swap his schedule for."

Mitchell unfolds his arms. He turns to see whether anyone is within earshot, then leans across the desk. "You could go out with me."

I make a sound like a duck choking on Laffy Taffy.

"Just one date," says Mitchell. "I pick the time and place. And who knows—you may find after one date with me that this Adam Hood guy isn't really your type." He licks his bottom lip. "I have a way with the ladies."

Blech. I lean back in the chair and look at the ceiling. I cannot believe that I am even considering his offer. Really? Do I want that badly to become an Adam Hood stalker? I would counter with the suggestion of an early morning latte in the commons, but then Mitch and I would be seen together in public, a popularity quotient demolisher if ever there was one. And worse? What if Adam saw us together and thought I was already dating someone?

"How about lunch over Christmas break?" I offer.

Mitch stands firm. "A place and time of my choosing."

Perhaps someday, when Adam and I are walking hand in hand along a beach, the fresh flower that he just picked for me tucked behind my ear, I'll admit to the lengths I went through for him, and he'll love me even more for it. "Okay. It's a date."

Mitchell's face lights up. He pulls out a cell phone. "Phone number?"

"E-mail address," I counter.

He shoots out a hand and we shake. I recite my e-mail address and he adds me to his contact list. He hums the tune "We're in the Money" as he taps on the computer keys to bring up Adam's schedule, which I jot down in my planner.

"Well, good-bye." I stand to leave.

"Not good-bye," says Mitchell with a sly smile. "See you later. And remember, I pick the time. I pick the place." He points at me with his thumb and forefinger cocked like a pistol.

Oh, Adam. I hope you come to appreciate this.

As I hurry toward the guidance counselor's office I run through the facts to consider possible flaws in my game plan.

Fact: I dumbed down my schedule in the first place because I didn't want Chelsey or any of the other Monarchs to think I was some cheerleading poser—a smarty-pants who actually belonged at the loser table.

Fact: Switching into Adam's classes completely messes with that original plan.

Think, Nora. Think! I close my eyes, grind my mental gears and *thunk!* I've got it. I'll blame Mom. I'll tell people she's forcing me to switch to higher level classes. People will pity me, but in a good way.

I arrive to find Ms. Ostweiler busy with another student, so I take a seat outside her office on a square leather ottoman. I fish around in my book bag and am surprised to come up with the book Dad sent for my birthday. Joshie shoved it in there with a Post-it note on the cover:

Read this and you will get smart at chess.

The little turd.

With a few minutes to kill, I flip through the book and come to a page where Dad has shoved an MIT bookmark. Now I see why he sent this particular book. It's not just instructions about how to play chess. It's filled with chess anecdotes and history. And here, on page 178, a reprint of Benjamin Franklin's essay "On the Morals of Chess." Of course—the perfect accompaniment to the Revolutionary War chess set that Dad and I played on a million times. No, a zillion. Highlighted is the quote that Dad copied into my birthday card, the one in which Ben Franklin basically says that there are all kinds of parallels between chess and life. I skim down a couple of paragraphs:

The game of Chess is not merely an idle amusement. Several very valuable qualities of the mind, useful in the course of human life, are to be acquired or strengthened by it, so as to become habits, ready on all occasions.

He goes on to talk about three qualities of the mind. First, there's *foresight*—basically looking into the future and paying attention to the consequences of a planned move.

Franklin's second quality is *circumspection*—taking care to look at all circumstances and their possible outcomes.

And finally, *caution*—notmaking moves too hastily.

I consider the move I am about to make, switching into Adam's classes. Foresight? Circumspection? Caution?

I snap closed the book. All I'm doing is switching into the classes I should have been in in the first place. What could go wrong?

Finally it's my turn to see Ms. Ostweiler. She's at her desk sipping coffee from a mug that pictures a shaggy dog and the phrase, "Does the name PAVLOV ring a bell?"

"Aren't you supposed to be in class?" she asks.

"Well, yes, but my classes are what I'm here to talk about."

Once again I choose the nothing-but-business chair. "I'm sort of thinking about tweaking my schedule. Maybe I should switch back into precalculus and the AP classes I was originally supposed to take. And add AP US History."

She blows steam off her coffee and takes a sip. "Why the sudden change?"

"You were right. The classes I switched into are way too easy. And I should be working up to my potential, right?"

She holds her chin and taps her upper lip. "You seemed pretty certain that you wanted to take it a little bit easier this year. And now in addition to the classes you would have been taking, you want to add AP US History? That's a pretty heavy load."

I pick up a pair of magnets sitting on her desk and pull them apart. Snap them together. Pull them apart. Snap them together. She's right. AP US History will be awful. I am total crap at memorizing dates and names. But the only way I stand a chance with Adam is by being in his classes.

"I think I can handle it. These are the sections I want to get into." I reach into my book bag and open my planner to the notes I made in Mitch's office.

Ms. Ostweiler taps on her computer keys and talks to me with her eyes focused on the screen. "The AP classes move at quite a clip and you've missed a full week. It'll take some work to catch up."

"I'll be fine."

After a few clicks of her mouse, Ms. Ostweiler shows me what the new schedule would look like. While I can't have everything I want at the time I want it, Adam and I will have two classes together, AP biology and AP US History. In AP bio he'll be amazed by my scientific dexterity as I dazzle him with dissections. In AP US History—well, that will take a little bit more work. But I can do it!

GO! (clap, clap) NORA!
FIGHT! (clap, clap) NORA!
WIN! (clap, clap) NORA!
GO, FIGHT, WIN! (touchdown stance)

Eight

MOM IS DELIRIOUS ABOUT THE schedule change and tapes the printout from Ms. Ostweiler on the fridge.

> Period 1—AP Biology
> Period 2—Precalculus
> Period 3—Honors English
> Period 4—AP US History
> Period 5—PE
> Period 6—AP French

She runs her finger down the list of classes. "AP US History," she says, shaking her head. "That's a little surprising. You've never liked history much."

Never liked? More like hated. Whatever. "I'll be fine. I downloaded a syllabus and picked up the books. I figure I can use the weekend to catch up with what I've missed."

Mom pours us each a glass of lemonade and we clink glasses. "I'm so proud of you," she says. "Janis Joplin, who was such an independent, free-spirited woman, said, 'Don't compromise yourself. You're all you've got.' And with this schedule change, you are absolutely living up to your capabilities. Maybe cheerleading wasn't such a bad idea after all."

I smile, then guzzle some lemonade. I have Janis Joplin's album *Pearl* on my iPod. I know she also said, "You've got to get it while you can." And the way to get Adam is to rock some AP classes before his very eyes.

Nora!
Rocks those classes!
Kicks AP tests
In their asses!
(fast patter of hands on thighs) Goooooo, NORA! (T
stance)

The weekend flies by with barely a moment to crack open a book. There's the game Saturday against the Lions (VICTORY!), where the Teapot, Tallulah and a bunch of other drama people are dressed like gay Las Vegas lion tamers. Adam is not there, and I enjoy a full two hours of not obsessively overanalyzing, wondering whether he is, at this very minute, being fondled by Tallulah. There's a party at Gillian's house Saturday night where Jake insists I be his partner in a game of Twister against Krista and Dex.

No no, Jake. *Left* foot blue.

Then, on Sunday, it's six hours at the PCC parking lot washing cars to raise money for the cheer competition next spring.

Come Monday morning I am completely unprepared for my classes. I am also unprepared for the looming conversation with Krista. I had at least a thousand opportunities this weekend to tell her about my schedule changes, but kept chickening out. First, she would find my reasoning insane. While she has come around a little bit on Adam's position on the hottie scale, she's still convinced that I should be hooking up with Jake. Second, it means that we will no longer be in the same French class—the only class Krista and I had together. And finally, there is the fact that I have never come clean with Krista about my former life as a larva, and I fear that any discussion about AP classes might lead us there.

Krista dumps a Splenda into her latte and stirs. "I didn't read my chapters for French," she says. "Fill me in, in case Monsieur Tervuren calls on me."

Here we go. "Wow, I can't believe I forgot to tell you." I smack my forehead with the palm of my hand. "I switched to a different French class."

"What?" Krista's eyes go wide. "It was the only class we had together, you traitor. Why'd you switch?"

"Um, I needed to take AP biology. I had to switch some other things around to get it."

"AP biology? That's nuts. Don't you need to be a junior or a senior or something to take that class? And don't you need to take normal biology first?"

I nod. "I know. It stinks. It's all because of my mom. She's making me take it. She hasn't given up on me going to some top-notch school like Phil did." I practiced that line all the way to school, and fear that's exactly how it sounds.

Krista wilts. She strokes my wrist and looks at me like I'm an injured kitten. "You poor baby! That'll be really hard. Your mom really needs to get that you can make your own choices."

Oh, the irony.

When the bell rings, Krista calls after me, "Meet me by the doors at lunchtime. I want to make sure you're okay."

I am such a rat. And in true rat form, I totally forget what a rat I am as I walk into AP biology and spot Adam in the third row, all the way across the room. He's immersed in a book—it's another chess book. He moves his finger through the air up, then at a diagonal. Mental chess. I've seen it before when Dad worked out moves while driving—never a good idea.

Adam's fresh-from-the-shower hair lies flat on his head and I can tell that even without hair he would be hot, in a bald-guy way. As he studies the book he nods, slowly, a pencil clamped between his teeth. I want him to study me the way he studies that book.

"Well, look who's here." Coach Avery, who teaches AP biology when he isn't out on the football field, greets me as I enter the classroom. He hardly looks like himself without the Cutthroats cap, and wearing a white lab coat that hangs just below his knees. While I'm sure he's got on shorts underneath it, the look—lab coat, bare legs and sneakers without socks—is slightly creepy. "I hardly recognized you without your pom-poms," he says. "What can I do for you?"

I hand him the slip of paper Ms. Ostweiler gave me and sneak a glance at Adam. "I've transferred into your class."

Adam looks up at the sound of my voice. I feign surprise at seeing him. His surprise, on the other hand, is genuine. The pencil falls from his mouth and bounces on the floor. He looks behind me, as if checking to see whether I'm alone. I have taken great care to wear a sophisticated, but very cute, A-line skirt and a conservative silk blouse that say, "I am smarter than you think I am."

I waggle my fingers at Adam. His smile is tentative, confused. He scrambles for the fallen pencil. Coach Avery gives me some paperwork to hand back at the end of class, and I make my way toward Adam.

"So, really? You're switching into this class?" he asks, the pencil now tucked behind his ear. A wisp of hair traces the outline of his cheek, the curve of his jaw. The tiniest vestige of whisker stubble is visible above his lip and along the sides of his chin.

I shrug. "I was in regular biology, but you know how it goes, it was a little 'been there, done that.'"

His brow furrows. "Um, sure. Well, I'm glad we have a class together."

He doesn't know the half of it.

"Avery is a good teacher," he continues. "I think you'll like it."

I breathe in his air. "I think I will, too."

His gaze wanders from my eyes to my toes and back again. "That's a really cute, um"—he is basket-of-bunnies adorable when he's flustered!—"a really cute outfit."

He noticed! I smile and am working on a pithy reply when, from out of nowhere the Teapot bounds toward us in a purple tracksuit, and clutching a can of Diet Dr. Pepper.

"Hey, y'all were fantastic at Saturday's game!" She mimics our singsong, two-note battle cry, "Go-oooooo, Cutthroats, Be-eeeat the Lions." She laughs, sending her curls into spasms. She holds her hand out to Adam for a fist bump. He obliges. "Seriously," she drawls, "I know *every* one of y'all's cheers." She downs the soda and tosses the can a good ten yards into the recycle bin. Nothing but net. "I noticed that *you* were not at the game." She scolds Adam with a finger wag. "Where's your school spirit, young man?"

Adam offers no explanation.

Crowd avoidance?

Dumb cheerleader avoidance?

The bell rings. Coach Avery blows his whistle. "People, find your seats."

All of the desks anywhere near Adam are already gone. What did I expect? It's been a week—people have already figured out where they're sitting, and I'll just have to pick through the leftovers. But how can I have intelligent conversations with Adam if I am not even sitting near him? Searching for a seat I notice that, aside from Adam and the Teapot, I don't know anyone in this class except for the third-string kicker from the football team. While I will certainly not revert back to my larval smarty-pants self, I can safely raise my hand from time to time and answer questions when called on, and my PQ will take virtually no hits. Instead, I will impress upon Adam that Nora Fulbright is in the game.

I grab a seat a few rows from the back. Inches away, on the shiny black section of countertop that juts out and serves as a lab table, a large white rodent sits on its haunches in a glass tank, nibbling a chunk of carrot. The rat stares at me with pensive pink eyes. I scooch my chair a few inches away. I love biology. I tolerate insects. I am not big on rodents or reptiles.

"Let's get settled in please." Coach Avery moves front and center. PeopleE pull laptop computers or spiral notebooks out of their backpacks. I open my notebook to a blank page and glance around at the classroom décor. Hanging from the ceiling, a construction paper DNA strand runs all the way around the room. Up at the front there's a trough-sized sink with three faucets, two soap dispensers, and instructions in five languages about how to wash your hands. Posters presumably made by last year's students hang on the walls: MAN'S EFFECT ON WATER QUALITY; PLANT SURVIVAL IN DIFFERENT BIOMES; and TAP WATER: SAFE OR SERIAL KILLER? The ceiling crawls with smoke detectors.

"We have a new student," announces the coach. "Nora can cheer us up if class gets a little too boring." The class is split between amused chuckles and groans. "Check my website for assignments. There's a lot of reading you've already missed. Speaking of reading, any questions from last night's assignment?"

He responds to a couple of quick questions, then wanders to the window and looks out at the football field. He turns to face us, rubbing his hands together like he's trying to make fire. "Okay, I got it. Let's put this play into action. So. The quarterback is standing at the ten-yard line poised to throw the ball to his wide receiver." He draws back his arm, holding an imaginary football. "As he releases the ball"—Coach pauses for dramatic effect—"he farts."

Someone in the back row provides a sound effect. Coach Avery ignores him and goes on. "Within a few seconds, the center, who is closest to the quarterback, smells the distinct odor of methane."

Coach then makes eye contact with me. I have no idea where this is going but have the distinct feeling I'm not going to like it.

"Moments later, Miss Fulbright, who is several yards away—"

"Falls off her pedestal!" someone shouts from the back of the room.

"Nice underpants," yells another guy. The class erupts in laughter. So much for Krista's argument that no one would remember my fall at that first game.

Coach Avery winces and throws me an apologetic look. "All right, all right. Enough of that. Like I was saying. The quarterback farts, the center smells it immediately, and several seconds later cheerleaders on the sidelines plug their noses. Class, what biological principle is at work here?"

There is a rapid-fire exchange of remarks.

"Quarterbacks shouldn't eat beans before a football game," calls out a guy I've seen carrying around a sack of fencing gear. I'm pretty sure he's friends with Mitchell.

"Cheerleaders don't like the smell of farts," yells someone else.

"Cheerleaders don't like anything but football players and other cheerleaders," says a girl a couple of rows in front of me. She turns, and flashes me a catlike smile. Meow.

All eyes are on me, and there is so much blood rushing to my face that my eyebrows throb.

Coach Avery holds up a hand, and raises his voice. "Excuse me! This is AP biology. If we can't talk about bodily functions without acting like a bunch of seven-year-olds then we need to rethink whether we're ready for this class."

Hello? I don't think you could use the word *fart* at a retirement home without asking for trouble. What was he thinking? And why bring me into it?

He repeats his original question. "What biological principle is at work?"

I go right into my head. What I need to do is call out the right answer, defuse the situation, and immediately establish mental dominance, but I'm too flustered to think straight. I know that I know this. Think, Nora! While I didn't get a chance to study this weekend, I read the entire book over the summer and this was in there. A correct answer will defuse the situation and get me started on the right foot to show Adam that I am an AP kind of girl.

A girl in the front row raises her hand, and simultaneously calls out the answer. "Ooh! Ooh! Diffusion."

That larva beat me to it!

Coach thanks her and goes on to describe diffusion as the natural movement of molecules from places where they're in higher concentration to places where they're less concentrated. Diffusion, he explains, can take place through solids, in liquids, and of course, in gases, e.g., farts. He moves from diffusion into an overview of osmosis. While I'm already familiar with the terms and the concepts, he takes it to a level of detail, and talks so fast, that pretty soon I'm scrambling to take notes.

Before I know it twenty minutes have flown by and Coach has us call off numbers one through eight, asking us to sit at lab tables with the people who share our number. Wait, they've not yet assigned lab tables? Crap! What are the chances Adam and I will have the same number? Well, duh, one in eight.

"Six," says Adam.

I am almost done racing through the numbers to figure out whether we'll be in the same group when the guy next to me says, "Seven."

I let out a defeated sigh. "Eight."

With thirty-one people in the class, and me being an eight, I wind up at a table with just three people, and, yes, one of them is the girl with whiskers and claws and an abysmal opinion of cheerleaders. We hardly speak as we set up an experiment with beakers, plastic bags, and liquids with higher and lower concentrations of solutions.

Adam sits at a table of four. The Teapot is across the table from him. They're with a girl who just might be an albino, and the fencer. If I can't sit beside Adam in class I at least want to be at his lab table. That's where all the conversation happens. I want long lab hours debating the finer points of enzyme catalysis. I want to sit side by side and explore mitosis and meiosis.

Cat Woman pretty much runs our lab, talking over everything I try to say. She makes a few more snotty comments:

"Here, you'd better let me pour that. You don't want to mess up your nails."

and

"I guess you probably thought AP stood for Advanced Popularity."

Meanwhile, the guy we're paired up with may as well not have a tongue for all he contributes to the conversation. I have got to find a way to switch tables. I look over at Adam's group and begin to formulate a plan.

By the time the bell rings my plan is fully evolved. People jump from their seats and race for the door. Adam, who is instantly flanked by a couple of girls, seeks me out with his eyes and waves before leaving.

I hurry to the coach's desk, drop off my paperwork, then sidle up to the fencer. "Hey, got a minute?"

He looks around to see who my question was intended for, then points to himself, "Me?" His hands are bladelike—unusually long and thin. If he's ever unarmed during a fencing match he'll still do fine.

"Yes, you." I smile and nod.

He brushes his bangs off to the side. "Um, okay."

The classroom is empty except for Coach Avery who appears to be giving a pep talk to the rat. I keep my voice low.

"I'm having a really hard time at my lab table and I was wondering if maybe you would switch groups with me."

His eyes narrow. "What kind of hard time?"

I've got it all worked out. "Well, the guy at my table is really quiet, but I get the distinct feeling he's crushing on me, and it makes it really hard for me to focus. He's totally not my type, and I don't want to hurt him, you know?"

It's Swordhands's chance to be chivalrous. My knight in shining armor. He's a fencer, for crying out loud—they eat that stuff up, right?

Swordhands looks over at my lab group's empty table.

"You mean Frank?"

I nod. "I think that was his name." In fact, I know that was his name. It was the one word he uttered during the entire lab, in response to my question, "What's your name?"

Swordhands leans in. His breath reeks of coffee. "Frank is the president of the Gay and Lesbian Alliance. He brought a *guy* to the sophomore dance last year."

Inwardly, I wince.

Swordhands slices his hands into his front pockets. "What's really going on?"

I glance over at Coach Avery who's carried the rat to the back of the room where I notice, for the first time, another tank. This one contains a snake that could make a snack out of Copernicus. Swordhands waits for an answer.

"Okay. The truth. I don't think Sherrie (aka Cat Woman) likes me."

"Sherrie is a bitch," he says. "She doesn't like anyone. Everyone knows it. And I don't want to work with her any more than you do. Look, I've gotta go."

"Wait!" I grab Swordhands's shirt. "I just, I really want to sit at that table."

A slow smile spreads over his face. "Ah! I get it. You want to sit with Adam."

A twinge of paralysis creeps into my cheeks. "Um."

"You're so full of crap," he says. "Mitch is a friend of mine. He told me about how he showed you Adam's schedule. And about your date. So. How badly do you want to sit with Adam?"

Really? A date with Swordhands, too? I believe the word my mother would use is *trollop*. "Okay. I'll go out with you. But just once. Someplace public, preferably far away from here."

Swordhands laughs. "Get over yourself. No offense, but I don't want to go out with you."

I hear a scraping sound, and turn. Coach has removed the lid from the snake's cage and is dangling the rat into the tank by its tail. My stomach lurches.

"I want a date with Chelsey," says Swordhands. "Make that happen and I'll swap tables with you."

The cheek paralysis spreads to my lips. It takes a moment to make them work.

"Chelsey? Head cheerleader, Chelsey?"

He nods. "Yep."

He's a fencer, but I was not counting on this mental parrying. There is no way I can make that swap happen. But if I don't, then the swap with Mitch will have been completely pointless.

"I don't see how I could—"

He throws up his hands. "All right. Never mind."

I have to let this go. I can't get Chelsea involved in this craziness. But on their own, my hands reach out and grab him before he turns to leave. Have I no shame? "Okay! I can make it happen."

"Really?" he asks me.

Really? I ask myself the same question.

"How are you going to pull it off?" he asks.

I have no idea. I swallow before answering. "Chelsey and I are really good friends. I know she'll help me out."

He's impressed. "I figured there was no way. I mean, I thought she had a boyfriend."

Boyfriend, as in the starting quarterback. "I think they're having some trouble." Which is true—trouble tearing away from each other during long between-class lip-locks.

"Okay," he says, with a distinct note of skepticism in his

voice. "You're on. But I want a written contract."

The bell rings.

A written contract?

"Don't you kids have another class to get to?" asks the coach, still back by the snake tank. All at once the boa flings itself at the rat, then coils around it.

"We were just leaving," says Swordhands. I grab his hand and shake it.

"You're on," I say. And as I turn to leave I hear a muffled squeal from the snake tank.

"Ain't easy being a rat," says Coach Avery.

He's got that right.

Nine

AT LUNCHTIME, PEOPLE FLOOD in and out of the commons as I wait for Krista near the double doors. Not that I could eat anything. Thoughts of rat—broiled, fried, or swallowed whole—keep me from feeling hungry. And as much as I want to see Krista, it gnaws on me that I lied to her and made my mom sound like a bitch.

I text Krista. No reply. I wait five seconds and try again. Nothing. Meanwhile, Chelsey sashays by, arm in arm with her boyfriend. "We'll save you a spot at the table," she calls over her shoulder.

"Thanks." What I could possibly do to make it worth her

while to go out with Swordhands?

"Hey Nora!" Jake's voice booms as he makes his way into the commons. His entourage of ninth- and tenth-grade girls shoot me dirty looks.

"See you at the table?" he asks.

I give him a quiet thumbs-up.

He replies with a double thumbs-up, the tips of his index fingers touching to form a goal post. "Field goal!"

His entourage giggles.

"Nora!" Krista navigates the crowd at high speed like it's a human obstacle course. She reaches me with her hand hidden behind her back and her cheeks flushed. "I was worried I'd miss you. There was a huge line at the school store." She pulls her hand from behind her back with a flourish and hands me a giant bag of Skittles. "All morning I've been thinking about how awful it must be for you being forced to take such a hard class."

I try to hand her back the candy. "You really shouldn't have."

Really!

"What are friends for? Come on. Let's grab lunch. Dex told me Jake was hoping to catch up with you."

"Yeah, I just saw him."

As we head to our table I spot Adam in the sandwich line where the Teapot is laughing as Tallulah, in cowboy boots and supremely short shorts, playfully lassoes Adam with her long, ropelike braid. Where's a red-hot branding iron when you need one?

When we reach our table, Jake is already there. I slide into a seat across from him, and Krista slips in beside me. I open my tub of yogurt, then push it away. How am I going to pull off the swap with Swordhands? I can't eat. I can't look

Chelsey in the eye.

Krista whispers, "You okay?"

I nod. I am a liar. A rat. A snake.

Chelsey dominates the conversation, griping relentlessly about her *Hamlet* paper. "I wanted to write about how different it would have been if they'd just given Hamlet Prozac, but Mr. Pawlosky was totally not into it."

Jake lightens things up with some jokes that are pretty funny despite the fact that they're like the ones you'd find printed on a Popsicle stick. He tries a couple of times to lean in for a one-on-one conversation with me, but each time we're interrupted. First by Chelsey who moves on from *Hamlet* to discuss the party she's hosting after homecoming. Then Gillian goes on and on about how she'll wear her hair. Becca and Jazmine pull out their phones and have a show-and-tell with pictures of the dresses they're considering.

Homecoming. It's less than a month away. Last year, Krista went with Dex, and I went with a bunch of JV gymnastics girls. We danced in a group. We drank countless cups of punch. And we watched the Riverbend High glitterati flit across the dance floor. Even as juniors, Chelsey and her fellow Monarchs ruled the day. This year I want to be right there with them. Me and Adam. I will be dazzling in a dress that says, "I want you more than you could ever know," and Adam will be heart-wrenchingly gorgeous in his tux. We'll have our pictures taken beside the ice sculpture of a trout in a football helmet. The DJ will spin something slow and tender. Adam will cup my chin in his hand. Our eyes will meet and he will see the depth of my yearning.

"I've been waiting a long time for this," he'll say. He'll pull me in close. His breath, sweet and warm, will mingle with mine as there, beneath the disco ball, we share our very first kiss. The first of many.

I sigh, and smile dreamily at dust motes dancing in the air above my untouched yogurt. Something touches my foot. My eyes jerk into focus on Jake, who is across from the table absorbing my smile like there is weight to it. Oh my god. He thinks my smile was for him! Again, his foot caresses mine. His foot caresses *MINE*! He reaches across the table and, before I get what is happening, takes my small hand in his giant one. God, is it true that that there is a correlation between the size of a guy's hands and his—?

"There's something I want to talk to you about," he says.

Oh, crap! I freeze.

"It's about homecoming," he says.

Oh. Bigger pile of crap!

Krista, despite the fact that she is turned away from me, fully engaged in a conversation with Becca, elbows me in the ribs. Meanwhile, Gillian puts the finishing touches on a hairstyle she's testing out on Chelsey that involves braids and gel. Chelsey opens a makeup case and admires Gillian's handiwork. "Yup," she says. "This will be a homecoming we'll never forget."

I try to swallow, but my throat has gone on strike. Nora, what is wrong with you? Going to the homecoming dance with Jake Londgren would have been a dream come true last year. Hell, it would have been a dream come true a little over a week ago.

Despite the noise and activity, there is no way anyone can miss the hands comingling in the middle of the table.

Brrriiing! I am literally saved by the bell.

"I'm so sorry, but I really need to get to class." I tug my hand away and scramble from the table like it's a capsized boat and I must swim to shore before the sharks smell blood.

"Um, sure." Jake's left bicep bulges as pushes himself to standing.

Oh, if only he had blatant dandruff or an oozy eye infection. It would be so much easier to reject him!

"Later?" he says.

I give him a panicked smile and run.

"What's the rush!" Krista chases after me. "Did you see that? Jake Londgren was holding your hand!"

I stop and face her. "Did I *see* it? Uh, yeah. It was pretty hard to miss—seeing how it was *my* hand he was holding. Look, I've really got to go. I need to find a seat in my new history class."

"This is going to be the best homecoming ever!" Krista calls after me.

AP US History. What was Adam thinking? What was *I* thinking? Numbers and scientific theories are my friends. We can chat for hours. In binary. But memorizing names and dates? What do I even remember from other history classes? As I jog down the hall I move imaginary pom-poms through the air:

Columbus sailed the ocean blue
In fourteen hundred and ninety-two
That's all I know from history class
This AP stuff will kick my ass

The classroom is still half empty when I arrive. The teacher isn't even here. I drop the transfer slip from Ms. Ostweiler onto Ms. Harrington's desk and scan the room. People areeither looking at their notes or talking to the person next to them. In the front row, one girl explains to another some details about a worksheet.

Where will Adam sit? Are seats assigned? Even if they're not, after a week of classes everyone has most likely slipped into a routine of sitting in the same place. I hover close to the sidewall pretending to study a Bill of Rights poster, but subtly watch as people file into the classroom. When Adam sits down, I'll zoom to the closest empty desk. Beside him, behind him, even in front of him will do. I just want to be close enough for random moments of idle chitchat. Maybe we'll build up to note passing. Maybe someone will try to kick me out of "their" desk when I sit. Maybe Adam will tell them to get lost.

Chairs fill up. I move from the Bill of Rights to a series of world maps where the country sizes are adjusted to show income, population, and age of death. I saunter past a cheesy poster dotted with photographs. It's a Periodic Table of the Loved and Admired, which is conveniently hung beside the Periodic Table of Dictators, Despots, and the Despised.

Finally, Adam arrives. As he enters the classroom, a girl just ahead of him drops her planner. Adam stoops to pick it up, taps her shoulder, and returns it. She gushes about how sweet he is. It's a planner, for crying out loud! It's not like he picked up her nasty, soiled handkerchief. And it's not like she didn't drop it on purpose. In response to her over-the-top praise, Adam swivels his chin in an it-was-nothing gesture. She grins like a baboon and wrinkles her nose at him. I roll up my sleeves—the competition in here is going to be fierce.

I wish Adam would just sit down! Instead, he stops and says something to the girls still hovering over a worksheet in the front row. The three of them laugh.

Come on, Adam, find a seat! The bell is about to ring, a final wave of people will rush in and there will be no chance of our sitting near each other. In the front row, one of the girls slides out of her desk, motions to it with her hand, and Adam settles in. What the huh? The girl sitting to Adam's right flips her perfectly highlighted hair, allowing it to cascade halfway down her back.

I want her seat! I want her hair!

Okay, Nora. Move into action. Highlights is to Adam's right. Some nondescript guy is to his left. The seat behind him is free. I move toward it. But then I notice that the flirt who just gave Adam her chair rifles through papers on the teacher's desk like she owns the place. She's alarmingly cute. Pointy chin. Bobbed blond hair. Excellent clothes. She picks up my transfer slip and shoves it to the other side of the desk. My transfer slip! Who does she think she is?

"Excuse me." I wave my arm. "Please don't mess with that—it's for the teacher."

The classroom sounds like a laugh track for a lame sitcom. People turn to see who made the hilarious joke—I am the only one who doesn't get it. Adam's eyes connect with mine and he stops laughing. It's a toss-up as to which of us looks more confused.

The girl at the teacher's desk smiles and glances at the transfer slip. "Nora Fulbright?"

I cross my arms. "Yes." I flash her a wanna-make-something-of-it look.

"Kathleen Harrington," she says. As in Ms. Harrington. As in the teacher. Oh, US historical crap! She must have gone to college when she was thirteen! "Come on up and I'll let's find you a place to sit," she says.

I join her at her desk. The bell rings. "Everyone, go ahead and pull out the worksheet you did over the weekend," says Ms. Harrington. "I'll just be a minute." She pulls out a chart with rows and columns, lines and arrows, crisp lettering.

There is a perfect little square labeled "Adam Hood."

"It's a pretty full class," says Ms. Harrington. I look back at the classroom, avoiding Adam's gaze, and notice the desk right behind him is still empty. I point it out.

"No, that seat is assigned, but the student who sits there is absent today." She taps one of just two empty boxes on her seating chart. Both of them are in the last row, about as far from Adam as I could possibly be. What to do, what to do! I scratch my left foot with my right.

"I'm not sure what I should do," I say. "I have a really hard time seeing things unless I'm in the first couple of rows. How about if I sit there for today, and then tomorrow we can ask"—I peek at the seating chart—"we can ask Zeke Shinebock if he'd mind moving."

"Hmmm." She scans the classroom. "Class? Nora needs to be close to the front. Could I impose on someone in the first few rows to switch to the back of the room?"

It is a test of will to keep from rolling my eyes. Sure, I might get into the second row, but what if I'm all the way at the other side of the room? I look beseechingly at Highlights.

In the end, it is Adam, of course, who leaps to his feet. "You can sit here, Nora."

"Thanks." I groan under my breath—the sound of a plan backfiring.

"No problem," he says, as he shuffles his papers into his courier bag. He smiles at me like he has just offered me his spot in a lifeboat. We pass close to each other as I make my way to his seat, and he heads to the back of the classroom. "How crazy that you're in *two* of my classes," he says, shaking his head. "What are the odds, right?"

"Yeah. Crazy." I cannot believe I am going on a date with Mitch for this. I plop into the chair that is still warm from Adam's body, and that thought, his body heat warming mine, makes a lopsided wave roll through my abdomen. I reach into my bag for a notebook and see that I am still carrying around Dad's chess book, with the bookmark poking out at Ben Franklin's "On the Morals of Chess." So much for foresight, circumspection, and caution.

Ms. Harrington suggests I get notes from another student for the days I missed, and gives me until Thursday to complete the worksheet the rest of the class is handing in today. Settled in, I glance around the classroom. Geoff, the mascot, sees me and waves. He's a pretty sweet guy. He practices with the cheerleaders once a week and he's like everybody's favorite teddy bear. He's wearing his home jersey from last year, from before he got injured and switched to a fish suit instead of shoulder pads. I was so fixated on sitting with Adam I didn't notice him. Or that he's sitting with a couple of the Cabbage Whites. Vanessa smiles. Simone nods. I nod back.

Huh. So Vanessa and I are not the only cheerleaders taking AP classes. But Vanessa is the only cheerleader Chelsey makes life difficult for. So it's not just about the fact that Vanessa takes AP classes—it's that she takes AP classes *and* she's a lame cheerleader.

Wow. Has it really taken me this long to figure that out? I make a mental note to suggest to Vanessa that she blame her mother.

After lecturing, Ms. Harrington says, "All right. Let's chat a little bit about your biography projects." There is a bowl on the table behind her desk filled with names of characters from early American history. Each of us is to pick one. For the next three weeks we're to learn everything about that character and prepare a presentation that accurately demonstrates that character's attitudes, attributes, and interests. Then we'll have debates in which we'll dress as our characters and argue everything from abortion to zoology as though we really were that person.

She points out a row of biographies and autobiographies lined up on a shelf by the door. "After you choose your character you're welcome to take one of these books, or visit the library to find source material to get you started."

Someone complains about having to choose a character from the bowl. Ms. Harrington explains that last year she had eleven Thomas Jeffersons, which got a little boring during the debates. She fields a few more questions about the biography project.

Highlights kicks my foot. "He's going to notice if you keep staring at him," she whispers.

"What?"

"Come on, it's obvious. You've totally got it for Adam. I know that's why you wanted to sit up front."

"No. It's because I have a hard time seeing."

She looks at me incredulously. "You seem to have a pretty easy time seeing the back of the classroom."

I squirm in my seat.

"Don't worry, I'm not after him," she says. "I've already got a boyfriend." She takes a quick glance over her shoulder. "I can see why you like him. He nice. He's cute. And *really* smart. I heard a rumor that he already has, like, twenty credits toward medical school and spends his summers dissecting monkey brains searching for a cure for cancer. Did you know he performed CPR on some girl who had a heart attack in the commons?"

Ms. Harrington claps. "Okay, so come on up and pick your biography character."

People race to the bowl at the front of the room. It's like

a piñata has burst and everyone is battling for the best candy. Adam somehow gets there ahead of me. He closes his eyes and fishes around in the bowl. I hurry to get next to him, and when I arrive, he holds out his open hand, with two folded slips of paper.

"I took the liberty of grabbing one for you," he says, with a smile that's pushed a bit off to the side.

I take one from him. "Thanks."

He looks intently at my left eye, and then at my right. "I hate to bring it up, but if you have trouble with your eyes that could explain why you almost ran into that guy in your car. Have you thought about glasses?"

Highlights reaches into the bowl. "Glasses. There's a concept."

"Well, I'm glad I was in the front row so I could give you my seat," Adam says.

I swallow my disappointment.

"Let's see who we picked." Adam unfolds his paper and smiles. Not at me, at the paper, but close enough. "George Washington."

George Washington. I think of the chess pieces sitting on their black and white squares back at the house where the king is a little statue of George Washington. I can *so* picture me as Martha Washington and Adam as George, debating the ethical use of slaves as spies during the Revolutionary War. Wait—at least I think they had spies. Did they have slaves? Or was that just the Civil War? This class is going to kill me.

"Adam, the first man, gets to be George, the first president," I say. "From fig leaf to powdered wig."

He laughs. "Let's see who you got." He moves in closer. I'm acutely aware of the sound of his breath. The warmth of his proximity. The fact that he towers over me, making me feel delicate more than short. I fumble with the paper. Please be Martha Washington. Please be Martha Washington. On the day we do our presentations, I would look so cute in a Martha Washington dress. I unfold the paper. We read the name together. My shoulders sag.

Adam grins. "It's not so bad. Benedict Arnold was a really good guy. Until he messed everything up." Adam's smile is easy and relaxed. I could swear his dimple winks at me. This is why I am so insanely into him—moments like now, when conversation flows and I feel like we are, cliché as it sounds, made for each other. When he sees me as the girl he met that first day, not a ditzy cheerleader. But the moment doesn't last.

Geoff snatches the piece of paper out of my hand. He barks out a laugh. "Nice! You get to be the bad guy. Check it out." He hands me his slip of paper. Geoff will be Martha Washington. Sigh.

"Sweet, huh!" he says.

I force a smile. "Sweet."

He laughs, starts to walk away, then stops. "Oh, by the way," he says. "Jake was looking for you. He wants to ask you something." Then, Geoff turns his back to us, wraps his arms around himself so that his hands grip his own upper back and makes loud face-sucking sounds. "Oh, Jake," he moans, in his best Nora Fulbright voice.

Vanessa and Simone, who have joined us, crack up. Simone, wearing a CHEERLEADING IS MY LIFE T-shirt, squeezes between me and Adam and drapes her arm over my shoulder. Her fingernails still alternate purple and gold from the mani-pedi convention the day before school started. "Isn't Geoff funny?" she exclaims, looking from me to Adam.

My face is on fire.

"Hysterical," says Adam. And with his hands buried deep

in his front pockets, he moves toward the books and away from me and my fellow cheerleaders.

I want to hit Simone! And strangle Geoff. I'm finally having a semi-normal conversation with Adam and they come along to remind him: Nora is a lame-o cheerleader who only hangs out with other lame-o cheerleaders and jocks. Worse, between Jake's thundering on the car roof, his massive presence in the pizza line, and now Geoff's improv Nora/Jake make-out session, Adam probably thinks that I not only hang out with jocks—I'm dumb enough to be in love with one.

My stress attack is interrupted when Ms. Harrington calls out, "It looks like everyone's gotten a name. So, on your own, you'll get to know your characters—their background, their ethics, their morality. Then, in class, we'll work with a partner to come up with a set of debate topics that'll allow your character to really stand up for what he or she believes in. So while you're still out of your seats, take a minute now to choose partners."

Wait, what? It's another mad scramble as people seek out their friends. Vanessa pairs up with Simone. Geoff pairs up with some girl I don't know. I stand on my toes and peer around for Adam. Oh to be tall! Then I see him, over by the globe, talking with Highlights.

"Adam!" someone calls his name. I spin around. It's the girl who dropped her planner. "Partners?" she calls out.

No! Say no! I beg silently as I try to push through to reach him.

"No," he says.

I pull in a hopeful breath.

"I'm already partners with him," says Highlights.

My hopeful breath rushes back out.

Adam's eyes find mine, then look away. He gives the

globe an abrupt spin as a hand clamps down on my shoulder. I turn to see a tall, wafer-thin girl with kinky blond hair. "Partners?" she asks.

Why not. I nod, too flustered to speak.

Later, when school lets out, I'm coming out of the locker room bathroom when I see Highlights with her awesome hair pulled into a ponytail. She's sitting on a bench lacing up a pair of cleats. I walk right up to her and strike a Wonder Woman stance, my hands planted on my hips. "That was pretty crappy of you."

She looks up from her laces. "What?"

I check to see if the coast is clear and lower my voice. "You knew I liked him, but you sleazed right in and got him to be your partner!"

"Excuse me? I 'sleazed in'?"

"You already have a boyfriend!"

"Get over it, Nora. It's not like I asked him to crawl under the teacher's desk and have sex with me. I asked him to be my partner in the biography project. Like I told you, he's really smart, and I want to get a good grade. And, you know, you could have asked him to be your partner, but as I recall, when Harrington told us to find partners, you were busy blabbing with your cheer buddies and watching Geoff make out with himself."

I open my mouth to say something, but words fail me.

Highlights slips a shin pad into her sock. "So who did you wind up with?"

"Jolene," I spit.

Highlight's eyebrows arch. "You could have done a whole lot worse. Jolene is great. She's a history freak, and she's very laid back—really easy to work with."

She stands, shoving me aside as she piles things into her

locker and slams it shut.

"If Jolene is so great to work with then you work with her. Let's do a swap—I get Adam, you get Jolene. It would really mean a lot to me. Please?"

She raises her arms over her head, tugging first one wrist, then the other, watching me as she stretches. "Why should I?"

I am embarrassed to find myself blurting one of Mom's standard quotes, something said by Madeleine K. Albright, the first female secretary of state. "There is a special place in hell for women who do not help other women."

Highlights purses her lips. The locker room is filling up with girls from the soccer team and the volleyball team, and it sounds like Becca and Jazmine are yodeling in the bathroom stalls. A couple of Highlight's friends stop by. She tells them she'll meet them on the field. She watches them walk away.

"Okay, look. There's something you could do for me," she says, in a super-low voice. "Phil Fulbright is your brother, right?"

It takes me a second to respond. "Yeah. How do you know Phil?"

She smirks. "He was my counselor at math camp two summers ago. He's about the smartest guy I've ever met."

"Yep—that's my brother."

"He brought in a paper for us to read—the one he'd just won a mathematics scholarship with. Do you know it?"

Phil's paper, "The Improbable Probability of Using Mathematics to Solve Social Issues"—how could I forget it? My mother required that the entire family listen while Phil read it aloud—all forty-eight pages. I'm surprised she didn't have the thing bronzed.

Highlights motions for me to move in close. "I'm entering the contest this year. I'd love to get a copy of that paper. It's not like I'd steal any of it—I mean my topic will be something totally different. I'm not into plagiarism, but I'd like to look at how he structured it, and what level of detail he covered."

Phil wouldn't approve. Neither would Mom. And where would I find a copy of it, anyway?

"I'm sorry. I can't do that."

She shrugs. "Oh, well. Have fun with Jolene." She turns to leave.

How uncool would it be to share one of Phil's papers? What if I got caught? And even if I was willing to do this—where would I find it? How unfair that my brother, Mr. Computer-for-a-Brain, has something Highlights wants. Something I can't get.

Or can I? A lightbulb, halogen bright, goes off over my head.

"Hang on!" I chase after her. Mr. Computer-for-a-Brain will almost certainly have a copy of the paper on the computer he willed to Joshie when he left for Harvard. He'd made Joshie cross his heart and swear not to use Phil's AP English paper on the Brontë sisters to bump up his kindergarten GPA. But he never made *me* promise not to touch his work.

"Okay. I think I can get it. But you swear you won't copy anything?"

She draws a cross over her heart, her finger tracing up to down, then left to right. "I swear."

I offer my hand. She shakes it. "You're on."

She agrees to tell Adam that she'd forgotten she and Jolene had already agreed to work together.

The date with Mitch is looking like a small price to pay for the swaps I've set up so far. I've just got to find a way to get Chelsey to agree to a date with Swordhands.

Hah! Of course! A second lightbulb glows beside the first one. There's probably a whole lot more on Phil's computer than just the mathematics paper.

I find Chelsey in the gym, stretching, with one leg up the wall. She reaches for her ankle and presses her cheek to her thigh. Krista is over talking to a flock of Cabbage Whites. She sees me and waves.

"Got a second?" I ask Chelsey.

She smiles. "Sure, what's up?"

"I was thinking about your *Hamlet* paper."

Chelsey grunts. "*Hamlet.* I don't know why they have us read plays that are six hundred years old. I'll bet *somebody* has written another play since then." She sighs. "Maybe Mr. Pawlosky will let me do an interpretive dance instead."

"Don't get your hopes up."

She frowns. "It stinks. I need good grades to get into the University of Louisville. Do you know that they've won fifteen National Cheerleading Association championships?"

"I did not know that."

"But *Hamlet* is going to mess me up," she says. "It's a tragedy."

I pick a thread off Chelsey's tank top. "You know what? I might be able to help you out."

I tell her about Phil's A+ *Hamlet* paper. She desperately wants to see it.

"No problem," I say. "But there's something I need in exchange." And I spin a story I hope Chelsey will buy. "You see, I'm having a hard time in one of my classes, too. If my GPA tanks, I'll get kicked off cheer. Luckily there's a guy who'll help me get my grades up, but he'll only do it if you'll go out with him for a cup of coffee."

Chelsey shakes her head so fast that her ponytail whips around and slaps her in the cheeks. "No. I hate coffee."

"Well, you could have tea. Or juice or something. And how about this—I'll also throw in the *Tempest* paper you're going to need to write in the spring."

Chelsey groans. "Is that *another* Shakespeare thing?"

"Yup."

Chelsey's eyebrows knit together. She chews her thumbnail. "There's no way I'm going to risk losing you on the cheer squad. No way. My boyfriend wouldn't really need to know about the date. I guess I could drink apple juice. And I *do* need help with the *Hamlet* paper." She squints at the ceiling. "Okay. I'll do it."

We agree on the time and the location. All my swaps are in place.

Foresight? Check.

Circumspection? Okay, maybe a check minus.

Caution? What could go wrong?

Ten

JOSHIE'S ROOM LOOKS LIKE It was decorated by a team composed of a first-grade boy, a college math professor, and Charles Darwin. Lifelike prints of tropical birds and squirmy insects decorate the comforter draped on his twin-sized bed. Math gadgets, which he collects the way other kids collect seashells or Pokémon cards, cover his low dresser: a slide rule, a wooden abacus, and calculators of assorted shapes and sizes. The scrawly little-kid artwork on his walls feature a smeary oil-pastel drawing of a cheerleader who looks much like I would had I been birthed by a pair of trolls. The little set of pom-poms I made for Joshie out of paper from Mom's shredder dangle from a hook on the back of his door.

I enter on tiptoes, listening to Joshie and Bill downstairs laughing hysterically. They're spending Joshie's precious one hour of screen time watching some wildly inappropriate animated show they can only see when Mom is out of the house because she cannot tolerate the "flagrant misogyny." I need to work fast because once the show is over he'll be looking for me. He's desperately hoping, now that I have my license, that I'll drive him to Chess Kings, a kids' club that meets Monday nights at the library.

Curse the stupid law that allows me to drive with relatives but not with relatively hot guys!

But there is absolutely no way I'm going to drive him to Chess Kings. Especially because once we get to the library I know he'll insist that I stick around.

I ease closed the door, settle into the little wooden chair at Joshie's kid-sized desk and turn on Phil's computer. Today's math fact pops up on the screen. I click it closed and fire up Word. Moving the mouse, I nearly knock over the tank filled with dead leaves, rotting wood, and bugs. Lots of bugs.

It doesn't take long to locate the files I'm looking for because Phil's computer files are as organized as he is. Once, I needed to borrow a pair of socks because all mine were in the wash. His were sorted by color, within color they were sorted by type, and within type they were sorted by fabric content. What fourteen-year-old boy knows the fabric content of his socks?

I follow the directory path Senior_Year>English>First_Semester>Papers and send the *Hamlet* paper to the printer. Then I find and print the mathematics paper. The printer comes to life with a whir and spits out pages. I rifle through Joshie's desk drawers for a marker and some Post-it notes. I write "Chelsey" on one Post-it and "Highlights" on the other. It's tough work getting Joshie's little frog stapler through the thickness of the pages. I slap the Post-its onto the reports just as the door opens with a slow creak. I spin around. Copernicus greets me with a yawn. I resume breathing and quickly put away the marker and the stapler, but of course, where there is Copernicus, there is Joshie.

"What are you doing in my room?" Joshie points a corn dog at me menacingly.

"Nothing. Just. That's all. Nothing. I thought you were watching TV with Bill?"

"Dad had to get dressed for aikido." He squints at the bug tank. "Were you playing with my insects?"

"No! I just needed to borrow your printer. Mine is out of

ink." I gather the papers into a pile and get up to leave.

"How come you're printing some of Phil's stuff?" Joshie asks.

I stare at Joshie, then at the papers in my hand. How could he possibly know these are Phil's?

"'The Improbable Probability of Using Mathematics to Solve Social Issues' by Phil Fulbright," Joshie reads, and I follow his outstretched corn dog to the computer screen.

Crap on a stick!

"Oh. That. I'm just using some of his old papers to get ideas for something I need to write for school this semester."

Joshie tilts his head. "Chelsey," he says, reading the Post-it note fixed to the pages in my hand.

"Stop that!" I hug the papers to my chest.

"Chelsey is one of the cheerleaders," he says. "I read it on her megaphone."

God! He's like a little Sherlock Holmes!

"Phil said I would get in big trouble if I tried to hand in one of his papers," says Joshie.

"He was teasing. And besides, I'm not handing these in." Which is the truth, right? "It's fine, Joshie."

Joshie strokes an imaginary mustache. "Would Mom think it was fine?"

I don't like where this is going. Beneath that innocent-little-kid demeanor an evil genius is at work. I hesitate. "Mom isn't going to know."

Joshie shifts into a sitting position. He takes a bite of his corn dog. "If you take me to Chess Kings tonight I won't tell Mom."

"I don't want to go to Chess Kings. I have a ton of homework. Why can't Mom take you?"

"Mom has to grade papers. And Dad has aikido."

I cannot believe I am being blackmailed by an almost-seven-year-old. I run through my options.

> Option A: Joshie tells Mom, Mom wants to know why I was printing off Phil's papers, and the swaps with Highlights, Chelsey, and Swordhands are off.
> Option B: Suffer Chess Kings with Joshie.

I try Option C: "How about a trip to Molly Moon's for a hot fudge sundae?"

"Chess."

"How about a trip to the butterfly exhibit at the Pacific Science Center? We could go Saturday after my game."

We both turn toward the window at the sound of a car entering the driveway. Joshie hops off the bed. "I'm going to go say hi to Mom."

I slap the printouts onto the bed, making Copernicus jump. "Okay! Okay! Chess. Fine. But I'll bring a book and hang out in the corner. I am not going to sit there and play chess with a bunch of little kids."

Joshie grins. He holds out the corn dog for Copernicus to take a bite. "You'll like Chess Kings, Nora."

No, I won't.

Bill takes off for aikido. Mom, Joshie, and I eat Thai food leftover from a faculty luncheon in the Women's Studies department today. Mom squeezes a lime wedge into her glass of water and laments the fate of Cherise, the coworker who's leaving to have a baby, and in whose honor we're eating desiccated spring rolls and gluey clumps of pad thai, a food that does not age well. "So that's it," she says, a resigned look on her face. "Cherise has decided that she wants to just stay at home after she has the baby and become a full-time mommy."

By her tone you would think Cherise was staying at home to print counterfeit money, or start a drug cartel. I can't help offering an opinion. "It's her *choice*, Mom. You need to respect that. And besides, she'll probably come back in a few years after she figures out that hanging out with little kids isn't all it's cracked up to be." I shoot Joshie a look. He grins and dips a spring roll in his milk.

Mom jabs her empty fork in our general direction. "I'll tell you this. Cherise is a very bright woman and this stay-at-home-mommy game is one she will soon become bored of."

Joshie scores huge points for a nicely crafted and well-timed interruption. "Speaking of board games, Nora and me are going to Chess Kings at the library."

"Nora and I," says Mom. She plucks a wilted bean sprout out of her noodles but stops before it reaches her mouth. "Really? Nora is going with you to play chess? That's a little surprising."

"I'm not going to play," I explain. "Joshie was desperate to go, and he says he can't go without a grown-up, so in the end I offered to take him."

"Nora says chess is for nerds." Joshie spears a piece of chicken with his fork.

"Don't listen to Nora."

"Yeah, don't listen to me. In fact, you won't even need to talk to me, because I'll be in the back of the room doing my homework."

"Nora has a paper to write," says Joshie. I kick his shin.

"A paper?"

I jump up and clear my plate. "Yup. You know how it goes. School. Papers. So, Joshie, we'd better get going. God knows we don't want to miss a thing."

Joshie sets his plate on the floor for Copernicus to clean,

and we're off.

We arrive at the library about ten minutes before chess club is supposed to start. I wear a baseball cap with my hair tucked beneath to make myself less recognizable, just in case the library is crawling with high school students. Okay, so maybe not all chess players are nerds. Look at Adam. But there is definitely that general association. I think back to how Chelsey recoiled at the notion of a cheerleader joining chess club.

We wander back to the community room with bright orange walls, yellow chairs, and lime-green tables. I enter slowly, ready to run if I spot anyone I know.

"Oh yeah, Nora Fulbright? Sure, I know her. Isn't she the one that hangs out at Chess Kings on Monday nights?"

Nora Fulbright. Nerd Cheerleader. Give me an L! Give me an O! Give me an S-E-R!

In the Chess Kings meeting room, the small, square tables are covered with mats printed to look like chessboards. Chunky black and white plastic chess pieces are piled onto the chessboards. The room is packed with kids. A big guy with his back to us is hunched over a table. Based on the gaggle of kids watching him move pieces around the board I suspect he's the guy running the show. Where are all the parents?

"You told me you couldn't come here without a grown-up," I growl at Joshie.

"I forgot," says Joshie. "But isn't it good that you get to learn chess, too?"

He is exasperating! I do the math. By the time I drive home, then come pick him up, I might as well just stay here and get homework done.

I spot a Costco-sized tub of licorice on the counter. "Go grab me a piece of licorice and then watch what's happening at that table. I'll be right over in the corner, reading."

Joshie tightens his grip on my hand. "I don't know anyone."

For crying out loud. I'm seven chapters behind in history. Four chapters behind in biology. I have six sets of math problems to make up. "Look, it's almost seven o'clock. I'll stay with you until things officially start, then you're on your own."

A couple of more kids file into the room. We're raiding the licorice jar when I hear a familiar voice over by the door. I tug the brim of my hat down low.

"All right, little dude. Call Mom when you're ready to come home." Jake is with a miniature version of himself, but female. The same Jake eyes. The same Jake mouth. Sadly for her, the same Jake build.

"Man, I don't get how you can spend a whole night playing checkers with a bunch of nerds," he says.

"It's chess, you moron." Little Jake-ette scowls and makes a beeline for the table where all the action is taking place.

Jake doesn't see me. I wait until the coast is clear. "Let's sit here," I say, choosing a table at random. We plop into a couple of chairs. A cheer erupts from the busy table and the big guy receives pint-sized high fives all the way around. There's something familiar about that pearlike shape. He turns and I sink deeper into my chair. It's Chubby Stripes, the guy from chess club at school. The striped shirt should have been a dead giveaway. I don't want *anyone* from school to see me here—not even him.

He invites everyone to grab a seat and there's a mad musical-chairs moment as kids scramble for spots at a table, or at the counter that wraps around the room. Chubby Stripes rubs his hands. "Let's dive right in. Where are my helpers?"

Four of the older kids in the room raise their hands. Little Jake-ette is one of them.

"Either myself or one of these guys can help if you get stuck in a game. Ready to go?"

The kids cheer. I look at my knees. I want to slip away to one of the comfy chairs the ring the edge of the room, but moving now would only draw attention.

"Okay. Let's do it." Chubby Stripes moves to a huge felt chessboard taped to a wall. "I see we have lots of new kids here tonight. Is there anyone who has never played chess before?"

Half the kids in the room raise their hands.

"Excellent! So tell you what, before we start playing, let's do a refresher on the basics of play. Who can help me set up the board?"

One of the "helpers," a little girl dressed all in purple, runs to his side and places felt pieces on the board. Chubby Stripes describes how each of the pieces move, their strong and weak points. He explains that white always moves first. That *check* means you're in trouble. *Mate* means there's no way out of it.

Chubby Stripes invites different kids to come up and demonstrate basic openings and responses. I try not to watch. I try to read my book, but I get sucked in, both to the game in general, and to specific games that come rushing back at me. Hour after hour spent playing chess with Dad. Studying not just openings, but entire games played by masters. Dad and me, at the kitchen table, on the living room rug, or in that rickety little tree house he built for us when I was six and Phil was eight—two years before he took off. Dad and me. Me and Dad.

"Are you okay?" Joshie whispers.

"It's the air in here. Stop looking at me and pay attention to the teacher."

I open up my history textbook.

Joshie taps my arm and points to the felt chessboard. "This is cool stuff."

Chubby Stripes has moved from basic setup to basic strategy. He's teaching the kids about castling.

"So if the king and rook have not moved, and if the king is not in check, or passing through check, the rook slides next to the king—" Chubby Stripes moves the pieces into position. I lift the brim of the baseball hat to watch. "The king jumps over the rook, and now he's in a less vulnerable position on the board. When I play chess, I always castle."

No kidding. I remember the first time I castled Phil and he ran to Dad. "Nora cheated!" Dad rubbed my head. "Your little sister could teach you a lot about chess."

"So, anyway, castling is just one of those things that increase your chances of winning," says Chubby Stripes. "Like always looking ahead, always calculating what will happen if you move a particular piece, and always taking your time to think through whether this is really the right move to make."

Foresight, circumspection and caution. He's channeling Ben Franklin!

"Now, a quick refresher about the three steps you always take when you're in check, and then we'll split up and play some games," says Chubby Stripes. "What's the first thing?"

Joshie raises his hand and blurts out, "I ask myself if I can take the attacker."

"Right!" says Chubby Stripes.

I stare at Joshie. He grins smugly and flicks the brim of the baseball hat, which flies off my head.

"Hey!" I grab for the hat—too late. My hair falls around

my shoulders.

Chubby Stripes looks from Joshie to me. There is a flicker of recognition in his eyes.

Across the room Little Jake-ette calls out, "The second thing is I ask myself is whether I can move my king."

"Um, right. Yeah, that's right." Chubby Strips pulls his gaze away from me. "Anyone else? There's one more."

"I see if I can interpose," says a girl whose face is about two-thirds forehead.

"Meaning?" prods Chubby Stripes.

"I see if there's a piece that I can move so it's in the way and can stop the attacker from taking my king."

"Cool," says Chubby Stripes. "So unless anyone has any more questions, let's pair up—"

Interpose Girl raises her hand. "I finished my one hundred."

Chubby Stripes gasps and clutches at his chest. The kids laugh. Joshie laughs. I even laugh. What the hell, my cover is already blown. Chubby Stripes's eyes dart in my direction, then back to the little girl. "Bring them here, Lily."

Lily struts to the front of the room. She's wearing an impossibly cute sundress that would look awesome in an adult size four. She offers Chubby Stripes a packet of pages. He thumbs through them like they're one of those flip books. "Lily has completed all one hundred of the one-move-to-checkmate puzzles. Let's hear it for Lily!"

The kids clap like mad. Chubby Stripes opens a plastic filing box and pulls out a felt chess piece much like the ones he was just maneuvering around the felt chessboard. He pins the piece to Lily's dress. He also removes from the box a packet of papers, which he hands to her. "Now she gets to solve one hundred two-moves-to-checkmate puzzles!"

Again, the kids clap, then split into pairs. Lily invites Joshie to come to her table.

"Go ahead." I shoo him away, pick up my book bag and head for a chair in the corner.

Chubby Stripes blocks my path. "Nora, right? I'm Eric." His eyes narrow. "I think you know my friend Adam."

"Um, yeah, I do. We're in a couple of classes together."

"Adam?" Joshie turns and takes a couple of steps back toward us. "I know Adam. He comes over and plays soccer with me. He's really nice." Then, in a singsong voice, "I think Nora—"

I can see right where Joshie's headed. "Well then! Let's all play some chess!" I give Joshie a gentle push toward Lily's table.

"So you play?" Eric asks.

"She's not any good," Joshie calls back over his shoulder.

Eric laughs and settles into a chair, inviting me with a sweep of his hand to take the seat across from him. Crap. I pretty much just invited him to play, didn't I?

"I'm *really* not very good," I counter. "It's been a long, long time."

"It's like riding a bike," he says. "Let's see what you've got."

He sets up to play black. How does he know Adam knows me?

"You start," he says.

I struggle to push Adam to the back of my mind and I open with a pawn.

Eric moves. I move. We go back and forth, and Dad's voice plays in my head:

Control the center of the board!

Develop your knights before your bishops!

Castle early! The king's safety is crucial.

Fifteen minutes pass. Twenty. It's like Dad is sitting on my shoulder, and the weight of him is oppressive. Sweat trickles down the small of my back. We play slowly, methodically. A crowd of kids gather to watch. The clock on the wall is one of those obnoxious ones that seem to actually be ticking inside your head.

Tick! Move already! *Tick!* What's your problem? *Tick!*

No, no! Advancing too many pawns will weaken your defense.

Tick! Tick! Tick!

"I can't do this!" I jump up, knocking my chair to the floor. "Sorry. I just—I don't play chess anymore."

"But you were doing great," says Eric. His eyebrows shoot up. "Really great."

At that moment I'm thankful for the kid across the room that bursts into tears, crying because he's just lost his king. Eric hurries over to him.

My pits are sticky. This is ridiculous, I know. It's just a game. But it's a game with way too much baggage. I loved chess when I was Joshie's age. I was good. Better than good. But that was for me and Dad. Our special thing. And when he left, crazy as it sounds, he took that with him. There is nothing that could ever be important enough to get me playing chess again. Nothing.

The chess continues without me, and when it's time to go I've managed to just about catch up in my history reading. As we file out the door, Eric invites me to come back and try again next week. He offers me a packet of one hundred one-move-to-check-mate puzzles.

"No thanks," I say. "I'm plenty busy, and will continue to be busy well into the foreseeable future. Or longer."

Joshie gladly takes the packet of puzzles and shoves them in my book bag.

"See you around," says Eric.

And before I can reply, he's surrounded by little kids clambering to receive fist bumps and high fives as they say good-bye.

Joshie tugs my hand as we head for the door. "Mom said I could bring home a movie to watch tomorrow night."

"Okay—but choose something fast. I have a lot to do."

We paw through DVDs, and I hear my name. Jake and Jake-ette are right behind us. Crap-ette! I thought he said their mom was picking her up?

There is a tap on my shoulder. I turn and see that Jake has been out for a run. His cheeks are flushed pink. Sweat circles ring his armpits, and as gross as that sounds, he has a way of making sweat look hot.

"How's it going, Nora? I looked for you after practice but you were gone."

"Things are good." I nod toward Joshie. "I brought my brother to chess club."

"Yeah," he nods toward his sister. "Mom sent me to pick up the dwarf."

"Ork!" Jake-ette spits.

He ignores her. "My folks wanted me to stay and play. Chess? Give me a break."

"I know what you mean," I say.

Joshie chimes in. "But, Nora, you were really good at chess when you were little."

I bark out a laugh. "Yup, silly little Nora. Not anymore."

Jake chuckles. "I hear you. Hello? Is this the bus to Nerdville? My folks are, like, 'You should try playing, too. It's great brain activity.' And I'm, like, 'I get all the brain activity I need playing football,' right? Hey—I have a chess joke. There's this guy playing chess in the park with his dog. These people come by and they say, 'Man, that's one smart dog.' And the guy says, 'Not so smart—I'm beating him three games to one.'"

After Joshie and Jake-ette share a little giggle fit, she pulls him aside to rifle through her little purse for the felt chess pieces she's earned. As they focus on her purse, Jake steps in close. Pale streaks of dry, salty sweat line the sides of his jaw. "So I still need to talk to you."

He steps in closer. Bites his bottom lip. I swallow, hard. I would step back but I'm already pressed against the rack of movies.

Both our heads turn as Eric happens by.

"Good night, everyone. Oh. Sorry." Eric, evidently certain he has just interrupted something big, smiles sheepishly, waves and hurries out.

Crap! Will he tell Adam? Will Adam care?

I grab Joshie's hand. "We need to get home. It's a school night."

"Tomorrow?" says Jake.

I nod. "Tomorrow."

Joshie's arms are tight across his chest as I unlock the car door. His eyebrows are knitted tight, like boiled wool. "What?" I say.

"That guy has good jokes. But he thinks chess is for nerds."

I open the back door and Joshie slides into the car. He

uncrosses his arms to buckle his seat belt, then snaps them back across his chest.

I lean in. "Look. Chess is great for some people. Ben Franklin liked it enough to write about it, right? But some other people think that if you're into chess, you're kind of a loser. Okay?"

Joshie rolls his eyes. I close his door, get into the front seat and start the car. "You'll understand when you're in high school," I say, looking at him in the rearview mirror.

"I don't think so," says Joshie.

He's probably right.

Thankfully, Mom insists that Joshie goes right to bed when we get home, otherwise he'd pester me for the rest of the night to play chess with him. In my room, I dump the contents of my book bag onto my bed. God, why am I still carrying around this stupid chess book? There's the American Pageant books for history, my French workbook, the massive biology book that will eventually dislocate my shoulder. A packet of papers falls out with the books—Joshie's checkmate-in-one-move puzzles.

I pile the books onto my desk and plan my night. I'll start with the biology, then history. Then I can do some math problems, a write-up for French.

But those puzzles. It's like they're calling me.

"Oh, Noraaaaa!"

It's already nine o'clock. I need to start my homework. The stack of books seems to have grown taller. The puzzles crank up their volume.

"*Noraaaaa*!! You could have been the next Judit Polgár."

Shut up! I glance over at my dresser, and the framed picture of me, Phil and Dad at the Puyallup Fair. Phil and I are on the back of a horse while Dad feeds it a carrot. Phil is wearing a red cowboy hat and looks completely freaked out. So does the horse. Me and Dad, we look so happy.

The puzzles have got to be pretty easy. I could probably bang one out in under three minutes.

I grab a pencil. The puzzle takes only two minutes to solve. So I try one more. Just one more. Well, okay, two more. I mean three. They get progressively harder. When my phone chimes that I have a text, it's eleven thirty and I'm on puzzle number twenty-seven. The text is from Krista:

Homework sux!!!!!!

I reply:

Yup.

But you know what sux more? Not doing homework because you've wasted over two hours doing chess puzzles. Chess puzzles!

No. More. Chess!

Eleven

MORNING FEELS LIKE IT arrived three hours ahead of schedule as I sit slumped on one of the cement benches in the front courtyard sipping a triple shot latte in an effort to keep my eyelids open. By three thirty in the morning I still had not made it through the biology chapter on the evolution of populations. I never read the lab paperwork that Coach Avery handed out yesterday—hopefully there won't be any big surprises. The monologue I need to deliver in French sounds like the rantings of *un fou furieux*, aka; "a crazy person," and the few solutions I completed for precalculus look like I held the pencil in my teeth. At least I got all the history reading done.

It's a struggle to keep my half-lidded eyes peeled for Chelsey, but I can't go to biology without her signature on the contract that I scrawled this morning, while waiting for my deodorant to dry. As I wait, the parking lot fills with cars. Buses roll in, spit out piles of bedraggled teenagers, and roll back out again. People hurry past. I scratch out a few remaining math problems.

Over by the front door the ski club, in hats and goggles, sells hot chocolate to raise money for a trip to Whistler. A group of football players swill cups of cocoa, speculating about who is taking who to the homecoming dance. I hear a familiar voice and cover my face with my hand, like I'm shielding myself from the sun.

"Yeah, give me a cup of cocoa with a mess of

marshmallows," Jake says to a guy who's in a parka despite the fact that it's about sixty-five degrees and sunny. A bolt of panic shoots through me. I'm not ready for the conversation I know he wants to have.

"Nora?" he ambles over. "How's it going? Bet you were up all night playing chess, right?"

"You figured me right out, Jake." If only he knew.

He chuckles. "You look awesome today!"

Awesome compared to, say, mold? In a state of utter exhaustion I forgot to wash the conditioner out of my hair, which I only realized after I climbed into the car and discovered my hair was not only wet, but wet and slimy. I've cinched it back into a tight ponytail in hopes that it'll be less obvious. And sitting here, with crossed legs, I realize I only shaved the left one.

"What are you up to?" he asks.

"Just trying to catch up on some math problems."

Jake joins me on the bench. "I wish I was still in your math class." He feigns a pout that is as cute as his smile. Oh, Nora, you idiot. You could have this guy!

I can't help but smile back at him. "Actually, I switched out, too."

He wrinkles his nose. "No way! That stuff is hard, right? I mean, who is ever gonna need to calculate the sides of a triangle. Just about everything has four sides these days, am I right? Football fields. Windows. Toast." He plucks a gooey marshmallow from his hot chocolate and pops it into his mouth.

A crowd rushes past. I scan for someone, anyone to keep this conversation from going any further. The Teapot approaches in a purple-and-gold Hawaiian shirt and knee-length purple shorts. As she walks, she speaks to Tallulah with dramatic flourish, ". . . and I said to my auntie Jean, y'all are crazy! One week is just not long enough to call it a proper visit. You have *got* to stay longer . . ."

She sees me and waves. "Oh, hey!" she drawls.

They pull out of the flow of traffic and join me and Jake. "Are you ready for the biology lab?" asks the Teapot. "I wore just the right shoes!" She shakes the sky-blue sneaker on her right foot like she's doing the hokey-pokey. I didn't read the lab. We were supposed to wear blue sneakers?

Tallulah stands beside the Teapot looking bored—very bored. Her hair is piled on her head and dotted with pale yellow ribbons. She is stunning in a flowing yellow sundress that screams "Hollywood starlet." I hate her. And I hate that she seems to have no feelings toward me one way or the other. She obviously doesn't see me as a threat, and really, why would she?

"Dude, I heard about what happened," Jake says to Tallulah. "How's your appendix?"

She raises one eyebrow. "Fine. How's your spleen?"

She doesn't see me as a threat—but if my swaps go according to plan, she will.

Down in the front circle a black Lexus pulls up and Chelsey climbs out. "Gotta go," I say. "I need to check in with Chelsey about a—about a cheer."

"See you in biology," calls the Teapot.

"I'll look for you later," Jake calls after me.

Chelsey grabs my elbow and leads me to a less frequented entrance on the other side of the building. She slips on a pair of sunglasses, then holds up her hand and speaks behind it to make it unmistakably obvious that we are being sneaky. "Do you have the p-a-p-e-r-s?" she hisses.

"Y-e-s." I point to my book bag. "But first, this." I hand

her the contract. She wipes at a smear on the paper and smells her fingertips.

"Deodorant," I say apologetically.

She pulls a pencil from her bag and drags the eraser end of it across the page from left to right beneath each line as she reads, mouthing the words as the pencil passes beneath them. "You need to add a few rules."

I grab a pen from my bag.

"Number one, no questions about my family, my pets or about what I like and don't like."

I scribble onto the paper. "Check."

"Number two. No looking below here." With her finger she draws an imaginary line below her chin."

"No eyeballs below the neckline," I say as I write.

"Number three. No eye contact."

I start to write, then stop. "That's a little over the top. I mean, if he can't look at your chest and he can't look at your eyes, where is he supposed to look?"

She shrugs. "That's his problem."

"How about 'no *excessive* eye contact.'"

Chelsey considers.

I clarify. "It'll be a deal breaker if he can't even look at you when he talks."

"Okay. But no touching! If he touches me, fingers will be broken." She snaps the pencil in two.

"No touching." I add the line and throw on a pile of exclamation marks. Chelsey signs in purple ink on the dotted line. I swap her the printout of the *Hamlet* paper for the signed contract.

"The *Tempest* paper?" she says.

"You get that one after the date."

She considers, with pursed lips, then nods. "Fair enough.

Tell him seven o'clock, the Friday night before the homecoming game—my boyfriend will be going to bed super early. I'll be at Café Zoka in Kirkland." She looks at me over the top of her sunglasses. "I'll be the blonde in dark glasses."

In biology, I find Swordhands waiting by the rat tank. "Did you get it?" he asks.

I open my bag and nod toward its contents. He looks around, then reaches in and grabs the contract. He scans it. "What does 'excessive eye contact' mean?"

"She gets nervous when people stare at her."

He nods. "Got it." His teeth clench into a tight, nervous smile as he folds the contract in thirds and sticks it in his back pocket. "I can't believe I'm going on a date with Chelsey Oppenheimer!"

I give him the details about time and place, and the swap is on.

At the front of the classroom, Coach Avery grins and rubs his hands together. "I hope you all remembered your dancing shoes."

Dancing shoes? I *really* should have read the lab!

At my new lab table I find Teapot and Megan—who I've decided is not an albino, but is just ghostly pale—discussing homecoming. I explain that Swordhands and I swapped lab groups because he wanted to work with Cat Woman. The Teapot welcomes me like a long-lost cousin and assures me that the fourth lab partner, Adam, will be fine with it.

"Oh, I didn't know Adam was in this group." I'm a little embarrassed to find myself saying.

"Yeah, but he'll be a little late," she says. "Poor Tallulah has an owie on her arm and needed help carrying her books to class, and Adam is helping her out. Is that cute or what?"

Yeah. Really cute. She seemed to be managing her books

just fine when I saw her twenty minutes ago.

Up at the front of the room a small line of people wait to ask Coach Avery questions. The Teapot and Megan resume the conversation they were having when I arrived.

"So, anyway, like I was sayin', I'm dyin' to go to the homecoming dance," sighs the Teapot. "But a dance without a date? It just doesn't seem right."

Megan nods toward Adam's empty seat. "I wonder if Adam is going."

The Teapot glances at the doorway then leans in conspiratorially. "At chess club he told my friend Little Nate that dances aren't his kind of thing, and that even if they were, the girl he'd want to go with isn't available."

She draws out the word *available,* pronouncing each syllable like it is its own word. My heart picks up its pace. Could it be me? Maybe?

"I wonder who she is," says Megan.

I flush. It is a struggle not to appear overeager.

The Teapot raises a lone eyebrow. "Well, I can't say for sure, but I do know that Tallulah's got to go to her cousin's wedding down in Portland that weekend, making her about as unavailable as they come. What about you, Nora?" she asks. "You're a cheerleader. I'll bet y'all could go to the homecoming dance with any guy you want."

I wipe a hand across my conditioner-slick hair. "Maybe not."

"People, settle in, we need to get the video started," says the coach.

We're watching a video?

The Teapot is giddy. "Y'all, this is gonna be the best lab of the year." She repositions the faux diamond hairclip that keeps a swath of curls off her forehead. "Megan, who are you gonna mate with first?"

Wait. What? I *really, REALLY* should have read the lab.

Megan nods toward a buff Asian guy two tables away. "I think I'll mate with Takumi first. What about you?"

The Teapot laughs. "I'm not gonna be picky."

I look from Megan to the Teapot. "What are you two talking about?"

Megan pulls back her head. "Didn't you read the lab?"

"I didn't have time—"

"Sorry I'm late!" We all look up as Adam rushes into the room and apologizes to the coach. His hair sticks out at crazy angles. The bike helmet tethered to his backpack swings from its straps as he walks. Girls around the room greet him as he passes by, turning in their seats, waving.

"Hi, Adam."

"Howzit going, Adam?"

And

"I get to mate with you first, Adam."

Seriously. Do these people have no shame?

Adam smiles shyly and waves back at them. Finally he reaches our table. He spots me, then looks around the room checking to see whether it is me or him who is in the wrong place. "Nora? Are you in our lab group now?"

I chew my lower lip. This could be the moment where he demands to know what's going on, why I keep showing up everywhere. But instead, he has saved his best smile for me. It's like a little slice of the sun found its way into his body and is sending out beams of warmth from his lips, his eyes, his skin.

"She swapped seats with Greg," Megan explains. We all glance at Swordhands's new table. Sherrie is giving him crap about having touched her backpack with his foot.

The look in Adam's eyes tells me that he approves of the swap. In fact, I could swear that he is looking at me almost like I am edible. But is that how he looks at Tallulah, too? Or on the edibility scale, is she ice cream and am I just the sprinkles?

"Everybody should have their lab worksheets in front of them," Coach explains. "You should have filled out the hypothesis last night, and you'll complete the rest of the sheet as we go through the lab."

Megan feels compelled to point out to Adam that I didn't have time to read the lab or complete the hypothesis section. The Teapot pats my hand. She has dimples where knuckles should be. "Cheerleadin' is a busy life. Isn't that right?"

I can almost see my reflection in the shiny black tabletop as I avert the eyes of my tablemates. "Like you wouldn't believe," I say.

Crap! Switching into Adam's class was supposed to be about letting him see that Nora Fulbright has a subtle, yet highly developed brainy side. I should be touting my clever hypothesis. I should have read the lab ahead of time so I could be wearing dance shoes, or blue tennis shoes, or whatever else it is I should have done to be prepared. Adam doesn't know I was busy obsessing over chess puzzles. He probably thinks I was busy fluffing my pom-poms, ironing my pleats or making out with football players in the end zone.

Coach Avery blows his whistle. "People, quiet down and watch so you can learn the steps." He turns out the lights and projects a video onto the whiteboard. The scene opens with a bunch of blue-footed boobies from the Galapagos Islands. It features a male and a female bird. The male does his mating dance, stepping from side to side, lifting one pale blue foot and then the other. The female bird is unimpressed.

Another male approaches with a more energized version of the same dance. The female cocks her head, blinks her eyes. She looks—intrigued.

Coach Avery, his back to us, mimics the steps. In the near darkness Adam leans in close. His breath tickles my ear before I even register that he's speaking to me. I freeze. "Don't worry about not reading the lab," he whispers. "It'll all make sense as we go along. And you can fill in the hypothesis afterward—it's pretty easy."

I turn to ask a question and am stopped when I find him still facing me. His nose inches from my nose, his eyes looking directly into mine, his lips. Oh, his lips! The breath I pull in is almost a gasp. I struggle to remember my question. "But what do boobies have to do with anything?"

Adam smells freshly laundered. Oh my god. Did I really just say the word *boobies* out loud? Being this close in a room this dark with a bunch of sex-crazed birds dancing around on the screen, I have to turn my face away from him. What if I lost control and stroked his cheek, pushed my fingers through his hair or gently planted my mouth on just his lower lip the way the elf hottie tenderly kisses Aragorn in the Lord of the Rings movie that Phil made me watch seven times.

"Avery is just having fun," he whispers. "The lab is about how natural selection can change the ways that certain genetic traits occur in a population."

In the video, boobies come and go as Adam explains that Coach Avery is going to give each of us four little slips of paper, two of the slips have a small letter *a* on them and two have a capital *A*. The little *a*'s and big *A*'s represent certain genetic traits. We're going to randomly hook up with other people in the class and 'mate' with them, meaning that we hold our slips of paper behind our backs and, without looking, pull one out. Our partner does the same thing. The combination of our little *a* or big *A* with our partner's little *a* or big *A* describes the genetic makeup of our baby. We're going to keep track of all the 'babies' and see whether there is a trend in their genetic makeup. The whole dancing bird thing is just a goofy way to get everyone psyched up for the lab.

I can't believe that I am here, in the dark, with Adam Hood whispering to me about making babies.

The video ends and Coach Avery says, "Okay, let's see what you've got!" He plays some lame nineties dance tune and distributes the little slips of paper. The laughter in the room is crazy and loud as everyone bobs, boobylike, from one foot to the other. The Teapot hams it up, big-time. Megan is almost balletlike, hopping daintily from one foot to the other as she makes her way toward Takumi. Adam's dance is adorable. There is nothing like watching a six-foot-something guy plod from foot to foot like a giant toddler taking his clumsy first steps. He looks more flushed now than when he first arrived in class.

"I'm not big on dancing," he says apologetically.

"Think of it as practice for the homecoming dance," Coach Avery says as he passes by.

Adam looks away.

Then, the music abruptly stops. "Everybody mate!" calls out Coach.

The classroom is a frenzy of people laughing, making obscene comments and swapping big and little *a*'s. Before I know it's happened, a girl, the one who asked Adam to be with her first, grabs his arm. "Let's do it!"

"Um, okay." Adam throws me an apologetic look and fumbles in his back pocket for his big and little *a*'s.

I mate with a random stranger, and when the music

resumes, Adam is yanked off in another direction by a girl from the next table over. There are no shortage of girls waiting to swap DNA with him, and in the end, I have six different partners and none of them are Adam.

There in the almost dark, while blue-footed boobies danced across the video screen, did he feel it, too? The sense of being pulled by each other's gravity? Did he have to sit on his hand to keep from brushing the back of his hand against my cheek? Did his heart bruise itself trying to pound its way out of his chest?

Or is it just me?

As I drift down the hall to my next class, I replay Adam's words: *I'm not big on dancing.* Was he telling me that dances in general, and homecoming dances specifically, are not his thing? Does he sense my longing and is trying to let me down easy? Maybe the Teapot is right, if Adam can't go to the dance with Tallulah, he's not going.

He was so sweet to me in class. He said not to worry. He explained the lab. But the truth makes my insides clench. That's just who he is. He's sweet to everyone. He helped me because he feels sorry for me. Dumb Nora Fulbright who didn't even read the lab ahead of time.

Nora (stomp, clap)
Is so lame (stomp, clap)
Her brain's defective (stomp, clap)
What a shame (stomp, clap)
Adam Hood (stomp, clap)
Needs someone smarter (stomp, clap)
Which means that Nora (stomp, clap)
Will just try harder (stomp, clap)
(hand roll) Go, Nora! (single fist punch)

Okay. I wasn't prepared for biology, but in history, I will shine. At two o'clock this morning I reread everything there was to read about New World beginnings, which covers pretty much everything from the dinosaurs to La Salle's French expedition down the Mississippi River. I took copious notes. When Ms. Harrington asks questions about last night's reading my hand will be the first one in the air. Hold on to your seat, Adam Hood, Nora Fulbright is about to fly!

I spend lunch squirreled away in the library reading my history notes one last time, and conveniently putting off any conversation with Jake. Now, I take my front row seat beside Highlights and hand her a manila folder containing Phil's paper. "Thanks so much for letting me borrow your notes," I say, perhaps a little louder than necessary. "They really helped a lot."

She shoves the folder into her book bag. "Always happy to help a fellow female."

The swap is nearly complete.

Adam comes in and Highlights calls him over. "That was a crazy biology lab, wasn't it?" he asks, focusing only on me. "I'm sorry we never got to, you know, mate."

Highlights holds up her hands. "Too much information!"

The look on Adam's face is a cross between a grimace and a smile.

"You were right," I say. "It made total sense once we started, and the hypothesis section was *ridiculously* easy. Thanks for helping me out."

"My pleasure," he says.

Highlights clears her throat noisily. "Hey, I hope you don't mind, Adam, but I forgot I'd promised Jolene that I'd partner with her on the biography project. Are you okay swapping partners?"

"No problem. Who will I be working with?" He stands and looks around the room.

I slowly raise my hand.

"Really?" Adam Hood wears "baffled" better than anyone I know.

Highlights looks from Adam to me, then back to Adam. "Is that okay?" she asks.

"Oh, sure. It's just kind of a funny coincidence," he says. "Nora got switched to my lab table in biology, and now we're biography partners." He half smiles at me. "Weird, huh?"

"Weird," I manage to squeak out.

Highlights hums the Twilight Zone theme song. "It's almost like someone is trying to get you two together," she says.

I laugh too loud.

Adam bows. "It will be a pleasure working with you, Major General Arnold."

I salute him. "Indeed, Mr. Washington."

I pull out my notes. I am ready to impress—to make up for having been totally unprepared in biology. The bell rings. Ms. Harrington jots tonight's reading assignment on the whiteboard, then poses a question. "Class, for the last four sessions we've discussed what the textbook says about the beginnings of the New World. Let's wrap up the discussion today with some thoughts about what the textbook—"

My hand shoots into the air. I am willing to take the risk of behaving slightly pupal. I can answer anything about the reading. Anything. Watch this, Adam!

"Um, how about letting me finish my thought, Nora."

I nod and lower my arm.

"Let's share some thoughts about what the textbook might *not* be telling us about this topic?" She sweeps her hand toward me. "Nora?"

I hesitate. "Wait. What? You want to know what the textbook *didn't* tell us?"

She pauses. "Ah! You missed the first day of class. We talked about how the textbook provides a good understanding of commonly held beliefs about history. But more important for AP students, in my opinion, is to have an understanding about the truths that have been left out, and to delve into an exploration about why, in textbooks, our history is often whitewashed."

If a vampire were to swoop into the room and sink his fangs into my throat he would go away hungry, because every drop of blood in my body has rushed to my face. "Oh."

"But don't let that stop you from responding. What do you think? Based on what you read do you have any feelings about what the authors might *not* have shared?"

I lower my hand. Is she kidding? I don't have any feelings about what they might *not* have written about. In fact, I do not have any feelings at all. I am numb with embarrassment.

"I think I can help out here." I turn. The chair that was empty yesterday is occupied by a guy with glasses so thick that behind them, his eyes look like raisins. Tight, wiry springs of hair point in every direction. He smells like wet wool.

"Go ahead, Zeke," says Ms. Harrington.

Zeke talks excitedly. "There's this sense you get from the textbook that the reason Europeans set off in search of spices was because the Turks were evil and had cut off their trade route. In actuality the Turks had every reason to keep those trade routes open—I mean it was all about making money, Right? So it felt to me like something was missing. Know what I mean?"

I do not know what he means. Not even a little bit.

From the back of the room, Adam chimes in. "It was actually the Portuguese fleet that blocked trade along the old route because *they* controlled the new route that went around Africa. So the Turks had nothing to do with it, but I agree, they were made out in the textbook to be bad guys."

"Excellent points," says Ms. Harrington. "Do the rest of you see what I'm looking for?" She asks the class, but looks at me. Somewhere in my ancient reptilian brain my autonomic nervous system recognizes that in order to survive I must nod.

"Great," says Ms. Harrington.

When class ends I shove my notes into my book bag like I want to hurt them. So much for impressing Adam. For the biography project I will learn everything there is to know about Benedict Arnold. I'll read about his strategies during battle. I'll study up on his early family life. I'll find out what he liked to eat for breakfast. Adam and I will meet after cheer practice at the library. Or at my house. Yes. I will invite him to my house, and to my room, and there, I will throw facts at him like they are darts whose tips have been dipped in love potion.

People are filing out of the classroom, and I am still collecting my stuff when Ms. Harrington calls Adam to her desk. Zeke is there, twiddling a mud-colored mole on his neck. "Zeke was absent yesterday and missed choosing a biography partner," says Ms. Harrington. "Everyone is already paired up. Would you mind letting him join your team?"

Adam looks lost. I plead with him telepathically: Say no! Say no! We need to be alone, Adam! Just you and me in the library, in my kitchen, in my bedroom, talking about George, Benedict and us. Say no!

Finally, he replies, "We should really check with my

partner, Nora."

Ms. Harrington raises her eyebrows. "Nora? Would you mind adding another person to your team? It would really help me out."

Beside me Highlights smiles sweetly. "There's a special place in hell for women who don't help other women."

I force a smile. "No problem."

Zeke squints, exposing rabbitlike front teeth as he pushes his glasses higher on his nose. "Thanks." He gloms on to Adam for help with what he missed yesterday.

Beside me, Highlights sniggers. "Nothing like a three-some."

Twelve

VANESSA CATCHES UP WITH ME on the way out of class. "Look," she says flatly. "You might want to wait to take this class. I can't imagine having taken it anytime before my junior year. It's a ton of work and Harrington is a real ball-buster. Plus you have cheer taking up way too much time."

Did I really seem *that* clueless? If I had hackles, they would rise. "I can handle the work. I didn't know about the other reading, that's all."

"Well, if you decide to stick it out, you can e-mail me if you need anything. My contact stuff is on the cheer roster. I love history. And I'd be happy to help."

It occurs to me that this is our first real conversation. I've sort of avoided Vanessa, afraid of what Chelsey would think of me if she thought we were friends. Maybe that's been a mistake. "Thanks. Maybe I could help you with your Herkie jump sometime?"

Vanessa rolls her eyes. "I'd like to ram a Herkie jump up Chelsey's—never mind. I'm just counting the days until cheer is over. I hate it."

I stop walking. She despises cheer. And Chelsey isn't crazy about her. "So why do you do it?"

Vanessa studies something invisible on the back of her hand, then looks away. "It's complicated. Sometimes you just don't have a choice. Let's go." She continues walking. "So, practice starts late today, right?"

"Yeah, there's some big teacher's meeting about home-coming. Sports teams, after-school clubs—everything is pushed back a half hour. I figured I would just hang out in the commons. Want to come?"

She laughs. "No, thanks. I've seen who you hang out with. Don't take this the wrong way, but you and your 'sa-lami' twin have really latched on to the cheer squad dimwits. I mean, they're popular as hell, but—" She hesitates. "You seem smarter than that."

She backpedals at the look on my face.

"I'm sorry. I shouldn't have said anything. Obviously you get something out of hanging out with them. Who knows, maybe I'm just jealous." She smiles. "I'm going to kill time in the library. I meant what I said—let me know if you need help with history."

Big, wet clouds accumulate in my brain as I make my way to the commons. Is she just jealous? What's wrong with be-ing popular? Am I smarter than that?

I find the commons packed with people waiting for their after-school activities to start. I narrowly avoid the soccer guys who stand in a misshapen circle playing hacky-sack with an orange. And I steer clear of Mitch, who sneaks around like a tabloid paparazzo, snapping pictures for the yearbook.

"Nora!" Krista sits at a table by the drink machines with Dex. She is beaming. He is beaming. They are always beam-ing. I fully expect them to be married the day after Krista and I graduate. They've been dating since Krista was twelve and Dex was thirteen, when they met at some church camp. Krista has their future all mapped out. They'll have six kids. Dex will be a very tall accountant. Krista will be a very short super-mom. She'll take her kids on crazy outings and make homemade bumbleberry jam. My mother must not, for any reason, be allowed to make a speech at their wedding.

"Hey, how's it going, Nora?" Dex grins and his braces, which he's also had since he was thirteen, dominate the landscape. Krista says that she pines for the day that he doesn't taste like a box of paper clips when they kiss.

"It hasn't been a great day." I slump into a chair.

Krista rubs my arm. "AP biology?"

I stiffen.

"Poor baby."

"Well, I think your day is about to get a whole lot better." Dex lifts his eyes toward someone behind me. I spin around. Jake approaches with a gait like a gorilla that has just sniffed out a mother lode of bananas.

"Hey, I've been looking for you," he says.

"I was right here." Dex, with a wide smile, opens his arms for a hug.

"Not you!" Jake balls up a napkin from a nearby table and hurls it at Dex. Krista giggles. Jake pulls out the chair closest to me, spins it so it's facing backward and sits. "So, I've been trying to catch you alone but it hasn't worked out. So I'll just go ahead and ask you right now."

Jake Londgren's face is less than eight inches from mine. His jaw is wide, and angled. His eyes sit close to the bridge of his nose giving him an almost pantherlike appearance. He is strong and powerful, and there isn't a girl at Riverbend who wouldn't want to be his prey.

It stinks that in the brains department he's at least three yards short of a first down.

And he is not Adam.

Krista claps her hand to her mouth. Jake fidgets in his chair. For the first time ever he looks a little unsure of himself. "I didn't want to ask you too early, but at the same time I

want to make sure I beat all those other losers to the punch."
Jake punches his fist into his open hand. "So, what do you
think about going with me to the homecoming dance?"

What do I think? What *do* I think?! I think that I want to
go to the homecoming dance with Adam.

"We'll double-date!" squeals Krista.

"Well?" says Jake. He thrums his wide fingers on the back
of the chair. "Your move."

An interesting way to put it. It is my move, isn't it? Benjamin Franklin would tell me to make my move with foresight,
circumspection and caution.

> Foresight: Going to the dance with Jake Londgren will
> shoot my popularity quotient through the roof. It'll
> make Krista deliriously happy. Chelsey will probably
> crown me future Queen of the Monarch butterflies.
> Circumspection: Adam was *so* sweet the day we first
> met. He was so sweet by my locker—until he realized
> I'm on cheer. And even with his poor opinion of cheer-
> leaders and my boneheaded maneuvers that keep prov-
> ing him right—he's still been really nice to me in class.

But he's nice to everyone. He carries injured girls' books
to class. He picks up dropped notebooks. He saves lives. And
he is not going to the dance because the only girl he would
want to go with is unavailable.

Tallulah is pretty and smart and a senior, and she'll be at a
wedding during homecoming. She is undeniably *un*available.

I, on the other hand, am available. I am *so* available. If
only Adam knew how available I am!

> Caution: Wouldn't it make my chances with Adam even
> worse if I went to the dance with Jake and Adam found

out? Yes, but if Adam is not at the dance, he won't know I was there with Jake. And at the dance, I would make it clear to Jake that we're just friends. No damage done.

Mr. Franklin, I am ready to make my move.

I smile at Jake. "I—"

Click! A flash of bright white light leaves me temporarily blinded.

"I think what Nora is trying to tell you, Jake, is that you need to take the sucker's walk to the far end of the field because she's already agreed to go to the homecoming dance with me." Mitch stands inches from the table, his camera still pointed at my face.

Jake shakes his thumb toward Mitch. "You agreed to go the dance with this freak?"

Krista's jaw is slack. "You did?"

I swallow hard and manage a squeak. "I did?"

Mitch does a bug-eyed wink. "Remember? I asked you when you stopped by the attendance office. And you said yes."

There is an interminable moment of silence before Jake erupts into laughter. Krista and Dex join in. Jake slips an arm over my shoulder. "That's a good one," he says. "You and this flea going to the dance together. Hah!"

It is soon apparent to everyone at the table, even Jake, that Mitch and I are not laughing. One look at Mitch's eyes, narrowed beneath his invisible eyebrows, and I know the deal: I try to worm my way out of the homecoming dance, he tells the world about our swap. Adam would peg me as desperate and I would never stand a chance with him, ever.

Mitchell may be a flea, but he is not the only lowlife in the room. My wings begin to recede as I return to my larval state. Perhaps we were made for each other.

The laughter fizzles out. "It's true." My voice breaks. "Mitch asked me and I said yes."

Jake pushes back from the table and holds up his hands in surrender. "Wait a minute. Let me get this straight. This little flea, this head lice, this dust mite—"

"I think *vermin* is the broad category you're looking for," I say.

"This vermin beat me to the punch?" He drops his arms. His hand curls into a fist.

"And you said yes?" God, the look on Krista's face! I'm going to the dance with him, not marrying him.

My eyelids drift closed. "I guess I did."

When I open my eyes, Dex shakes his head like I've been given a terminal diagnosis. And I have. Terminal unpopularity.

Mitch does not look like the cat that got the canary. He looks like the cat that got the forty-eight-pound turkey. He pumps his elbows and does this vulgar little hip thrust. The camera hanging around his neck bounces on his chest and nearly knocks the wind out of him. "Ciao," he says, and he swaggers away.

Jake, Krista and Dex stare at me. I want to cry. I want to throw up. I want to be the size of a chess piece and jump into my own pocket. The commons has mostly cleared out. There's a squashed orange on the floor where the soccer guys were.

Krista glares at me. "You didn't bother telling me, your best friend, that you're dating the biggest leech at school?" Her face is stony.

"I'm not dating him!"

No one cares. Jake crosses his arms hard over his chest. His biceps bulge. "Have a good time on your date." He spits out the word *date* like it's a broken tooth.

I walk to the locker room alone.

> *Hey, hey, what do you see?*
> *A PQ that's a minus three*
> *Hey, hey, what do you know?*
> *Nora's future's looking low*
> *Hey, hey, what do you say?*
> *Nora's wings have gone away*

Homecoming will be a complete bust. Jake hates me. I've completely pissed off Krista. I am going to be seen in public with Mitch. And what if Adam hears about it and thinks there's something going on between me and Mitch? Crappiest-crap-of-all-time! How did things go so wrong?

We spread out in a circle near the bleachers and Chelsey leads us in stretches. We play a few rounds of Simon Says— *Simon Says touchdown stance! Simon Says High V! K-Motion!* I mess up every time. Krista shows up late, and when I step back to make room for in the circle her she squeezes into a nonexistent space between Becca and Jazmine instead.

We jog a few times around the track, then run stairs, sprinting to the top of the bleachers, and quick-stepping back down. Krista keeps her distance. I pause at the top step and catch my breath. Down below, on the football field, Jake is doing a drill where he hurls his body against a padded, movable post and it looks like he wants to kill the thing.

On the track, Chelsey presses the megaphone to her mouth, "Come on, girls! Faster! Lift those knees!" It's hard to run, let alone move, with your stomach twisted in knots. I stop halfway down the bleachers to catch my breath beside Vanessa, who's doubled over, also breathing hard.

I manage to pant out a sentence. "Are you okay?"

"This"—*pant, pant, pant*—"sucks."

We spend the entire practice working on the cheer that Chelsey has chosen for the homecoming halftime show. "This is going to be the best homecoming game ever!" she assures us. "The guys are super stoked, the snack bar is selling football-shaped cookies and marshmallow pom-poms, and—"

Vanessa drifts into the conversation like a rain cloud. "I heard Coach Avery is actually kind of freaked out because Highline has this whole new defensive strategy and they're expected to shut us down by halftime."

Chelsey glares at Vanessa. "Well. Then we're just going to need to cheer a little bit harder, aren't we."

Vanessa waves a dismissive hand. "I'm just saying."

If Krista were standing beside me, we'd talk in a gossipy whisper about the Vanessa/Chelsey dynamic. Instead, I look over at Krista and when she catches my eye, she stabs the toe of her shoe into the grass. I should have told her about the Mitch thing. But she's been so intent on me hooking up with Jake that even when I've tried to talk about Adam she has shut me down. She would have given me three-hundred yards of crap if she knew I'd swapped a date with Mitch to get into Adam's classes. I guess it doesn't take a genius IQ to see that it wasn't my best move ever—a move that turns out to have been a little thin in the foresight department. But I never thought the "date" would be the homecoming dance! I didn't think anyone would ever need to know.

Chelsey huffs at Vanessa's remark, then smooths her tank top over her stomach and tucks a loose strand of hair into a clip at the back of her head. "Like I was saying. The homecoming game is our most important one of the entire season for—" Chelsey counts silently on her fingers, then gives up. "For a whole bunch of reasons. First. Everyone will be at the game watching us. Everyone!

"Second. The football players are counting on us to get that ginormous crowd cheering. And three . . ." She bites her bottom lip and widens her eyes. You would think she was about to reveal the age-old secret to the perfect pike jump. "You guys—I heard a rumor that the coach from Louisville will be here to watch us cheer!"

Chelsey hoots and does, in fact, demonstrate the perfect pike jump.

Becca looks reverently at Chelsey. "She'll see you in action and snap you up on the spot for the Louisville squad!"

"You're going to college nationals!" squeals Jazmine.

Chelsey throws her arms over her head, hoots and gyrates her hips, then turns serious. "Well, I can't do it alone. That coach needs to see that we are the best cheer squad ever! So let's hammer this thing!"

Chelsey teaches us dance steps she found on YouTube from last year's nationals. She demonstrates with Becca a cool move where she slides behind Becca, they hook elbows and Becca rolls over her back. We partner up and I try it with Vanessa. It's like rolling a corpse over my back. Then there are a few more twists, spins and jumps. We try it again. And again. Chelsey is super smooth as she glides through the steps. We do the whole thing as a group, and eventually even Vanessa gets it. Chelsey may not be fluffiest pom-pom in the locker, but she really knows how to lead the squad. I shudder to think how we would do if we ever had to cheer a game without her.

Chelsey wants to finish with a tumbling routine, and it would be the perfect addition if I could get it right, but I just can't concentrate. There's Krista, talking behind her hand to Gillian, whose eyes bug out in response. There's Jake, standing with a crowd of guys. He points at me and says something. They laugh. How long will it be until everyone in school knows about me and Mitch?

Everyone. Even people with one awesome dimple.

"Get in the game, Nora!" Chelsey chides.

My body is in the game. It's my brain that is someplace else, and it has taken my heart with it. I can't believe I am going to the homecoming dance with Mitch.

After practice, I find Krista sitting on the hood of my car. She watches me cross the parking lot and stands to face me when I reach her.

"Okay. What's going on, Nora?"

I unlock my car and toss my bag into the backseat. "How are you getting home?"

"Dex is picking me up in a couple of minutes. But you and I need to talk. There are too many weird things going on and I can't figure out how they connect. First, there's the whole schedule change thing."

"I told you—my mom made me switch into AP biology."

"Baloney, Nora. Do you remember the day we went to Molly Moon's for ice cream?"

I nod, recalling my double scoop of Theo's Coconut Kiss.

"We compared our schedules that day. You were taking algebra two, biology, US History. And, okay, sure, your mom made you switch it up a little bit and take AP biology. I get that. You want to do science stuff in college. But Dex's friend Gunner says that you're in his precalculus class. And when you switched out of history I thought you needed to shift things around to get the AP biology thing to work, but Vanessa mentioned that you guys are in AP US History together. You hate history. So, what's up? Your mother made you switch *everything*? Or is there something else you aren't telling me."

My tongue feels dipped in lead. I cannot move my lips. I am furiously dog-paddling in a deep pool of lies and there is no one to throw me a life ring. When I came to Riverbend High I vowed that I would never tell anyone that I am a born-again normal person. I almost slipped a couple of times. I almost told Krista, "If you had known me back in middle school you would have hated me, because everyone did." I am trying so hard to figure out how to be smart and popular at the same time and clearly there is a step in the process that has managed to evade me completely.

"My family has this hang up about academic excellence," I finally say. "Mom was all freaked out about me not living up to my potential. She wanted me taking harder classes."

"And you needed to lie about it? To me? What—you're afraid that if I know that your mother is pushing you too hard I'm going to like you less?"

Krista doesn't wait for a response.

"And what is up with Jake? You have totally messed with him. You knew that he liked you. You've been flirting your ass off at lunch, and during breaks at practice. You held his hand at lunch."

"I did not! He held mine!"

"It takes two, Nora! You could have pulled your hand away. You could have told him that you're not into him. He's totally hot, but you'll notice he doesn't have a girlfriend, and you know why? With everything he's got going for him he's actually kind of nervous around girls he likes. So he finally works up the nerve to ask you to the dance and it turns out you're already going with Mitch." She pokes her index finger halfway down her throat. "Mitch! Who is only the skeeviest jerk in the entire school. Do you know that he asked permission to take pictures for the yearbook in the second floor girls' bathroom? That is just gross. What possessed you to agree to go to a dance with him? There has *got* to be something you're not telling me."

I sand my cheek with my fingertips. I could tell her about the swaps. But I can't implicate Chelsey. It's bad enough that I'm helping her cheat in English—it's because of me that she's effectively going to be cheating on her boyfriend, who's friends with Dex.

Highlights. Swordhands. I've got all these other people involved. And what about Adam? He absolutely cannot find out what I have done to get close to him. He would never want to have anything to do with me. Ever. And while I don't think Krista would tell him outright, secrets are slippery little fish that have a way of jumping out of the water when you least expect them to.

Krista folds her arms over her chest. "Dex and I think you're making some really bad choices."

Something inside me clicks. I mirror her stance. "Oh, so you and Dex think I've made bad choices? You sound like my mother!"

Krista is taken aback. She mouths a silent "What?"

"Look," I say, my voice louder than I intend it to be. "You're entitled to your opinions, Krista. But any choices I've made are my own and I stand by them. As far as Jake goes, you told me yourself that he may be about the nicest package that boy guts were ever poured into, but he's dumb as dirt. You can't blame me for not wanting to go to the dance with him. And I only flirted with him because he started it. He can just take his shy butt to the nearest branch of the Jake

Londgren Fan Club and find a different date for the dance."

Dex's little blue VW Bug chugs into the empty spot beside my car. "Hey," he calls from his open window. "What's up?"

"I was just leaving!" I climb into my car and slam shut the door. Krista runs around to the passenger side of Dex's car and clambers in beside him. Even with my window rolled up, I can hear Krista crying. And even with NPR cranked up to top volume, I can hear myself doing the same.

Thirteen

MY LIFE HAS BECOME AS BORIng as the instructions on the back of a shampoo bottle. School. Practice. Homework. Repeat. I arrive at school each day just as the first bell rings to avoid running into Krista in the latte line. At practice and games she looks through me like I am not there. I don't see her, Jake or the Monarchs at lunch because I eat alone, sneaking food into the library. Or I find an empty classroom. Last Tuesday, desperate for solitude, I found the steps leading to the rooftop chessboard, but the door at the top of the stairs was locked so I ate my tuna sandwich alone in a dank stairwell.

None of the Monarchs ask me out for pizza at lunchtime, or invite me to movies on the weekend, or encourage me to come to postgame parties. At practice, Chelsey is nice the way you are nice to people with a debilitating handicap. As long as I shine in the cheer lineup, she wouldn't care if I were going to the homecoming dance with a weasel.

Oh, wait, I am.

Gillian, Jazmine and Becca aren't as forgiving. Becca pops up out of nowhere, "Click!" and pretends to take my picture. Jazmine asks me if I'm the spokesperson for some charity that promotes cheerleader/dork relationships. Gillian has offered to dye my hair and shave my eyebrows so my date and I will match for the dance.

Even the Cabbage Whites have gotten a little frosty. It's

like I have given cheerleading a bad name and no one is quite sure what to do about it. Vanessa, on the other hand, has only gotten friendlier. She talks to me like nothing has changed, and then, it's usually about history or to make disparaging remarks about cheerleading.

I consider my current larval state and can't help wondering about all the crazy swaps.

Was it worth it?

Then, I go to history class, and Adam stops by my desk to talk and he flashes that adorable smile; and as we talk, he scours my face with his eyes and his collar is pointing the wrong way and I fix it for him and his ears go pink; and I say, "Yes, it was worth it!" Emphatically, yes.

But there are other times in biology, like when we were supposed to collect gametes from male and female sea ur-chins. Someone asked Coach Avery whether female sea ur-chins are genetically predisposed to prefer males with big spines. Sherrie, aka Cat Woman, quipped, "Just like cheer-leaders are genetically predisposed to like football players with big muscles."

I suppose it could have been worse. She could have made an announcement about me and Mitch, a gossip item that never seemed to reach the biology crowd. But still, I jerked at her words, squashing my sea urchin, sending guts all over Adam's blue hoodie.

When Megan laughed, and the Teapot gushed, "Hell, I'd be happier than a dead pig in the sunshine if I had the genetics to attract boys like Jake Londgren," Adam froze. He coolly wiped the goopy guts from his shirt and didn't say a word the entire lab. It seems like the world conspires to remind him, constantly, that I am nothing but a ditzy cheerleader.

Was it worth it?

On a random Thursday I see Adam by the bike rack where Tallulah, in hot-pink Lycra shorts, is locking up her bicycle beside his because she has started riding her bike to school, but of course she needs him to manage the lock for her because her favorite role is that of the helpless twit. Doesn't he notice? Then, I overhear her in the library asking, with a dramatic sigh, for help finding volumes of romantic poetry. Finally, I read the sappy-ass story she wrote for the school paper talking about her near-death experience in the lunchroom. She likens herself to Sleeping Beauty, Adam to her Prince.

How could any of this possibly be worth going to the homecoming dance with Mitch?

Now, the dreaded Saturday has arrived and once again that question nags me as I stand in the shower and I lather, rinse and repeat. Was it worth it?

Mom pounds on the door. "Leave some hot water for the rest of us!"

Homecoming. The parade, the game, the dance. I heard that Jake got invited by a dozen girls and in the end, Dex chose one for him. Mitch e-mails me daily wondering about the color of my dress. Sadly, the one I wore to my grandmother's funeral is tight across the chest so I'll wear a salmon pink creation Mom got from Cherise, whose baby belly may never again fit into a size four.

I lather up my hair a fourth time and remember that Chelsey had her coffee date with Swordhands last night. I hope it all went according to the terms of the contract.

Joshie bangs on the door this time. "Mom says you're going to look like a prune with pom-poms."

It's eight thirty in the morning when Mom, Bill and Joshie drop me off at the school parking lot, where the parade will both start and finish, doing a one-mile loop through downtown in between. They head off to find good seats for the parade. The parking lot is a zoo, with throngs of people scrambling into position. The drill girls, dressed in slinky gold lamé dresses and ankle-high boots, twirl giant purple flags festooned with leaping golden trout. Over in the front circle, the marching band, in simulated military tunics with fluffy-plumed hats, warms up. The trumpets play a marching tune, the clarinets blast the school fight song and a little Latino guy on sax wails a bluesy rendition of "Stairway to Heaven." The place is lousy with convertibles, buffed and shiny, ready to transport the homecoming court through the downtown parade route.

And the class floats, each attached to a green-and-yellow tractor, get touched up with last-minute balloons, crepe paper and Astroturf.

I finally find the cheer squad. They, we, are stunning! The special homecoming uniforms look rich, like the anonymous person who donated them. There is a damp chill in the air and I am grateful for the matching purple jacket. I scan the sea of purple and gold sequins looking for Chelsey so I can find out how the date went.

Becca, with her hair in a bun for the parade and her foot on the bumper of an SUV, stretches, with her nose pulled to her shin. Krista, who chats with Jazmine, catches sight of me and turns around. Vanessa leans against a lightpost sipping from a Starbucks cup. She gives me a little nod.

"Where's Chelsey?" I ask no one in particular. I call her name, and Chelsey appears from behind the senior float.

"There you are!" she shouts through her megaphone and marches toward me like she's on her way to put out a fire. "I've been looking for you!"

Krista and Jazmine stop talking. Becca drops her foot off

the back of the car. Vanessa straightens and tips the dregs of her coffee onto the pavement. The entire squad closes in.

"He kissed me!" shouts Chelsey. "We're talking full-on lip to lip, taste bud to taste bud." She gags and spits. "He broke the rules!"

Everyone stares bewildered, looking first at Chelsey, then at me for an explanation. "Well, technically, no kissing wasn't a rule," I say. "The rule was no touching."

Chelsey fumes. "If he blew me a kiss it would have been one thing. But no! That's not what he did. There we were, talking about the weather this summer. Then we talked about the weather last summer. The next thing I know he's pressing his lips onto my lips and his tongue is halfway down my throat. He touched me with his lips and his tongue! Kissing counts as touching!"

Becca sides with Chelsey. "Yeah. Technically, I think kissing could be considered touching." There is some back-and-forth about kissing versus touching, then Krista raises the obvious question: "Who kissed you?"

Chelsey waves her hand at me. "Nora asked me to go out for coffee with this guy from the sword club."

"The fencing team," I say.

"And we agreed that there would be no touching. And to me, touching includes kissing. I mean, I have a boyfriend, for crying out loud! Not to mention the fact that this guy has really skinny lips and one of those skeevy bunny-hair mustaches."

Jazmine, who towers above me, cocks her head. "Why did you ask Chelsey to go out with a guy who has no lips?"

"He has lips! They're just thin." I hesitate before going on. There is no telling what kind of trouble we could get into if anyone found out I gave Chelsey my brother's papers.

"There's this guy from the fencing team in my biology class. I asked him for, um, extra help. It turns out he's totally crushing on Chelsey, and the only way he would help me was if Chelsey would go out with him for a cup of coffee."

"But there were rules!" Chelsey says. "No talking about personal stuff. No looking at my girls"—she points to her chest—"and NO TOUCHING!"

Krista slowly winds a loose strand of hair around her finger. "Hang on. Chelsey, you agreed to go out with this guy. This guy who has no lips—"

"He has lips!" I say.

Krista keeps going. "And you did it just to be nice? Really? There was nothing in it for you?"

Chelsey's mouth is stuck open.

"I helped her . . ." I hesitate. "I helped her with a paper she had to write for English."

"The *Hamlet* paper for Mr. Pawlosky?" asks Gillian.

"Yeah." Chelsey strokes her megaphone absently.

Gillian narrows her eyes. "But you're a sophomore, Nora. The *Hamlet* paper is for senior English. How were you able to write it for her?"

"I didn't write it for her. I just helped her. And I know a lot about *Hamlet*." Which is true. The last summer that I visited Dad in Cambridge, when I was twelve, he was dating a Danish woman named Gertrude, who was playing the role of Ophelia in a summer stock production. We read the play out loud a bunch of times and certain lines really stuck with me. "Foul deeds will rise, / Though all the earth o'erwhelm them to men's eyes."

The sweat glands in my armpits kick into overdrive. Krista takes a step closer to me. "And this guy. This fencer. Exactly what did he help you with?"

I raise, then lower my shoulders. "You know. Just some stuff in class."

Krista purses her lips. "Uh-huh. Just some stuff in class."

Chelsey jumps in. "But the point is, he stuck his disgusting coffee-flavored tongue down my throat. I don't even *like* coffee."

The conversation comes to an abrupt stop when Stuart Shangrove announces over a loudspeaker fixed to the top of a gold Hummer that the parade is about to begin. We grab our pom-poms and line up. I can feel Krista's eyes on me as the parade gets underway. If we were not marching in the formation that we've been practicing all week, I am confident that, except perhaps for Vanessa, I would be marching all by myself because no one wants to be near me.

The drill team steps and twirls their way out of the parking lot followed closely behind by the marching band, who blast out a jazzy version of "Mack the Knife." We fall into place behind the band, running through our repertoire as we jump, cheer and shake our pom-poms through the town.

Mitch and the rest of the yearbook crowd snap our pictures as we pass by. "See you tonight," he shouts, and I pretend not to hear him.

"Nora!" Josh waves like crazy from out in front of Small Fry's Hardware (need live bait?) where he, Mom and Bill sit in lawn chairs. Copernicus strains at his leash.

"Woohoo!" The Teapot waves from in front of the Steelhead Coffee Company—the fish metaphor in my town runs deep—where she stands with a bunch of the drama crowd. Their faces are painted purple with gold stars, and they're wearing medieval dresses and robes. After the uproar caused by last year's drama club float (a tractor pulling a trailer upon which they performed a mostly nude scene from the show

Hair), they were banned from this year's parade.

Tallulah, attending the out-of-town wedding, is conspicuously absent.

"Go, fight, win!" shouts the Teapot. "You look great, Nora!" It's hard to smile, but I do.

Behind us, from their perches on the backs of convertibles, the homecoming court tosses candy into the crowd. Chelsey officially took herself out of the running for queen because she couldn't bear the thought of not marching with the cheer squad in the parade. The junior class float, a papier-mâché Spartan being eaten by a giant fish, becomes disconnected from its tractor and there's a five-minute slowdown while they reattach themselves.

We're almost back at the school when my heart does a little hiccup. Adam and Eric are sitting side by side on their parked bicycles. Adam's hands are tucked into his armpits against the morning chill. He's wearing shorts and a Brown hoodie—the college, not the color. We chant a cheer as we pass by. Eric, whose shirt is striped purple and yellow in honor of the day, makes eye contact with me and smiles. He leans over and says something to Adam, who smiles shyly and waves. What did Eric tell him? Something about Chess Kings? Something about how adorable I look in my special homecoming uniform? Something about how lucky Adam would be to go out with a girl like me? Crap! Or is he sharing a little bit of tittle-tattle about a certain cheerleader and her eyebrow-deficient dance date?

I have noticed that over the past few weeks the circle of girls that surround Adam has gotten smaller. Like me, I guess they've noticed that Adam is rarely seen without Tallulah. But unlike me, they've given up.

As we pass Adam I serve him up a crisp salute, hoping he

gets the General George Washington reference. He laughs and salutes in return. I peek back over my shoulder when we've passed. Eric is watching the girls' soccer team, who follow us in the parade. But Adam is not watching the soccer girls. He is still looking. At me.

We return to the school parking lot as people begin to arrive for the big game in hopes of finding seats in the bleachers. The cheerleaders stop by the locker room to freshen up before following Chelsey onto the sidelines. When we reach the field, Chelsey starts us off with a chant, and before long the entire stadium drones along in long, drawn-out syllables:

GO, CUTTHROATS!
BEAT THE SPARTANS!

Chant, breathe, repeat.

There is not a free seat in the stands. Halfway up the parent section Joshie sees me and shakes his shredded paper pom-poms. A few rows up from him the Ultimate Fan, in her cheer jersey and a tiara, waves her arms wildly over her head. The courtyard beside the field is filled with fans in purple and gold and the line at the popcorn trailer is a mile long.

In front of the bleachers a section of chairs have been setup for special guests. The principal. The vice principal. The barista from the lunch room who was elected grand marshal for the parade. But the person who really stands out is a stocky lady with beehive hair and a Louisville sweater.

"The Louisville coach!" squeals Chelsey.

The football team jogs onto the field amid a roar from the crowd. The band blasts out the fight song. We jump onto our pedestals and shake our pom-poms like they're filled with bugs. The football captains go to the middle of the field for a coin toss, and as we climb down from our pedestals I notice some commotion in the special guest section. A guy with a fistful of papers shakes them, and shouts at Mrs. Esposito, the vice principal. Mrs. Esposito looks my way.

I lean over to Gillian. "Who's the guy yelling at Mrs. Esposito?"

"Mr. Pawlosky, the English teacher."

I look over at Chelsey, who blanches. Mrs. Esposito motions for us to join her. The sandbags in my stomach and my feet make it hard to walk.

"I need you girls to join myself and Mr. Pawlosky back in my office," says Mrs. Esposito.

"But the game!" shrieks Chelsey. "The game is about to start."

"Not for you!" Mr. Pawlosky looks like he would pop if pricked with a pin.

The walk from the field to the school is torture, with thousands of eyes on our backs and questions racing around in my head. What are my mother and Bill thinking? Is Adam at the game? How did Mr. Pawlosky figure out that Chelsey looked at my brother's paper? Isn't the penalty for plagiarism expulsion? Beside me, Chelsey weeps into her hands.

The walk down the hall to Mrs. Esposito's office is like a scene from a death row movie, with no sound except for the footsteps of the prisoners and the guards making their way to the execution chamber. The silence is broken by excited screams from the crowd. The game has started.

What have I done!

Mrs. Esposito motions for us to sit as she flattens the *Hamlet* report on her desk. The name Phil Fulbright has been painted over with white-out, and Chelsey Oppenheimer is written over it in swirly purple ink. The *i* in Oppenheimer is dotted with a wide purple heart.

Oh god, Chelsey. Really?

"I have never seen such flagrant cheating in my life," roars Mr. Pawlosky.

Looking at the paper, I still don't see how I have been implicated. Chelsey at least had the brains to cross out Phil's name. Then Mrs. Esposito turns the page. My eyes drift to the bottom of the paper: "P. Fulbright—page 2." His name appears on every page. Forty-eight pages of inescapable incrimination.

Mr. Pawlosky rants about suspension, and expulsion. Mrs. Esposito replies with grim-faced nods. I should never have tried out for cheer. Who was I kidding? I am Nora Fulbright, sister of Phil, both of us fruit of a family tree called the giant nerdwood. If I'd stuck with gymnastics, I could be up in the stands right now, sitting beside Adam, who probably thinks gymnasts are pretty cool. We'd lean in close and he'd make some wisecrack about the cheerleaders. I would giggle and agree. Instead, I sit here with tears streaming down my cheeks, barely able to breathe. Beside me, Chelsey is racked with sobs. I need a tissue really badly.

"Girls?" says Mrs. Esposito. "What do you have to say for yourselves?"

"It was all my fault," I say through tears. "I gave her the paper."

"But she's the one who handed it in and tried to pass it off as her own work," says Mrs. Esposito. I notice for the first time that there is a streak of purple in her otherwise asphalt-black hair. I sit on the edge of the seat and can barely feel it beneath me.

"Look," she says. "I don't know yet what disciplinary steps we're going to take, but there will certainly be some action taken right now."

I picture Chelsey and I cheering in handcuffs, dragging a ball and chain behind us as we somehow manage to muscle through and cheer on our boys:

> *Block that kick!*
> *You gotta—*
> *Block that kick!*

Perhaps we'll be banned from the homecoming dance! Even the most water-logged cloud can have a silver lining.

"It's completely inappropriate that they should be allowed to represent our school out on the field," interjects Mr. Pawlosky. "They should be kicked off cheer effective immediately."

"What?" Chelsey and I say at the same time.

"No! No, please!" Chelsey drops to her knees, groveling with her hands at her chest, prayerlike. "Cheer is my life. It's what I do best. I want to cheer at Louisville. I want to go the college-level nationals. Please!"

Chelsey's begging reduces my heart to a pile of thumping crumbs.

"A committee will decide on Monday what the long-term ramifications are," says Mrs. Esposito. "But I agree that they can't go back out on the field today."

Chelsey moans. There is so much more at stake for her than there is for me. I have ruined her dream. I put my arm around her and she jerks away.

"Please," I plead with them. "This is the most important game of her life. The Louisville coach is out there. Chelsey is so good—they need to see her in action."

Mr. Pawlosky stands stock-still, his hands clasped behind

his back. "A little foresight would have gone along way here, Ms. Fulbright."

Foresight. Circumspection. Caution. Oh, Mr. Franklin, why didn't I listen to you?

"I'm very sorry girls. I truly am, but Mr. Pawlosky is right." Mrs. Esposito pulls a little packet of tissues from her purse and hands it to me. "Why don't you both stay here for a few minutes and collect yourselves. Then, you can go home, or stay and watch the game. Your choice."

Chelsey speaks through rattled sobs. "Can I at least go back out there to tell Becca what's happened and give her the set list so she can lead the cheers?"

Mr. Pawlosky opens his mouth to speak but Mrs. Esposito beats him to it. "Yes. Then right off the field."

I stand up and adjust the elastic from my spanks, which cuts into the bottom edge of my butt. Chelsey struggles to get up. I offer her a hand and she swats it away. "What about the dance?" she asks when she's finally gotten to her feet. "We can still go to the dance, can't we?"

"Look," says Mrs. Esposito. "I know this is a first-time offense for both of you, and that the pressure of keeping your marks up while playing on a varsity team can get to kids sometimes. Missing the game is punishment enough for today. Go to the dance, and on Monday we'll figure out what to do."

Where is the justice in that?

"This is all your fault!" Chelsey berates me as we walk back to the field. Despite the tissues her face is slick with tears and snot. Somehow, she still looks good.

"I should never have given you the paper, I own that. But you're the one who handed it in with my brother's name all over it. You were supposed to use his paper to get ideas, not try to pass if off like it was your own work."

"Now you tell me," Chelsey practically screams. "I am so mad. SO mad!!" She stomps back to the stadium with me several steps behind her. We enter the gates and walk toward the stands and I can't even look into the bleachers. The cheer squad rushes to surround us. Becca reaches over and wipes the purple mascara streaks off Chelsey's cheeks. Jasmine grabs a water bottle for her. Gillian smoothes her hair. "What happened?" they ask.

Chelsey points at me. "She got us kicked off the squad for the rest of the game!"

"It wasn't my fault!" I argue, but no one pays me any attention.

"Maybe for the whole rest of the year!" Chelsey explodes.

The rest of the girls demand an explanation. Chelsey gives them the Chelsified version. I supply important details. Screw the details—they're livid.

"So that's how you 'help' people with their paper? You get them kicked off of cheer for the most important game of their life?" snaps Becca.

I have nothing to say. I want to go home, but I'm stuck here without a car and I don't have the guts to walk up into the bleachers to ask Mom or Bill for a ride. They'll ask what's wrong and I'll cry. Instead, Chelsey and I sit on folding chairs at opposite ends of the cheer pedestals and watch the game. A shame-fueled fire rages inside me, and the eyes of the wondering crowd keep me from ever turning around to face them. Out on the field, without Chelsey running the show, we lack our usual edge. Some of the cheers go on too long. Some of them end at the wrong time. The halftime show looks off balance and completely loses its punch without my tumbling piece.

Vanessa's inside scoop about the homecoming game turns out to have been correct—the Cutthroats are slaughtered. Chelsey's friends surround and console her. And my friends? Oh, right. I don't have any.

Fourteen

BACK AT HOME, MOM IS FURIOUS. It turns out that a pretty accurate version of the truth made its way into the bleachers by halftime. I am sick, thinking about what Adam's reaction must have been: Wow, she's dumber than I thought. To Mom, I try to sell it as the act of a Good Samaritan. One woman helping another. Wouldn't Elizabeth Cady Stanton have done the same for Susan B. Anthony? Mom doesn't buy it.

"Do you know how seriously plagiarism is taken in the academic world?" she asks, for the tenth time.

I sink into a fresh round of tears. "I really didn't mean for her to steal his work. I meant for her to use it to get ideas."

I expect Joshie to hug me or bring me a sloppy glass of chocolate milk. Instead, he runs to his room. Mom, Bill and I all start at the sound of his bedroom door slamming shut.

"Let me go to him," I say. If nothing else it gives me an excuse to get away from Mom and Bill. But there's no escaping. Walking up the stairs I still hear Mom back in the kitchen describing to Bill the depth of her disappointment. She's suffering a triple whammy of humiliation, embarrassment and mortification. I am suffering those same things and more.

I find Joshie on his bed, using Copernicus as a pillow. He stares up at the butterfly mobile that hangs over his bed. "You lied to me. You said they only wanted to borrow the papers to see how Phil had written them," he says flatly.

"I didn't lie on purpose. That was what I thought she would do with it." I sit in his little desk chair, fiddling with a freakishly lifelike rubber snake. I explain that Chelsey, who is an amazing cheerleader and the most popular female of her species, was off perfecting her straddle jump the day that God doled out brains.

Joshie considers. "And what were you doing that day?"

Ouch. "I was right at the front of the line with a five-gallon bucket. But I guess I must have tripped and spilled some out somewhere along the way."

Joshie wrinkles his nose. "That's gross." He sits up and we're both aware of a crinkling noise coming from his pocket. He reaches in and pulls out a couple of Jolly Rancher candies. "Want one?"

Apparently he is on the road to forgiving me. I take the green one. "Who gave you these?" I pop the candy into my mouth.

"Adam. He was with my chess coach. They got the candy when everyone was throwing it at the parade. Adam said to say hi to you. Hi."

The candy drops from my mouth and Copernicus is on it after just one bounce. "Did you see Adam before or after the game?"

Joshie's forehead wrinkles as he mulls over my question. "Before."

If I had any fingernails left, I would chew them. Word of the *Hamlet* paper debacle spread to the parent section of the bleachers, but did it make its way to the student section, too? Then again, the fact that my biology class still seems to be in the dark about me and Mitch—Cat Woman would certainly have said something by now—supports the hope that not all news reaches all ears.

Still, I groan and drop my head into my hands. What would Adam think of me if he knew?

"Are you okay?" Joshie's blue-raspberry breath is sticky and sweet.

"I could be better," I tell him.

"Can I remind you about something that will make you happy?" he asks.

"Sure."

He lights up. "You get to go to a dance tonight!"

Slipping the dress on over my head it hits me just how ridiculous this is. I agreed to a date. How did that get turned into a date for the homecoming dance? And after this disaster of a day, how can I possibly go to the dance with Mitch, or anyone else? All the cheer squad will be there, still angry, except for Chelsey who will not be merely angry, but completely furious. I pop open my e-mail and craft a quick note to Mitch:

I am very sick. Could be contagious. I'd better stay home.

Mitch's reply is instantaneous:

I wonder what Adam would think about you begging me for his schedule?

I write back:

See you at 7:00.

I lumber down the stairs and find Joshie by the front door with a book of math brain teasers in his lap and the bug tank by his feet. He's all set to be the official greeter. He glances up and his eyes pop. "Wow! You look pretty."

"Thanks." I'd thought about letting myself look like crap. Why dress up for Mitch? But like it or not, people will be staring at me. All night long they will watch and whisper:

> Look! Someone told me Jake Londgren was hot for that cheerleader. So why is she here with Mitchell Wiencis?
> Look! There's the cheerleader who got Chelsey kicked off cheer for the most important game of her life.
> Look! There's Nora Whatsername. Wasn't she popular once?

So instead of looking like crap, I spent most of the last hour primping like I've never primped before. Thanks to the magic of heated rollers my hair tumbles in soft waves onto my shoulders instead of hanging straight. I looked up makeup tips on the Internet and figured out how to do *alluring*—it turns out it's all in the eyes. And while Cherise's dress looked like a big pink oven mitt on the hanger, it fits me like a glove. Mom even loaned me some of her jewelry—the good stuff.

Mom and Bill come out of the kitchen. "Va-va-voom!" says Bill, shaking his hand like he's just touched something hot.

"So who is this boy that you're going to the dance with?" asks Mom again.

"Mitchell Wiencis," I say—again.

Bill probes for a little bit more. "And he is?"

"Just a guy."

"Football player," says Mom, bitingly.

I laugh. "Hardly."

Mitch arrives wearing a powder blue tuxedo with wide lapels, a frilly white shirt, and a yellow polka dot cummerbund and bow tie. His shoes are pointy, shiny and black. His hair, slathered with product, is slicked back vampirelike, accentuating his dearth of eyebrows. He holds out what looks at first glance like a small, transparent casket.

"Yowzah! You look hot!" He hands me the box that contains a corsage big enough to be a funeral wreath for a cat. Salmon-colored roses surrounded by baby's breath and shrubbery. Mom inserts herself with an outstretched hand.

"Well, you must be Mitchell." She forces a smile. I can practically hear the gears churning as she struggles to figure out—What is Nora doing with this guy?

"Mitch," he corrects her.

He takes her hand and kisses it.

Bill just waves.

I remove the corsage from its box. I didn't even know they made pin-on corsages. It would take a staple gun, a glue stick and a pile of rivets to get it to stay on my dress. And, since my dress is strapless, where would it go?

"We can make this work." Mom takes the corsage from my hands. "We'll be right back."

Bill heads off to find some pins and we leave Mitch by the front door with Joshie, who is eager to introduce Mitch to his insect friends.

"Quite a looker," says Bill.

Mom pokes him in the ribs. "Stop that." She examines the corsage and Bill hands her a pile of pins. "So. Why are you going to the dance with this guy?" she asks.

I give her an answer that is technically not a lie. "He was the first person who asked me."

"Hmmm. Hold this." She pushes the corsage into the waistband of my dress and I hold it in place. "Saying yes to the first boy who asked you. That was—"

"Noble?" offers Bill.

Mom shoves a pin into the corsage. "I think I was look-ing for something along the lines of shortsighted, but noble is nicer." In the end she manages to anchor the corsage to the waistband of my dress, off to the side so it won't get squashed when we slow dance.

I assure her there will be no slow dancing.

Mom doesn't offer to take pictures as we head out the door, and I am relieved. The last thing I want is permanent evidence that this night ever took place.

Mitch has borrowed his mother's minivan, and wants to go for dinner at The Barking Toad. But I overheard Krista telling Becca that she and Dex are going there with Jake and his date. I tell him that I really do not want to go to dinner, and he insists that it will not qualify as a date unless dinner is involved. In the end we settle on burgers and fries at Dick's Drive-In. As we head from Dick's to the high school, Mitch-ell puts his hand on my thigh and I slap it. I should have demanded a contract.

I am grateful to find the commons dimly lit, and the mu-sic playing loudly enough that conversation will be close to impossible. People gather in little clusters around the tall, round café-style tables that line the edges of the room. The tables are covered in tablecloths that look like remnants from the drill team's dresses, and in the center of each is a plas-tic trout anchoring a half-dozen helium balloons, purple and gold, of course.

The long, rectangular food table sees a lot of action. It's covered with standard party food—sandwich-y stuff, chips, faded carrot sticks with dip. There are tubs filled with as-sorted soft drinks, and the centerpiece is a cake in the shape of a giant fish. Someone has given the fish a sexual identity with a well-placed carrot stick and a couple of radishes.

"The place looks nice," shouts Mitch.

I nod. It looks like the commons, disguised as a cheesy dance hall. Purple and gold streamers loop from the walls to a spot in the center of the ceiling where lights bounce off a mirrored disco ball.

"Do you want to dance?" he yells.

"No."

Just a few brave couples have ventured onto the makeshift wooden dance floor. Chelsey slow dances with her boyfriend even though the DJ is spinning a hip-hop tune. Beside them Frank, from my original lab table, dances with his date. They look very cute in color-coordinated tuxedos.

"Let's sit over there." Mitch points and I follow him to a table near the food. "Punch?" he shouts, making a motion like he is drinking from a small cup. I nod, and sit by myself, watching groups of people arrive. Krista and Dex show up with Jake and his date. Krista's hair has seen some serious beauty parlor time and looks like it has more hidden nuts and bolts than my corsage does. That said—she is stunning. The red corsage on her wrist matches her not only her dress, but her shoes, her hair clips and the boutonniere pinned to Dex's lapel.

Jake, in a basic black tuxedo, could be the cover boy for *Hot High School Football Player* magazine. His date, who is pretty in an emaciated fashion-slave kind of way, is one of the freshmen I always see in his wake. Wearing a trancelike smile, she clings to Jake's arm like a piece of lint. I watch people watching them and a pang of jealousy zaps me. That could have been me.

Jake turns to say something to his date and sees me. Instead of flashing me the eager grin I'd have gotten from him a few weeks ago, he simply shakes his head. I drop my chin.

As awful as I feel for myself, I'm glad for Jake that he's with someone who truly wants to be with him.

Over by the punch bowl, Mitch talks to Swordhands, then points back at me. Swordhands is with a mousy-looking girl from the fencing team. I should warn her about his invasive, coffee-flavored tongue.

All at once I feel powerfully sorry for myself. What have I done? The Mitch date couldn't possibly get any worse. After the Chelsey ordeal I am a cheerleading pariah with a PQ that has plummeted into negative numbers. And I'm no closer to Adam. If anything, I've driven him further away.

The evening with Mitch drags on. Whenever anyone walks by our table Mitch leans in close and laughs like I have just said something pithy and amusing. The kind of thing you might say to a guy you actually like. Highlights wanders past with her date and does a double take. A freshman from the yearbook committee stops and takes a picture—Mitch scootches in and plants his lips on my earlobe just before she snaps the photo.

Gaak! Mitchell's lips, his pale, disgusting lips, are touching my earlobe! I jerk my head away and grab an antibacterial wipe from my purse.

"That'll go right into the center spread," he says, beaming, totally oblivious to the fact that I am practically scrubbing the skin off my earlobe.

Two different guys from my French class stop by the table and ask if I would like to dance. Each time Mitch throws his arm around my shoulder. "She doesn't like to dance."

I need a break. I slide out of my chair. "I've got to use the restroom."

"I'll walk you there."

"I am fully capable of getting myself to and from the

bathroom," I insist.

A look of concern flashes across his face. "You'd better come back." He taps his watch. "This date isn't over until eleven."

"I wouldn't dream of leaving," I say, dreaming of leaving.

While I'm in the bathroom stall a couple of girls come into the restroom to gossip and fix their makeup. I come out to wash my hands and find Becca and Gillian standing at the mirror. It's like a scene from a bad teen novel. Gillian stops brushing her hair and gives me a frosty look. "Really hot date," she says. Becca laughs and smoothes on some berry-colored lip gloss. They're still laughing as I leave.

I take a long, circuitous route back to the table, finally cutting across the dance floor, which has gotten packed. I am literally run over by Jazmine when she spins into my path. I land, sprawled on the floor.

"Oh, look, someone spilled something on the floor," she says, then spins back into her boyfriend's arms.

Lying there, facedown, it's like falling off the pedestal all over again, complete with the audible gasp of the crowd. Only this time, Krista doesn't race to my aid, though I'm sure she sees me. Instead, Frank and his date scrape me off the floor. And when I get up, nobody claps.

Mitch looks at his watch when I finally return. "That took seventeen minutes."

"I have my period," I tell him.

He flinches. "Oh. Do you, uh, need some more punch?" he asks, because everyone knows that girls who are menstruating need extra punch.

"Sure. Thanks."

He has just left the table when the DJ takes a break. The dance floor clears. Across the room Krista is on Dex's lap. She sees me, says something to Dex and looks away. Jake peeks at me over Lint Girl's shoulder. Can I possibly make it until eleven o'clock? I fold my arms on the table, rest my cheek on them and close my eyes.

"Nora?"

My eyelids drift open. I roll my head to one side.

Adam, sitting one table over, points to the chair vacated by Mitch. "May I?"

Adam. Is here. Adam Hood is here, at the dance?!

I jerk upright.

And he wants to come sit by me? Nora the Mitch Dater? Nora the Hamlet Paper Cheater? To quote the Bard from Act 1, Scene 2: "It is not, nor it cannot come to good."

What do I do? I look from him, with his warm, generous smile, to the empty chair, to the line for punch, which is huge. Mitch is at the end of the line chatting with some yearbook people. I lick my finger and smooth my eyebrows. I give my strapless dress a quick up-tug. I gesture toward the empty chair.

"Of course."

Adam joins me. His hair is tucked back behind his ears with tapered waves that play peek-a-boo from behind his earlobes. Back in late August, when his skin glowed with a summer tan, I didn't notice the three little freckles that line up to create a perfect isosceles triangle, cheek, cheek, chin. He's freshly shaven and smells coconutty and clean. If Jake is the cover boy for *Hot High School Football Player* magazine, Adam is the cover boy for the magazine titled *Hot Every Other Category of Guy.*

Black jacket with satin lapels, black pants with a side stripe in matching satin—I am mere inches from the luckiest tuxedo alive because it sits this close to his skin.

"Wow. You look really pretty," he says.

I smile, grateful for his kindness. "Thanks. You don't look so bad yourself."

He pinches his lapels. "Think I should buy one?"

"Absolutely." I watch my finger trace nervous circles on the tablecloth. Adam breaks the silence. "Are you having a nice time?"

I consider. "*Nice* might be too strong a word."

He is intrigued. "Really?"

"Really."

I swallow, afraid to ask, but I have to. "Were you—were you at the game today?"

His grin is sheepish. "Will you forgive me if I admit that I wasn't?"

My whole body exhales. "Forgiven," I say. "Totally forgiven."

"Eric and I went to his house and played chess," he says. "It's not that I have anything against football, but that first game was a little—crazy."

"Not every guy is hounded by girls asking him to sign their foreheads," I say.

His blush is visible even in this dim light. "I think I've mentioned before—I don't like crowds. I enjoyed the parade, though," he says. "Did Joshie tell you I saw him there?"

"He shared his Jolly Ranchers with me."

Adam smiles. His gaze drifts out to the dance floor. "I'd ask you to dance, but you already know I'm a pathetic dancer. Anyway, I would never drag you onto the dance floor without asking Jake's permission."

I sit up straighter. "Jake?"

"Yeah. You know, the big, burly football player I always see you with?" he says—half smile, full dimple.

I am quiet. The fractional smile leaves Adam's face. "Aren't you and Jake—?"

I look down at my lap. The roses at my waist are broken and bruised from my earlier fall. "No."

"I see."

That's all he says. Unasked questions hang in the space between us. Was I going out with Jake but we broke up? And if I'm not here with Jake, then who am I here with? I choose to leave the unasked questions unanswered. Instead, for this brief blip of time, I pretend that I am here with Adam. That we started the evening with a fabulous dinner at a restaurant with booths, candles and gossipy waiters who tittered about young love at the very sight of us. That we arrived here in a limousine, and after the dance, we will go back to his house, which is conveniently empty because his mother, the oncologist, had to race out to perform an emergency cancer surgery and his father, the shrink, is out talking some heartsick girl off a bridge. All alone. Me and Adam. Adam and me.

I glance up at him. If only it really was just the two of us, but I'm here with Mitch, and—wait, who is he here with? "So, I suspect you're probably not here alone," I say.

When he shakes his head, his hair untucks from his ears, framing his beautiful face. "No. I wouldn't come to something like this by myself. I knew how much Sarah wanted to come, and that she'd only come if she had a date. So here I am."

I am stuck. Sarah? He says her name like I would know who she is. Is she the little redhead who sits the next table over in biology lab? Or maybe the blonde in history who always wears pink? What would Tallulah say?

"There she is." He waves to someone over at the refreshment table. The Teapot, resplendent in acres of gauzy purple fabric, waves back.

Sarah. Of course. This explains Adam's purple cummerbund and tie, and the spray of purple and yellow freesia tucked into his lapel. Who but Adam would agree to be the Teapot's date simply to be nice. Is that why he's here now, sitting with me? Is he just being nice?

But this is a question I cannot dwell on because the Teapot is not the only one who sees us. Mitch surges through the crowd, punch splashing out the sides of the two cups he's carrying. He slams them onto the table and one tips over.

"You're in my seat." He glares at Adam.

Adam holds his hands up in surrender as he shifts to standing. "Whoa. Sorry. I was just saying hi." He looks at me, confused.

"'Just saying hi.'" Mitch mimics him. He raises his voice. "You can just go say hi to someone else, pal. This is my date. You understand that?"

Oh my god. Where is the high-volume DJ when you need him? People at nearby tables stare as Mitch erupts into a full-on tantrum.

"You know, just because a girl is sitting by herself at a table doesn't mean she's available for every other guy to hit on."

"Calm down," says Adam. "I wasn't hitting on her."

"No? Not hitting on her? Then what do you call sitting two inches away from her face and making googly eyes at her? You think I didn't see you? I saw you! She's with me. Got that? So back off!"

I have not seen behavior like this outside the checkout counter at the grocery store where there is always a lollipop or candy bar involved. Mitch's face goes crimson, and I fully expect him to flop onto the floor and pound it with his fists. Adam looks from Mitch to me, trying to figure out who is crazier, the guy having a fit or the girl who came to the dance with him.

For the second time today I am completely and thoroughly embarrassed. Humiliated. Ashamed. And what's more? I'm done. Done! I cannot put up with another second of Mitch's mitchiness. I paid my dues. I came on a date with him, and now, the date is over. I rip the corsage off my dress, pins go flying, and I hurl the thing into the puddle of spilled punch.

"We're done!" My voice is low and deadly serious. "This date is officially over."

Mitch stabs at his watch. "It's only ten eighteen. The date ends at eleven."

My arms are so rigid at my sides that they shake. "Wrong. The date ends now."

"Fine!" shouts Mitch. "Just go ahead and spend the rest of the dance with your little boyfriend. See if I care."

The Teapot is conspicuously quiet, keeping her distance. Adam speaks in a calm, collected voice, "I'm not her boyfriend."

"Oh-HO!" says Mitch. "But she wishes you were. That's how this whole thing got started."

"Stop it!" I shriek. It's like an accident scene. All around us, people gape over one another's heads and shoulders, eager to witness the carnage.

Mitch snarls. "The date was supposed to end at eleven. You broke the date; you broke the deal."

"The deal?" Adam looks to me for an explanation but I have none to offer. Could it make things any worse if I stuck my fingers in his ears and sang, "LA LA LA LA LA" to keep him from hearing what Mitch has to say?

Mitch stabs his finger in my direction. "She agreed on a date if I would give her a copy of your schedule so she could switch into your classes."

I suspect Adam looked dumbfounded. I suspect the cheerleaders hovering nearby wondered how a loser like me ever made it onto the squad. I suspect Mitch wiped his hands on his jacket, happy to be rid of me. But I didn't see any of it because I ran for the door.

Fifteen

OF ALL THE NIGHTS TO LEAVE home without my phone! I beeline to the office to call Mom for a rescue ride but the office door is locked. I try to slink past the side doors leading to the commons, hoping I can find a phone in the library, but I'm stopped by the wood shop teacher, Mr. Schoonover. He's a serial chaperone at school dances, and I find him kicked back in a chair by the door watching a movie on his phone.

"Whoa, there. Slow down. Are you Nora?" he asks.

"Um, yes, that's me."

"A fella was just out here looking for ya. Hang on, I'll go find him." He presses his hands to his knees, preparing to push himself up.

A fella? Mitch? Adam?

"No!" I insist. "No—don't go get him."

Still sitting, he takes in my red-rimmed eyes. My wet cheeks. He does a head-to-toe scan and stops at my waist. The waistband of Cherise's dress is shredded where I tore off the corsage. Mr. Schoonover stares at the torn fabric and shifts uncomfortably in his seat. "Is everything okay?"

"Not really." Crap! What a time to start crying! "I need to call my mom." I rub the wetness into my cheeks and swallow. "May I please borrow your phone?"

His face reddens. "Did that boy hurt you?" he asks in a hushed tone. I assure him that any damage was nonphysical, and my own fault. He hands me his phone and waits with me outside until Mom shows up in her bathrobe. We drive in silence for a couple of minutes. "I guess it didn't go so well with Mitch?"

I shake my head and am soothed by the familiar smells of Mom's car: curiously strong mints, leather cleaner, and the vanilla-scented cardboard pine tree that hangs from the rearview mirror. It has started to rain and the steady *thwap-thwap-thwap* of the windshield wipers helps to take the edge off.

Mom, who has been respectfully quiet, asks, "Want to talk about it?"

Another head shake.

"Guys aren't always all they're cracked up to be," she says. She quotes her favorite comedienne, Lizz Winstead: "I think, therefore I'm single."

It feels good to laugh a little bit.

We stop at a light and she studies me. "You're sure you don't want to talk about it?"

"Maybe tomorrow. I just want to go home and sleep."

Bill and Joshie are already in bed. Copernicus greets us at the door with a pair of Joshie's socks in his mouth. It's after eleven—my date with Mitch is officially over.

Upstairs, I toss the dress into a heap on the floor. I climb into bed too tired to wash my face or brush my teeth, but lie awake because my brain is a television that plays the world's worst reruns, over and over and over.

Adam being sweet.

Mitch having a tantrum.

Adam looking concerned.

Mitch blowing the whistle.

Adam contemplating whether he needs to get a restraining

order against me.

In desperation I flip on the light and rifle through my book bag for reading material that will make the reruns stop. My hand settles on the chess book from Dad, and I am curious. Ben Franklin has plenty to say about how to plan your moves, but does he have any wisdom to share about what to do when things have totally fallen apart? I scan his essay and find

> We learn by Chess the habit of not being discouraged by present appearances in the state of our affairs, the habit of hoping for a favourable change, and that of persevering in the search of resources.

Franklin says that no matter how crappy things seem, chess players should always

> Continue the contest to the last.

In that weird state between asleep and awake I find myself on the giant chessboard painted on the gymnasium roof. It's nighttime, and I'm dressed like a queen, in a crown and a salmon-pink gown with a bunch of radishes pinned to the waistband. I'm chased from square to square by a red-haired rook with no eyebrows. From the edge of the board I catch a glimpse of Benjamin Franklin dressed in purple and gold. He shakes a set of pom-poms and shouts a cheer:

> *Continue the contest to the last!*
> *Beat 'em hard!*
> *Beat 'em fast!*
> *Victory's yours! Use your skill!*

Who's gonna win?
Nora will!

Oh, Mr. Franklin. If only I had your confidence.

I wake at ten o'clock in the morning to the sound of pissing rain. Welcome to fall in Seattle. And winter. And spring. Mom brings me breakfast on a little wicker tray with foldable legs. She toasted a bagel and smeared it with an extra thick layer of cream cheese. A little bowl of blueberries sits at the back of the tray along with a cup of "energizing" tea that was a nice thought, but makes me gag. Perched on a plate, folded in half so it will stand, is a pale green index card with Mom's thought for the day printed on it:

> Being a woman is a terribly difficult task, since it consists principally in dealing with men.
>
> —Joseph Conrad

Joshie whisper-shouts outside my door wondering if I'm awake yet.

"She's awake, but she might want to be left alone," Mom cautions him.

Joshie throws caution to the wind and bounds into my room with the chessboard in his hands and Copernicus at his feet. If Joshie were not wearing cowboy pajamas and a pair of felt antlers I would send him and the chessboard packing, but he is eager and cute and he greets me with a kiss. "Mom said you had a hard night and I told her I knew what would cheer you up." He offers me the chessboard like it is a trophy.

"I don't know, Josh." I do know, actually. There is not a single molecule in my entire body that wants to play chess.

He grins mischievously. "Please? You won't be sorry."

What is he up to? His smile, his outfit and the fact that he felt so let down about the debacle with Phil's papers persuades me to give in. "Okay. But just one game."

I scooch to one side of the bed. Joshie snuggles in beside me and levels the board. Completely out of character, he insists that I play white, so that I get to go first. We line up our pieces, and I move e2 to e4. Joshie mirrors my move. We go back and forth a couple of times when Joshie makes the most blatantly boneheaded move ever, leaving me with no choice but to put him in check.

"Why did you do that?" I ask.

"What?"

"You let me win."

Joshie shrugs, coyly. His antlers tilt to the left. "I thought you needed to win something."

I choke back tears. Am I so pathetic that an almost-seven-year-old in antlers is compelled to let me win?

"Are you okay?" He rubs the little mound that is my foot sticking up beneath the blanket.

"I'm pathetic," I say. "Just pathetic." I pull the comforter to my face, and as much as I don't want to cry in front of him, I can't help it. My shoulders shake as I heave great snuffly sobs.

He removes the antlers from his head and places them on mine. "Poor Nora. Poor, poor Nora. When I'm sad Copernicus has me tell him about it. I could listen if you want to talk."

I peek over the top of the comforter. "Oh, Joshie. It's such a long story."

He manages a sympathetic smile. "I like stories."

"Are you sure?"

"Uh-huh." He flops onto his stomach, propped up on his elbows, his chin resting in his hands.

"Okay. Here we go." I start with the day Adam showed up and kicked a soccer ball with Joshie. "I hardly slept that night. I kept thinking about him and thinking about him. You know how sometimes you meet someone and you just feel an intense connection?"

Joshie nods. "I felt that way about a pill bug I found yesterday."

Whatever. I continue as though I am lying on a couch and Joshie has grown a goatee and is settled beside me in a leather chair, scribbling an analysis of my psychosis onto the pages of a notebook. "I wanted him to like me, you know? And I didn't feel like it was good enough to just be me. I needed to show him that I was cute, and popular and as smart as he was. But I had already switched into lower-level classes because I didn't want all the cheerleaders to think I was some know-it-all brainiac. Then I got this guy, Mitch, to show me Adam's schedule, but in exchange, I had to go on a date with him."

"Copernicus didn't like Mitch," Joshie says.

He is one smart little dog. I reach for a tissue, blow my nose and continue my saga. "Trust me, that was the first and the last time I'll go on a date with Mitch. So, anyhow, once I knew Adam's schedule I switched into his classes, which were a lot harder than the classes I was in. I figured I could lie and tell people that my mom is making me take AP classes."

Joshie scrunches his eyes. "I thought it was good to be smart."

I sigh. "It is. And it isn't. But I wanted to be someone different this year. I wanted everyone to know me as Nora Fulbright—fun, cute cheerleader."

Joshie looks like he is trying to puzzle out a solution to

Goldbach's conjecture—the unsolvable math problem that kept me and Phil busy during long family car rides. I keep going. "Anyhow, I switched into Adam's classes but I wasn't sitting anywhere near him, which made the swap with Mitch sort of pointless. So I swapped seats with this guy in biology class but he wanted a date with Chelsey, and so I swapped Chelsey a couple of Phil's papers to get her to go out with him."

"Ahhhh." Joshie's "ahhhh" sounds so—professional.

"And there is this girl with totally amazing hair in AP US History, and she agreed to swap project partners if I would give her one of Phil's papers, too. She was entering a scholarship contest and wanted to get ideas about how to write a killer paper."

"Highlights," says Joshie.

"Right, Highlights."

"Did she win?"

"No. It turns out Phil's paper was so over-the-top good all it did was make her feel bad about herself. In the end, she never even entered the contest. So, anyhow nothing has worked out. Chelsey got caught cheating, and everyone knows that I'm the one who helped her. God only knows what's going to happen Monday. I might even be suspended. But worse than that, Chelsey hates me. The whole cheer squad hates me because the halftime show looked like crap, and Chelsey missed her shot performing for the cheer coach from Louisville. Krista hates me, and she should, because I've been a terrible friend. And the most ironic thing of all is that I've been trying so hard to be the girl I think Adam would like that I have become a girl that nobody could like. Ever."

As I cry, I shake so hard chess pieces tumble off the board. Copernicus yips when Betsy Ross smacks him squarely on the nose.

"Oh, Joshie. How do I fix things? How do I let people know how sorry I am?"

Joshie knits his eyebrows and blinks a couple of time. "Is this a trick question?"

"No."

"Really?"

"Really."

"Why don't you just say 'I'm sorry'?"

I shake my head. "If only it were that easy."

Joshie slaps the bed and Copernicus scrambles up. "Copernicus ate my hot dog again this morning, and then he said I'm sorry." He kisses the tip of the dog's long black snout. "See? And we're still friends. That's just the way friends are."

So all I need to do is tell Krista I'm sorry and kiss her snout? Could it work? We sit in silence. I pull Joshie into a hug and rub his cheek with mine. "You're so smart."

"It runs in the family," he says, then wriggles away and bounds from the room.

I lean back into a pile of pillows. Again, I pick up the chess book and flip from chapter to chapter, reading the epigraphs that appear in italicized print below the chapter headings. I read the one on chapter thirteen twice:

> We cannot resist the fascination of sacrifice, since a passion for sacrifices is part of a chess player's nature.
>
> —Rudolf Spielman

Do I have a chess player's nature? And what exactly does that mean? Dad sacrificed a family to take a job all the way across the country. Phil sacrificed popularity by being a head's-down science and math geek, and settling for a social life that revolved around his computer, Zeebo and Louis. And me? I have sacrificed my shot at having an off-the-charts popularity quotient by being obsessive about Adam. I sacrificed my friendship with Krista by lying. Maybe Joshie is right? There's nothing more to lose. Maybe it's time to sacrifice a little pride and tell people I'm sorry.

I text Krista: R U There?

It's almost noon. She must be back from church by now. Maybe her family went to brunch? Maybe she's with Dex? Maybe she's out scouting for a new best friend?

Sigh. I grab my bathrobe and head for the shower. I'm halfway out the door when my phone chimes, telling me I have a reply.

Why do you want to know?

I send a message right back. Can we talk? Now?

Krista's response stings. No. Busy.

I pinch the bridge of my nose to stave off another round of tears, but it doesn't work. I toss the phone, the evil phone, onto the bed, and as it hits, it rings.

It's Krista. "Okay, the curiosity is killing me. What do you want?"

Her voice, just the sound of it, is like a scoop from Molly Moon's on a sweltering day.

"How are you?" I ask.

"Pretty good."

The pause in our conversation is pregnant enough to birth an elephant.

"You texted *me*," Krista says.

"Right. Yeah, I guess I did." I pause for deep breath in

and out. "Look, I've been a real jerk."

"And?" her tone is sharp.

"And I want to say I'm sorry."

Without thinking, I launch into a history of my deceptions. "Do you remember when we met at freshman orientation and we started talking about when we were little kids and went to summer camp?" I ask.

"Yeah."

"And you told me you went to Girl Scout camp every summer?"

"Yeah."

"And I told you that until I was twelve I went to camp on the East Coast?"

"Uh-huh." She sounds skeptical.

"Well, they were these sort of kid-genius camps. So when you were at Girl Scout camp making lanyards and collecting firewood, I was dissecting pig hearts, learning what happens when you mix volatile chemicals and exploring how Hemingway uses dialogue to establish character."

"Blech," says Krista. "Why didn't you just tell me that?"

"I didn't want to seem like a show-off. At middle school I got picked on all the time for being a know-it-all. Kids were nice to me if they needed help with homework, or on a science project. That's it. You were the first person who seemed to like me for who I was, not for what I could give you, and I didn't want to wreck that."

"You're such a moron, Nora."

My heart skips a frightened beat.

"I would never judge someone that way," she goes on. "Especially not my best friend."

My heart picks up its lost beat, and I tell her everything. I tell her about switching classes this year because of what Chelsey said to Vanessa the day before school started, and that I didn't want the cheer squad to peg me as a brainiac. "And then I met Adam."

I can almost hear Krista's eyes, rolling in their sockets. "Yeah, Adam. What's up with *that?*"

I flop onto my bed and hug a pillow to my chest. "The first time I met him I felt this incredible zing. It's nothing I've ever felt before. But when I told you I thought he was cute, you almost gagged."

"Oh, crap, Nora. I'm sorry. It's not that he isn't cute. I just really wanted you to go out with Jake. Dex really likes him, and I had all these romantic ideas about the four of us hanging out and, you know, being the maid of honor and best man at each other's weddings. That kind of thing."

"You wanted me to marry Jake?"

"Well. You could have divorced him later. It's just that Jake is so hot! You have to admit he's hotter than Adam."

I'm a little bit offended. "There are different definitions of hot, Krista. I mean, there's temperature hot, you know, like the boiling point of tungsten. Five thousand, six hundred and sixty degrees Celsius, right? Crazy hot! But there's also spicy hot, like capsaicin."

"Cap—what?"

"You know. Capsaicin. The chemical that makes chili peppers fry the insides of your mouth."

Krista laughs. "Did you really think I never figured out that you're smarter than the average wildebeest?"

Outside, on the shades-of-gray scale, the sky has brightened from light charcoal to dark aluminum. I laugh, too. "Okay. But you have to agree with me that Jake and Adam are both hot. It's just that one of them will melt tungsten and the other will burn the crap out of your tongue."

Krista agrees—reluctantly, but I'll take it. I tell her about switching classes. About how I figured I could cover my brainiac tracks by telling people my mother was making me take AP classes. I told her about all of the swaps.

"Wow. For a smart girl you've had a pretty solid run of stupid," she says.

And how.

"Look," she goes on. "One of the reasons I always liked you was because you're different from most people. When you said we should try out for cheer, I wanted to because I thought about how awesome that would make us. I know, how shallow can you get? But at the same time, I didn't want to because I thought the girls would be a bunch of stuck-up snots. Then I figured it would be okay because you and I would have each other. So, yeah, some of the girls are pretty into themselves. But some of them are really nice. And I don't think there's anyone on the squad who would like you less because of how smart you are."

"I get that now. But Chelsey made that crack at practice and I guess I kind of panicked."

Krista groans. "Chelsey's super sweet. But if she went to medical school? You would not find me in line to have her take out my tonsils. I'd probably go home without an arm. So, yeah, she's a little dim, but come on, all she cares about is how well you cheer. So you can stop being all 'Poor me, my brain is bigger than a basketball.' If you weren't so busy stressing about what people think of you, you would have noticed all of this."

Krista is totally right. She and Joshie should partner up and open a therapy business.

"A lot of people are pretty angry at you," she says.

I hesitate before asking what I really want to know. "But what about you? Are you still angry at me?"

Krista says exactly the right thing. "Meet me at Molly Moon's in a half hour. I'll buy you a double-dip."

Sixteen

ON MONDAY, EXCEPT FOR THE forgotten disco ball still dangling from the ceiling, the commons is pretty much how it was before the dance. I wish I could say the same for myself. I search out a table far from where the football crowd gathers and hide behind my math book. It was Krista's idea to meet me for a pep talk. I'm not ready to face anyone from cheer. I don't want to see Mitch—what if he pitches a follow-up tantrum? And I'm prepared to fling my book bag over my head and become invisible if I spot Adam.

Joshie's advice worked great with Krista—but who else would be so willing to accept my apology? And do I even have the guts to try?

Looking around the commons it's like I've returned to a crime scene. There should be yellow tape marking off the place where Mitch had his fit. A corpse-shaped figure drawn in chalk, identifying the spot where I landed at Jazmine's feet on the dance floor. Even with my eyes glued to a book, I sense people slowing as they pass, whispering behind their hands.

I jump as Krista drops into an empty chair. She catches her breath. "Whew! Sorry I'm a little late! Is that mine?" She points to one of the two lattes on the table—the one with a straw.

"Double-tall half-decaf nonfat mocha, no whip," I say.

She smiles and sucks a sip through the straw, then takes a bite of my granola bar. "I didn't see you all the way over here.

You look . . ." She chews the granola bar slowly.

"Like crap? I know. I feel like it, too. How am I going to face these people?"

Krista's shoulders droop. "Look. You told me the truth. Do the same thing with Chelsey. If she's okay with you, her drones will be okay with you, too."

"I wrecked her chances at getting into Louisville!"

I wait for Krista to say something I hadn't thought of. To shine some hopeful glimmer of light on the situation.

She nods. "Yeah. That pretty much stinks."

I fold my arms onto the table and bury my face. "It's not just Chelsey I'm worried about. I should apologize, or at least say something to Mitch." I look up. "As skeevy as he is, I did agree to go out with him, right? And instead of it being his dream date it turned into a nightmare. And Swordhands—the guy who went out with Chelsey—that couldn't have gone worse! I've made all these other people miserable with my lame-ass swaps."

I bolt upright at the sound of familiar laughter from across the commons. Jake and a couple of other football guys laugh like mad at Geoff the Fish, who sits on the floor in the debris of a chair he just sat in and flattened. He gets up and rubs his butt. They laugh louder.

I groan. "I don't ever want to talk to Jake, either."

Krista rubs my arm. "Don't worry about Jake. According to Dex's report on the way to school this morning, Jake is completely over you. He had a great time at the dance with Fluffy, and spent all day Sunday with her, too."

"Stop it! Tell me her name is not Fluffy."

Krista crosses her heart. "They were made for each other. And for the record—no way will she be my bridesmaid. I—" Krista freezes.

"What?"

From where she's sitting, Krista has a perfect view of people lining up for coffee behind me. She leans in. "Adam just got into the coffee line. He's with Hair Girl."

I can't look. "God! I am *so* embarrassed! I've pursued him relentlessly and it's clear that it'll never work. He was *so* sweet at the dance. And he's been sweet in class. But he's that way with everyone." I pause. "And he thinks cheerleaders, me in particular, aren't smart enough for him."

Krista shrugs. "Look, we both know lots of people think that, and we also know they're mistaken. Well, mostly. And if anyone can prove Adam wrong, it's you."

If only. I tell her about some of my not-so-successful attempts to just that. "But even if I could convince him that I'm as brilliant as, I don't know, Judit Polgár—"

"Who?"

"She's an amazing chess player. Even if I could prove I was *that* smart, he's got Tallulah."

Krista's eyebrows go up as she looks past me into the coffee line. "She's obviously into him, but if you ask me, he looks a little uncomfortable."

I slowly turn and take a peek. Adam is at the front of the line ordering his drink. Tallulah, in knee-high boots and a short sweater dress slides her hand into his back pocket. He gently reaches behind him and removes it. She strokes his cheek and he pulls away.

"I know she clings to him like pond scum," Krista says. God, I love her! "But have you ever actually seen him reciprocating?"

I consider. "Maybe he just isn't into PDA?"

Krista shakes her head. "Please. I wouldn't be so sure. It's too bad you can't just ask someone."

"I know. But even then, how do I convince him that I'm

not a stalker, and not a complete idiot? And how will I do any of that if I can't even muster up the guts to talk to him?"

Krista offers nothing but a look of sincere hopelessness.

"Crap! And I still need to face Chelsey. And the other cheerleaders. And Jake." I groan.

Krista grimaces. "It sucks to be you." She glances at her phone. "Look—the bell's about to ring. Are you going to live?"

I drain my latte. "No."

She offers a hopeful smile. "I'll bring Skittles to your funeral."

"Orange ones?"

"Orange ones."

The first bell rings, and as we leave the commons Krista changes the subject. "Want to hear something Dex told me on the way to school?"

"Sure."

"He ran into Chelsey and Becca at the gym yesterday. They bitched about you. About the game. Becca moaned that it was such a bummer that Chelsey didn't even get to cheer in her fancy homecoming uniform. Then, Chelsey went on a rant about how the homecoming uniforms, while totally adorable, were not worth it."

"Worth it?" I ask. "They were donated by some rich alum."

Krista glances left then right and lowers her voice. "You know the Ultimate Fan?"

"The one who always wears a prehistoric cheer uniform to the game and cheers like crazy?"

Krista nods. "She's the rich alum. She's also Vanessa's mother."

"What?"

"She donated the uniforms in exchange for Vanessa making the cheer squad."

"But Vanessa hates cheer. Why would she even agree to that?"

"I know, right? But apparently her mother only allowed her to take AP classes if she did cheer. Crazy, huh?"

I shake my head. It's crazy, all right. If Vanessa wasn't a year older than me I'd wonder whether we'd perhaps been switched at birth.

"Don't you have biology?" Krista asks as we pass the hallway leading to the science classrooms.

"I have my meeting with Mrs. Esposito."

"Ouch. Good luck with that. Seriously. Are you okay?"

"Sure."

"Are you sure you're sure?"

The truth is I am not sure of anything. For all I know I may be getting kicked off cheer this morning. Or if Mr. Pawlosky gets his way, suspended, or expelled.

Krista pulls me into a hug. "Things are never as bad as they seem. It'll all work out, okay?"

I flash back to Ben Franklin shaking his pom-poms for me. Could there possibly be a move that I have not yet thought of? "You know what?" I manage a weak smile and paraphrase Ben Franklin. "I'm going to continue the contest to the last."

Krista rubs my head, mussing my hair. "Whatever. It sure is good to have you back."

Mrs. Esposito's office door is closed, with a heated, but muffled argument going on inside. Chelsey sits alone in the waiting area cradling a box of tissues.

"Hey," I say.

She huffs, crosses her legs and turns away from me.

"We need to talk."

"I have nothing to say to you," snorts Chelsey.

"Well, I have something to say to you, and it's this. I'm sorry. I'm really, really sorry." I go on, not sure whether she's even listening, and I tell her the whole sordid truth. The classes I dumbed down because I thought it would make her like me better. The trade with Mitch. The classes I smartened up because I thought it would make Adam like me better, and how I arranged the date with her and Swordhands so I could get closer to Adam in class.

Chelsey turns so that she's facing me. Her mouth is pinched and her short, angry breaths make her nostrils flutter. "So everything you did was about making someone like you better?"

When she puts it that way, I feel so small. So desperate.

"And you thought," she sputters, "you thought that I would like you better if you were dumber. More like me. Because I'm so dumb. Is that it?"

Oh my god. I just said that, didn't I? "Wow, Chelsey, I . . ." I am at a loss for words.

Chelsey looks so sad. So broken. She draws a shuddering breath. "You know, I may not be the smartest person in the world, Nora. I get that, but I have feelings. And you used me because I was dumb enough to do what you asked me to do. You used me in your stupid game. You played me like a—like a prawn."

Chelsey is right. Okay, I didn't play her like a water-dwelling crustacean, but I know what she means—I played her like a pawn. The pawns, the foot soldiers, the pieces we sacrifice in order to achieve our objective.

"God, Chelsey, I feel awful." Tears break through. Chelsey pulls a couple of tissues from the box and hands them to me. She's crying, too. "You're right, Nora. I am stupid. I'm the one who thought it would be okay to just cover up your brother's name on the first page and then I left it on all the others. Do you know that I have a tutor who helps me with math three times a week, and that he's only in the eighth grade? And that I took chemistry twice, and I only passed the second time because they let me do a final project where I made up a cheer for every element? I hate being so dumb." She pounds the seat of her chair with her fist again and again. "I hate it, I hate it, I hate it."

I grab her hand. "Chelsey, no! No, no, no. There are all different flavors of smart. Just like ice cream. I'm smart when it comes to things like math and science. But I'm not so smart when it comes to people. You're right. I used you, and I didn't even get it until now, until you pointed it out to me because you're smart. When it comes to working with people? You're brilliant. You make everyone smile. And when it comes to cheerleading? God, Chelsey, you're a genius! You write amazing cheers. You keep everyone in line. You're not stupid, Chelsey. In fact, I think you're one of the smartest people I know."

Chelsey blows her nose and smiles. "Really?"

"Really."

I'm sure I look like a train wreck. Chelsey, however, looks reborn. "When I hand in that *Tempest* paper," she says, "I'm going to make sure I take your brother's name off *all* of the pages."

I drop my head into my hands.

The volume behind Mrs. Esposito's closed door has fallen a few notches and we probably don't have much time before we're called in to receive our sentence.

"Trust me on this, okay? You can't hand in my brother's *Tempest* paper," I whisper.

"But that was part of the deal!"

"I know, but we don't want to take any chances of getting you into even more trouble. I could help you write a great paper that would be all yours, not my brother's. I'll just coach you. Trust me. We can do it. *You* can do it."

Chelsey chews on her thumbnail and considers. "I guess that would fix the *Tempest* paper problem." All at once she wilts. "It's too bad we can't fix the Louisville problem."

"But if I help you on the paper you'll get the grades you need to be able to even apply to Louisville, right?"

Chelsey fiddles with her ponytail. "I guess so."

The door to Mrs. Esposito's room flies open and Mr. Pawlosky marches past us. His glasses are askew and his spiky gray hair sticks up like little smokestacks that have just vented steam. He stops, glares at us and leaves.

Mrs. Esposito calls us in to deliver our sentence. We stand, because the two visitor chairs are taken, one by Ms. Ostweiler, who cradles her coffee cup looking deeply disappointed, the other by one of the senior English teachers. Mrs. Esposito says that in addition to missing the homecoming game Chelsey and I each get a zero factored into our first semester English grades. On top of that we're to clean the bleachers after every home game until the end of the season.

Mrs. Esposito looks hard at Chelsey. "Mr. Pawlosky expects a miracle on the *Tempest* paper."

Chelsey's eyes flick toward me, then back to Mrs. Esposito. "I am a miracle-making machine."

Back in the waiting area, Chelsey hugs me. "Yes! We're still on cheer!" She texts Becca the good news. "And by the way," she says, "I accept your apology."

"Thanks. I just wish there was something I could do to make up for you missing your chance to show the Louisville coach your stuff."

"You're pretty smart," says Chelsey. "If anyone can think of a way to fix things, it's you."

The success with Chelsey combined with the fact that I'm still enrolled in high school gives me a surge of confidence and I swing by the attendance office. Thankfully, Mrs. Turner does not require that I date her in exchange for Mitch's schedule. I knock on the door of his geometry class and ask the teacher if I may have a moment with Mitch in the hall. He puffs his chest and struts out of class like I'm his nymphomaniac girlfriend who's pulling him out for a quickie in the hallway.

"I knew you'd be back." He hooks his thumbs through the belt loops of his jeans.

"I just want to clear things up. I made a mistake asking for Adam's schedule. I'm sorry I dragged you into it. I won't bother you again."

I turn to walk away.

"That's it?" he shouts. "That's all you have to say?"

I face him. "Um, yeah. Pretty much."

He steps toward me. "I thought we had something special."

I step back. "Sorry, Mitch. We don't."

I head toward biology and he calls out after me, "You'll regret this, Nora! That picture of us at the dance is getting cut from the centerfold of the yearbook!"

I turn the corner and do my best Herkie jump ever.

With just ten minutes left in first period, I skip biology and bide my time in the commons, happy to avoid any possible encounter with Adam before I've figured out what to say to him. Between periods I keep my eyes peeled for the Teapot, but never see her.

Later, at lunch, Krista insists I get it over with and take my chicken wrap and smoothie to the regular spot. The greeting I receive as I set down my food is stony, but Chelsey comes to my rescue. She extols my virtues, making sure everyone knows that in her swirly purple-penned book, I'm okay. By the end of lunch Jake, with Fluffy on his lap, calls me a dork and delivers a friendly blow to my shoulder. Jazmine apologizes for flattening me at the dance. Gillian brushes my hair to a high gloss.

It takes everything I have to force myself into history class where I swear I can feel Adam's eyes on the back of my head. As my rotten stinking luck would have it, today is the first day we're to meet with our partners to start planning our debate questions and responses. Perhaps Highlights notices that I am nearly hyperventilating because she passes me a note:

> *I saw what happened at the dance. Want to work with me and Jolene instead?*

I turn to her, momentarily dumbstruck. "Seriously?"

She shrugs. "Women are supposed to help each other out, right?"

I breathe an audible sigh of relief. After Ms. Harrington agrees to the change, I spend the rest of the period avoiding eye contact with Adam. But he catches me on the way out of class.

"Nora, wait! I thought you were working with me and Zeke?"

I look at his chin. If I go any higher I will lose myself in his eyes. "I switched groups. I've got to go." I hurry toward my next class knowing I am only making things worse, but not knowing what else to do.

In the locker room, for the first time in weeks, people talk to me, and it feels good! I do a quick change into shorts and a T-shirt. Chelsey announces that we're practicing in the upper gym today and I offer to wait for Krista, who hasn't shown up yet, to let her know where we'll be. I stop Vanessa on her way out.

"Can I ask you something?" I say.

"Sure."

"Is it true about the homecoming uniforms?"

Vanessa deflates. "I thought you were the one person who wouldn't give me a hard time about it."

"And I won't. Really! I just wanted to say that I know how it feels to want to do something that your mom thinks is ridiculous."

She shakes her head. "It's not that my mom thinks AP classes are ridiculous. It's that cheerleading was her whole life in high school. In college, too. She was convinced that if I would just try it I would love it, but I would never have made the squad without her—assistance. So here I am, and I hate it. I hate giving up Saturdays when I could be at the library. I hate standing in front of a crowd. And the worst part? The US Intellectual History Conference will be at the Seattle Convention Center the same weekend as our last game. I have to miss it because I'll be jumping up and down, cheering on some testosterone-engorged lunkheads fighting one another over a pointy ball."

Wow. I wish I were taping this for Mom. "Blow off the last game! Tell your mom you're capable of making your own choices, Vanessa. That's what she did when she was in high school, right? She chose to be a cheerleader? And you can choose not to be one."

Vanessa purses her lips and shakes her head. "Chelsey

would kill me. She gets all freaked out if someone misses a game because we're off balance in our stunts. I may be totally lame, but at least with me out there we look balanced. Crappy, maybe, but balanced."

"I wish I could help you."

She smiles. "Thanks, but I think I'm stuck. Listen, I'd better head to the gym. Chelsey will think I'm down here doing my AB homework."

Vanessa and Krista nearly collide as Krista races into the locker room. "Sorry! I had to help Dex carry a bunch of basketball gear to his car. It's pouring out there!"

I grab a towel out of my locker and hand it to her. "We're practicing in the upstairs gym. I'll wait for you."

She pulls her hair into a sloppy ponytail. She peels off a pair of wet jeans and a saturated shirt, and slips into gray yoga pants and a dry tank top. She looks at me like she's checking for wounds. "How did the rest of the day go? You seemed good at lunch."

"Thanks to you and Chelsey."

She drops onto the wooden bench and pulls on a pair of dry socks. I tell her about my conversations with Mitch and Swordhands. About Highlights coming to my rescue in history. About totally avoiding Adam.

She laces up her sneakers. "You should talk to him. Tell him how you feel. Look what happened when you came clean with me and Chelsey. Hang on, I need to pee."

Krista and I talk through the stall door. "When I talk to you and Chelsey, there's a clear line of communication between my brain and my mouth. Sometimes when I talk to Adam, when I'm nervous, there is this bizarre internal rerouting where my thoughts leave my brain and reach my mouth via my feet. I'm just not ready to talk to him yet."

Krista flushes and comes out to wash her hands. She looks at me in the mirror. "You'll need to talk to him eventually."

She sticks her hands in the high-speed blower thing. Little droplets fly out and hit me in the face. "Right?" She shouts to be heard over the steady whir.

"I don't know," I shout back. "Actions speak louder than words. I need to figure out a way to show him that I'm worthy."

Krista laughs. "Worthy?"

"Yeah. Worthy of his respect. And his affection."

She rolls her eyes. "Worthy of his affection. How romantic. Come on, let's go."

We pass by the student activities board on the way to the upper gym. The ski club is showing a movie to raise more money for their Whistler trip. The anime club is hosting a fall fashion show. There's also a flyer posted by the chess club announcing a tournament. I stop to look at it.

"Come on." Krista tugs my arm. "We're already late."

"Hang on."

At the bottom of the flyer there's a sign up list with sixteen slots—all of them are filled in. I glance at the list. Maneesh. Nathaniel. Corinna. Eric from Chess Kings is on there. Adam is there, too. Go figure.

Krista, steps in to take a look. "A chess tournament?"

"I actually used to play a lot with my dad. I was good. I never thought I'd want to touch it again—but who knows. Maybe one day."

I pull her over to the glass trophy case and point to a plaque at the back: RIVERBEND HIGH SCHOOL STATE CHESS CHAMPIONS. "See the third name from the left?"

Krista puts her hand over her eyebrow to cut the glare from the glass and reads it out loud. "Jonathan Fulbright.

Wait. Your dad?"

I nod. "He used to call me his little Judit Polgár."

"The brilliant chess player."

"Yup. Polgár's dad set out to prove that geniuses are made, not born. So he did this experiment with his three daughters. He and his wife homeschooled them, but the thing they focused on more than anything was chess. All three daughters went on to become amazing chess players, but the youngest one, Judit, was the best. She broke Bobby Fischer's record and became the youngest grandmaster of all time when she was just fifteen years old. My dad harbored this crazy dream of me being the next Judit Polgár. And then he left."

Krista smirks at me.

"What?"

"Nora Fulbright, a chess geek," she says. "The things you learn about a person when they come out of their cocoon." She hooks her arm through mine and we run upstairs to the gym for one of the best practices ever.

Afterward, I'm cold and wet, stuffing my gear bag into the backseat of my car when I spot someone in a purple rain poncho waving like mad from over by the after-school activity buses. The Teapot. She motions urgently for me to join her.

I brave the monsoon and jog over.

"How are y'all doin'?" she asks.

I swipe rivulets of water from my eyes. "Wet. Very wet."

She replies in a theatrical voice quoting Portia from Shakespeare's *The Merchant of Venice*, "The quality of mercy is not strained / It droppeth as the gentle rain." She gives me a big, warm smile. Beneath her poncho hood, raindrops dot her cheeks like wet freckles.

"Y'all raced off before we ever got to shake our booties on

the dance floor," she says. "You're sure you're okay?"

I shrug. "Okay enough."

A bus roars into the circle. "Oh, shoot," says the Teapot. "I'd like to chat more, but I've got to make my bus."

Around us, people jockey into position competing to be first onto the bus. "Ordinarily I wouldn't mind missing it, but Tallulah's waiting for me." The Teapot holds up a bottle of glue. "She's trying to make a collage with pictures of her in all her favorite roles for her new boyfriend but she ran out of glue."

My heart attempts a standing double front somersault. "*New* boyfriend? But what about Adam?"

The Teapot waves a dismissive hand. "Goodness, no. That little crush has been over for"—she checks the yellow smiley-face watch strapped to her wrist—"four hours. At lunch, right between nibblin' her sandwich and chewin' her carrot sticks, Tallulah got a drop-dead romantic text from a guy she met at her cousin's wedding."

I blink. Twice. Everyone but the Teapot has boarded the bus. The driver revs his engine. She turns and shouts, "Hold your horses!" Then to me she says, "I love Tallulah and all, but if you ask me, Adam could do better than trying to play Romeo to her particular brand of Juliet."

"They never seemed like a perfect match," I offer.

She nods vigorously causing raindrops to fly off her hood as she climbs aboard the bus. She pauses on the first step and turns back to face me. "Hey! Speaking of matches, there's a chess match coming up. Little Nate is playing. So is Adam. Maybe y'all should bring your pom-poms and cheer on your favorite player?" Her wide eyes, lifted eyebrows and pursed lips speak volumes. She totally knows I've got it bad for Adam Hood. She gives me a frilly wave and says, "Ta ta!" as the bus driver shuts the door.

I match her wave and call out, "Ta ta," though I know she can't hear me.

I'm freezing. My clothes are soaked. My sneakers are wet through. But I feel great!

Back at my car, I climb in and listen to rain pattering on the metal roof. There is no way that I would ever show up at a chess tournament in my cheer uniform and cheer on my favorite player. It would send completely the wrong message. But if my favorite player were to see me hunkered down at a chessboard annihilating the competition? What would he think of me then?

Hmmmm.

Seventeen

TUESDAY AT LUNCH, IN HIS Striped shirt, Eric is easy to spot in the burger line. Before approaching him I sneak a glance at his usual table. There are only a couple of empty seats. Adam is already there with the Teapot on one side of him and Little Nate on the other. Tallulah is nowhere to be seen.

"Hey, got a second?" I ask Eric.

He looks left, then right. "Me?"

"You. Can we talk? Over by the tree?"

"Talk? By the hippie tree?"

"Uh-huh."

"Umm. Okay. Sure. I'll see you over there."

I walk as invisibly as possible to the tree growing by the art wing stairs. All the kids stuck in the 1970s congregate here. A guy with a long braid, scruffy facial hair and tie-dyed yoga pants juggles beanbags. A girl in waif attire picks at a guitar. The air is thick with patchouli. No one would think of looking for either me or Eric over here.

Eric arrives balancing a tray with a burger, fries, a chocolate milk and nine little bowls of ketchup. We sit on the low cement wall that circles the tree. I jump up and grab a chair for him to set his tray on.

"So, what's up?" he asks. "Need help with a chess puzzle?"

"A chess puzzle? You could say that."

He doses his burger with three of the ketchups.

"Seriously?"

"The puzzle is that I want to play in the chess tournament posted down on the student activity board, but there are no slots left."

He lifts the burger but doesn't take a bite. "Wait. You want to play in a chess tournament? I don't know when the last time was that you played in an actual tournament, but these days you're not allowed to knock over your chair and quit halfway through a game."

My face warms. "I got stressed out that night at Chess Kings. I didn't think I wanted to play chess again, but things have changed. I want to get back into it—to make it all the way through a competitive game. May I?" I gesture toward his fries.

"Sure."

I sweep a fry through some ketchup and pop it into my mouth. "Look, there are two weeks till the tournament. I know a lot of people on that sign-up sheet have played forever, but if I play nonstop between now and then I think I'll be able to hold my own. I was actually a pretty good player when I stopped."

"Pretty good?"

"Excellent, actually."

Eric takes a bite of his burger, then chews, nodding thoughtfully. "Why'd you quit?"

I look up, into the tree. It's amazingly healthy for something that's being forced to live totally outside of its element. "Look, I don't really want to get into it. But I know I could get up to speed enough to at least make it through the first round."

Eric dunks a fry into ketchup as he considers. "You could sign up to be an alternate. If anyone drops, you take their place."

I shake my head. "Not good enough. I want to be in the tournament. It means a lot to me."

His eyes wander to the guy in a chain-mail shirt giving a shoulder rub to a girl in a velvet cape. "You'd need to persuade someone to drop."

I pull from my book bag the packet of red licorice twists I picked up this morning at the school store and place it beside his spent ketchup bowls.

He laughs, then his face goes blank. "Wait. You want *me* to drop?"

I nod, my confidence waning. I tighten my lips trying hard not to show it.

"That's nuts. I'm the top seed," says Eric. "And no offense, you may be a cheerleader and all, but in the chess club, you're a nobody. I can't just swap places with you."

The word *swap* clangs around inside my head, bruising my sensibility. No more swapping. NO MORE SWAPPING! No more dates, for me or anyone else. Unless—is it possible to do a trade where everyone truly wins?

Nearby, an iPod cranks out a tinny mix of Grateful Dead tunes. I make my pitch. "If you help me by giving me your spot in the tournament," I say, "maybe there's something I could do to help you? Maybe I could, I don't know, coach the kids at Chess Kings and give you a night off."

Eric picks up the packet of licorice and examines it. He taps his foot rapid-fire on the floor. His cheeks puff up trumpet-player style and he blows out a breath. "Okay, yeah. There's something I want, and maybe since you're a cheerleader, you could make it happen." He licks his lips, looks at his tray, then rubs his fingers over his mouth as he tells me what he wants. "I, uh, mmrph mivveph mmt."

I lean in to better hear him. "What?"

"I, uh, I would—" he speeds up the end of his sentence so I can barely make out what he saying. "I want to be the mascot at a football game."

Who would have thunk it? "Seriously?"

An eruption of sweat leaves Eric's face clammy. "Yeah. Okay, never mind. It was stupid."

"No! It isn't stupid. You would make a terrific mascot. Look at how you cheer on all the kids at Chess Kings. They love you. You make them feel really special. Really smart."

Patches of pink bloom on his cheeks.

"You would be awesome," I say. "I just need a second to think about how I could possibly make this work."

I gaze up into the branches of the tree as I give the situation a little foresight and circumspection. I'd need to get Geoff to buy in, which will no doubt require another trade. Eric probably needs to sign some kind of liability form saying that if he bends, folds or mutilates himself while running around in a fish suit the school is not liable. And what about caution? Is there any potential for disaster? If I can even get through the first round of the tournament, I have to believe that Adam would regain some respect for me. If I get trounced, I will only confirm what he already believes—that Nora Fulbright is a freak show. Nothing ventured, nothing gained.

I stand and brush dust off the back of my skirt. "Let me see what I can do. So just to make sure we're both clear—if I can get you a gig as the mascot at one of our football games, you'll see to it that I get your slot at the chess tournament?"

"Yes," he says. I follow his gaze to his usual lunch table. Little Nate is thumb-wrestling the Teapot. Adam, his elbow on the table, his head resting in his hand, is reading a book.

"The chess club guys are not going to like this," says Eric.

"Don't be so sure. For the first and only time someone other than you gets a shot at winning, right?"

His head does a little bobble-head thing. His smile broadens. "Yeah, I guess. Maybe. Although Adam—he's got a shot at top dog even if I play. The guy is pretty amazing."

We both glance over at Adam. He's amazing, all right.

"One more thing," I say. "Can we keep this between us? I don't want anyone to know until the day of the tournament."

He pops one last fry into his mouth and wipes a little dab of ketchup from his lip. "You're crazy, you know."

"Perhaps I am. But crazy or not, I've got to go. I need to go see a man about a fish suit."

From the hippie tree I head toward the football section of the commons.

"Nora!" Krista, sitting beside Dex, waves me over. Across from them, Chelsey uses a plastic knife to cut the crusts off a sandwich. Fluffy feeds the crusts to Jake who quacks like a duck. I join them and Krista offers me some smoothie. "Strawberry banana," she says, and points to an empty chair. "Why don't you sit?"

I inhale some smoothie. "No time. I'm on a mission."

Krista's jaw tightens. "Please—don't tell me you're going through with this chess thing." I revealed my plan to her last night over the phone.

"Chess thing?" asks Dex.

"Don't ask," mumbles Krista.

"Totally going through with it." I scope out the neighboring tables. "I need to talk to Geoff."

"The fish?" asks Dex. "He's right over there."

"Don't help her," says Krista.

I take another sip of smoothie and hand Krista her cup.

"See you guys later."

"Nora! Do not do something you'll regret later." Krista jumps to her feet.

I beeline for Geoff's table.

"Good luck," Dex calls. I turn and wave as Krista hits him on the head with her notebook.

Geoff is at a table with the Riverbend High defensive line. He crams a wad of sandwich wrappings into a brown paper bag as I reach his table.

"Hi guys." I receive a half-dozen grunted variations of hello in response.

"Geoff, can I steal you away for a minute?"

Geoff looks at the other guys for permission. Some primitive form of communication takes place between them and he says, "Sure."

I motion for him to follow me away from the table. "The bell's about to ring," he reminds me.

"I know. I'll cut right to the chase."

I consider the elaborate ruse I've worked out about my friend who's got cancer, and whose dying wish is to have Eric be mascot at a football game. But before I open my mouth I reconsider. It's like all the lies I've manufactured so far were made in China—cheap imitations of the truth, and quick to fall apart. No more lies. "I have a friend who wants to wear the fish suit at a football game," I tell him.

He laughs. "And what would I wear on the field? My tightie whities?"

Perish the thought—although it would be fascinating to observe a pair of underpants that large in their natural habitat. "No. What I mean is that this other person would actually be the mascot for a day. He would wear your fish suit, and get out there and dance around and do all the things you usually do during the game."

"Why would I let someone else be the mascot?"

"Because there's a really nice guy who would be extraordinarily happy if he could have a shot at being the catch of the day. And if that's not good enough, then you tell me. What would it take to get you to give him a shot?"

His eyes drift to my chest. I cross my arms. "Aside from that." Ben Franklin would applaud my foresight.

Geoff narrows his eyes. He absently picks at a little hole in the elbow of his Seahawks jersey. "Okay, if some other dude is out there in the fish suit, I want to announce the game."

"Really?"

"Yeah." He perks up. "I'm gonna major in radio journalism in college. I did this internship last summer with KUOW and sometimes they let me make the day sponsorship announcement. Maybe you heard me?" He clears his throat, and says in a crisp, affected radio-guy voice, "Today's day sponsors are Gustav and Lucretia Reisigdorf, celebrating twenty-five years of togetherness in the beautiful Pacific Northwest."

I stare at him. He looks embarrassed. "Sorry. I know you're not the type who listens to public radio."

I laugh. "You'd be amazed. And you'd also be terrific at the football game!"

He smiles. "You mean it?"

"I do! But no promises until I see if I can make it work."

The bell rings, we shake hands, and head to class.

After school I track down Stuart Shangrove in the front circle where he's waiting for his bus, which, thankfully, is late. Stuart Little, as everyone facetiously calls him, is the only guy at the school taller than Dex. I'm out of breath when I reach him.

"Stuart!" I pant and press my hand to my chest. "Can I

talk to you?"

"Sure."

I introduce myself, my head tilted all the way back on my shoulders in order to talk eye-to-eye. I feel like a hobbit.

"Come on, I know who you are," he says. "You almost took me out with your car the first day of school."

Oh, right. That.

"And I announce all the games," he says. "Of course I know who you are." He speaks into an air microphone in his announcer voice, "Ladies and gentlemen, for your viewing pleasure, Nora Fulbright! The cheerleader who fell down."

"Very funny. How about, 'Nora Fulbright, the cheer-leader who got back up.'"

"Yeah, that would work, too."

Around us, the crowd is growing impatient. "This sucks," says Stuart. "It's the third time this month that we've had to wait for the bus, and I've got a ton of homework."

Ah. I see a way in. "So, you don't have a car?"

"No. And it's a pain in the ass."

"I have a proposition for you, Stuart." My neck hurts from looking up at him.

"A proposition?"

"Yes. I have this friend who wants really badly to an-nounce one of the football games—"

Stuart starts to object. Something about needing to know football inside and out, needing to know the players, but I keep going. "Hang on. Hear me out. I'm talking about Geoff."

"The fish?"

"Yeah. And as you know, he played football until he blew out his knee his sophomore year, so he understands the game. And of course he knows all the players. Well it turns out that he did an internship at KOUW and wants to study radio broadcasting in college, and he'd be super stoked to have a shot at announcing a game."

Stuart pulls back his head so that his chin all but disappears. "So why are *you* telling me this? If the fish wants to announce a game he should swim over and ask me himself."

"Well, I'm the one arranging the swap."

"The swap?"

"Yeah. Long story, but it's sort of a specialty of mine. So here's the deal, you let him announce a game and I'll lend you my car."

The bus is still nowhere in sight.

"A scary silver Honda as I recall," he says. "Especially terrifying when it's heading right for you."

I roll my eyes. "Do you want to use my car or not?"

He looks at his watch, then at the empty bus lane. "Okay. One game for a month of car use."

"What? Anything more than a day and my parents would sort of notice that the car has gone missing. Here's the deal, take it or leave it. Geoff announces one game, you get the car for one twenty-four-hour period."

Stuart strokes his chin as he considers. "Lori and I are celebrating our seven-month anniversary in a few weeks. It would be pretty sweet to pick her up and take her out. Maybe grab dessert someplace. Then we could drive over to the lake. How big is your backseat?"

I kick his foot. "You're disgusting! Not to mention that you're like eight feet tall and my car is a Honda."

He laughs, but agrees to the deal. Geoff will need to meet with him ahead of time to go through the ropes and learn how to use the equipment—he'll broadcast the last game of the season, a home game that we're almost certain to win. I tell him that he'll need to squeeze into a fetal position to fit in the front seat of my car, and that the deal prohibits more than one occupant in the backseat, especially when the car is parked. The deal is sealed with a handshake, and Stuart waves from inside the bus as it pulls out of the circle.

Nora Fulbright, dealmaker extraordinaire, is on fire. Why can't I always operate with this kind of confidence whenever I'm near Adam? I should make a movie of me in my Adam-free moments and send it to him. But instead he will observe me in real life, in my role as chess goddess. I skip to practice. All the pieces are in place except for one: As much as I'd rather not do it, I need to play some chess.

Eighteen

BACK AT HOME, JOSHIE RACES to his bedroom, then skids back into mine with the chessboard. He arranges it on my desk and dumps the pieces from where he's been storing them in Phil's old Pokémon backpack. "This is exciting! You *never* want to play chess!" he gushes.

"Things have changed." I tell him about the upcoming tournament.

"But you hate chess," he reminds me.

"I know. And I'll probably still hate it once the tournament is over. But for right now, I need to get good, and the only way to do that is to play, right?"

"Right." Joshie spins the board so he'll be white. We play a couple of games. I go easy on him but, still, I beat him every time. While I'm impressed with how much he's learned, I'm more impressed with the fact that he doesn't cry when he loses.

He credits Eric with his newfound resilience.

"And does Eric also get the credit for teaching you to play so well?" I ask.

"Not all the credit." Joshie holds up three fingers. "I've read your chess book five times. And I've done eighty-six of the one-move-to-checkmate puzzles. And I play chess at recess with Theodore and Pratik."

I need to read the book. I need to do the puzzles. And I need some nerdlets to play on a regular basis.

Joshie cups my ear with his hands and whispers, "Plus I have a secret weapon."

A secret weapon? I'm intrigued. "And are you going to tell me what it is?"

"No. Because then you'll beat me even more. Want to play again?"

"Only if you let me in on your secret weapon."

He politely declines my offer. But not for long. At eight o'clock I wrap up my biology reading as Joshie bounds into my room. His freshly washed hair is slicked and parted, and he smells like he has rolled in baby powder. He hops onto my bed and a fine white dust flies up out of his Spider-Man pajamas. "I've decided to tell you my secret weapon." He hands me a manila folder filled with papers. I flip it open. Chess notes. Pages and pages of notes about strategies and play-by-play game descriptions, each with a detailed analysis that could only have been put together by one person.

"Phil is your secret weapon?"

Joshie nods. "I stole your idea and searched for 'chess' on his computer. I've learned a ton of stuff from him. You can borrow his notes."

Bill appears at the doorway. "There you are. Time for bed, mister."

"Okay." Joshie leans in close and we rub noses Eskimo style.

"Thanks for the secret weapon," I say.

His face gets serious—which is tough to do with no front teeth. "You need it more than I do." He's right. But he's given me an idea. I toss the folder onto the bed—I'll read those later. I can't believe that I have totally overlooked the fact that I have a secret weapon of my own just a phone call and a mouse click away.

It's a little past eight o'clock—after eleven in Boston, but Phil answers my call on the second ring. After the usual "hi, how are you" stuff, Phil asks how cheer is going.

"Cheer is good. How's school?"

"Good."

He loves his classes. He loves Boston. He loves being in love.

"What about you?" he asks. "Guys must be banging down the door to check out your pom-poms."

"Hardly."

"Come on. You're a cheerleader now. I thought they could go out with any guy they wanted."

"Well, that's kind of why I called. Got a minute?" I spill the whole sordid story—way more than a minute. I leave out details about precisely whose papers I shared with whom. "So what do you say? Will you give me long-distance lessons and be my secret weapon?"

Phil laughs. "Do you know how many times I've begged you to play chess with me?"

"Counting the times you wanted me to play with that little magnetic board on the airplane trips to visit Dad? Approaching googolplex. You didn't stop hounding me until you found Zeebo and Louis in middle school."

He laughs. "They were as chess obsessed as I was."

"All you ever wanted to do was play chess," I say.

"I know," he says. "I've thought about that. I think that, for me, chess kind of filled the hole that Dad left. It never made sense to me that you didn't feel the same way—that you became so chess averse. I mean, chess had really been your thing much more than it was mine."

Chess averse. That's me. I pick up a little ceramic Ben Franklin chess piece and roll him around in my hand. "I guess for me it was the opposite. Since Dad left, every time I look at a chessboard it reminds me that there's this gaping hole that needs to be filled. You know? Pawn to e2: *Dad left*. Bishop takes pawn: *Teaching at MIT beats having a daughter*. Queen takes bishop: *If I was really as good as Judit Polgár he would have stuck around*. I managed to safely avoid chess for years, then Dad goes and sends me that stupid Revolutionary War chess set for my birthday and it was like he ripped the scab off a gaping wound."

"Nice metaphor, Nora, but don't go all high drama on me. I think Dad was just trying to make peace with you by sending you that set. And you know as well as I do that you could have been a grandmaster by age seven and Dad still would have gone to MIT. His leaving had nothing to do with you. Or with me."

"Exactly," I say, my jaw tight. "He didn't think about me and he didn't think about you. All he thought about was himself."

Phil sighs. "Look, that's a conversation you can have with Dad."

"Then it's a conversation that is never going to happen!"

"Jeez—calm down, Nora. You know, I see him at least once a week for lunch. He misses you. He said that when he calls, you always keep it short. And I know it's been years since you've come out to see him. I don't know if you remember, but you and he were pretty tight back in the old days. He gets that you're still hurt, but you need to get over it. If you want to kick lover boy's ass in chess it's Dad you should be playing—not me."

I set Ben Franklin back on the board. "Are you finished?"

"Yup."

"Okay. Maybe someday I'll be ready to play chess with

Dad. But that's not today. So, are you going to help me out or not?"

"I'm in," says Phil. He laughs. "But I have to say, I find it pretty damn funny that you, a cheerleader, are hoping to win a guy by flaunting your chess prowess." In the background I hear Phil tapping on his keyboard. "Okay. Your secret weapon is online and ready to play. Go ahead and open up your browser."

Phil directs me to an online chess site. We keep a window open where we can see and talk to each other. We mostly play chess, but we also talk. About Dad. About Mom. About life. When it's one o'clock in the morning Boston time, we sign off.

"When is the tournament?" Phil asks.

"Two weeks."

Phil whistles, long and low. "You won't stand a chance unless we do this every night."

He's at Harvard studying premed. I'm taking three AP classes plus precalculus. Neither of us really has the time for this.

"So does that mean I stand a chance?" I ask.

Phil yawns loudly. "Yup. I'll see you tomorrow."

We meet online every night. Plus, Phil shows me a chess app and we keep a game going all day long, making moves from our phones whenever we have a couple of minutes to spare. Openings Dad taught me come rushing back. I recall long-forgotten attacks and counterattacks. I read the book Dad sent cover to cover, get a couple more books from the library, and study Phil's game notes. I start to feel like I might, indeed, stand a chance.

Joshie is unhappy about my newly rediscovered skills as I beat him by wider and wider margins. "How did you get so good?" he demands, his face set in a firm frown.

I cup his ear with my hands and whisper, "I have a secret weapon."

"No fair! You need to share it with me. I gave you mine!"

I tell him my secret. "And Phil promises that after the tournament he'll help you, too."

Joshie leans into me. "I won't need Phil. I have you."

One day, Joshie brings the nerdlets over for a match and it's like one of those Bruce Lee movies where I am the chess ninja surrounded by an onslaught of bumbling assailants. When Theodore leaves the house in tears I decide it's time for a more age-appropriate opponent. As enormously as the online games with Phil help, I needed some face-to-face chess time with someone who'll be hard to beat. I find Eric's phone number on the Chess Kings handout.

"Hello?"

"Hi, Eric, it's Nora."

Pause. "Cheerleader Nora?"

"Chess Champion Nora."

He laughs. "Okay. What's up?"

"It's just a few days until the tournament and I need some solid competition. Could you meet me at the mall for some chess?"

Long pause. "Look, you're going to get taken out in the first round. Are you sure you want to go through with this?"

"Do you still want to be the mascot?"

He assures me that he does.

"I've done a lot of work on my game," I tell him. "I've got this private coach and, yes, I still want to go through with the tournament. But there's actually another reason we should get together."

I remind him that the mascot does more than just stand

around in a fish suit. The mascot knows all the sideline cheers, and he spends a lot of the game cheering right there beside us.

"So how about this?" I say. "You play chess with me, I'll give you some cheer lessons so you don't stand up there and flounder. Pun intended. Deal?"

"Deal."

We agree to meet by the fountain at the mall at six o'clock. Eric is easy to spot in a red-and-white-striped shirt that makes him he looks like he's trying out for a part in a *Where's Waldo* book. He sees me and waves. We go outside to an empty corner of the parking lot and run through six of the standard sideline cheers, keeping our voices low. Eric has surprisingly great stage presence and is way more coordinated that I would have guessed. It turns out he did dance and gymnastics when he was a little kid but stopped because other boys teased the crap out of him.

I give him a pep talk like the one I gave Vanessa. I tell him about the dancercise club Krista and I did last spring when gymnastics was over. "There were a couple of guys in there and, yeah, they were a little out of shape, but the girls didn't give them any crap. In fact, we all thought they were totally cool because they were even giving it a try. You should sign up. And here's something else to think about. Geoff is a senior. It's time for a new fish to swim onto the scene. You totally have what it takes. What do you think?"

Eric types "dancercise club" onto his phone's notebook. He looks up at me and smiles. "Glub, glub."

It's chess time. We set up a board on one of the small square tables in the food court. Eric is suitably impressed with my playing. I don't beat him, but I come dangerously close. Close enough that I won't thoroughly embarrass myself at the tournament. I tell him about my secret weapon.

He pulls back his head like he needs to see me from a different angle. "You're Phil Fulbright's sister? I never put it together."

"You know him?"

"I sure do. He was the regional champ for two years running. But he didn't go to Riverbend."

"No. We moved my freshman year so my little brother could go to the all-day freakishly-smart-kid kindergarten over at Cascade."

He nods. "And here you are. Proof that brains run in the family."

I take this as a compliment. "You know, I'd sort of purposely forgotten that once upon a time I was actually pretty good at chess," I tell him. "Even better than Phil. And I still have a few more lessons with him before the tournament. I think I'll be okay."

"You'll definitely make it past the first round," he assures me. "And who knows? Maybe a cheerleader at a chess tournament will command the same respect that chubby guys get at a dancercise class."

We finish chess and still have a half hour till the mall closes. There's something I need to know. I hesitate, then ask, "Who picks out your shirts?"

Eric studies the hem of his Waldo shirt. "My mom."

Nooooo kidding.

"They're just shirts," he says. "Mom brings home clothes, I wear them."

"Obviously it's up to you," I say. "But I think Eric the Fish should have some say in what he wears. Want to look at some shirts?"

The concept intrigues him, and by the time the bell chimes

to announce that the mall is closing, Eric has four new shirts. I'm pleased to find him drawn toward solid colors.

On the way home from the mall I stop by Krista's house. She's in her room doing homework and is stuck on a math problem, which I help her figure out. She works at her desk. I grab my books from the car, then flop onto her bed to read for a while. Krista's room is like a shrine to Dex, with pictures everywhere. Dex doing a layup at last year's championship game. Dex sitting beside the giant troll under the Fremont Bridge. Dex and Krista grinning beside the ice sculpture of a football helmet–wearing fish at last year's homecoming dance.

My favorite picture of all is framed on Krista's desk. It's the one Mom took last year of me and Krista after our first gymnastics meet. You can tell by the way we're looking at each other that even though we haven't known each other long, we're going to be best friends.

Krista closes her math book and drops the pencil onto her desk. She stretches and lets out an earth-shattering yawn. "So. You're not still going through with this whole chess thing, are you?"

"Yup." I tell her about the lessons with Phil, the matches with Joshie and the nerdlets, and tonight's game with Eric. "I know it's a lot to ask, but any chance I could talk you into coming to the tournament? I'm going to be pretty nervous, and it would be great to have you there, cheering me on."

Krista slings an arm over the back of her chair. "I still think it's crazy, but okay. I'm in."

I hop to my feet and circle her chanting a repetitive cheer:

Way to go, Krista,
Way to go (clap, clap)

She shoos me away. "All I can say is that I sure hope Dex likes this Adam guy. The homecoming dance was a bomb, but at least we can all go to the sophomore prom together."

I pick up the stuffed plush basketball on her bed—an anniversary gift from Dex—and toss it to her. "So what's the plan for Saturday?" she asks. "What time does the chess thing start?"

"Three o'clock."

She looks at the heart-shaped clock hanging on her wall—a Valentine's Day gift from Dex—and moves her finger in clockwise circles, counting backward. "Wow. It's going to be a little tight. The football game starts at ten. And it's an away game."

"Yeah, but it's just over in Bellevue. We should be back by one o'clock, latest."

Krista looks again at the clock. "Yeah. I guess." She studies me.

I laugh. "What?"

"Do you really think you're ready for the tournament?"

"I know I am. I think. I mean, I won't win the tournament, but I'll make it through the first round. I hope."

Mom texts to remind me that it's almost ten thirty. I pack up my books, but can't help myself from flipping to the section of the chess book that I recently bookmarked. I read again Ben Franklin's thoughts about what to do when you've beaten a lesser opponent. Even if I don't win the tournament, I should be prepared to win a game or two, right? Ben says:

You must not, when you have gained a victory, use any triumphing or insulting expression, nor show too much pleasure; but endeavour to console your adversary, and make him less dissatisfied with himself, by every kind of civil expression that may be used with truth.

He gives suggestions about what you could say to console your opponent. I run Ben's suggestions past Krista to see which she thinks I should offer my opponent if I win a game:

> "You understand the game better than I, but you are a little inattentive."
> "You play too fast."
> "You had the best of the game, but something happened to divert your thoughts, and that turned it in my favour."

Krista doesn't like any of them. "How about, 'Too bad you suck!'" She laughs and returns to her book.

I moan and lie back on Krista's bed for a moment. The chess book weighs heavily on my chest. I picture myself in my first game of the tournament, beads of sweat on my brow as the clock ticks down and I scan the board like mad trying to save my king.

My opponent grins sadistically. Pointy little teeth part as his laugh echoes through the room and he cries, "Checkmate!"

I gasp for breath. Adam looks up from across the room, his game still in progress. Our eyes meet just as my opponent points at me with a long bony finger. "Too bad you suck!"

Nineteen

FRIDAY NIGHT, PHIL AND I meet for our final official training session. I'm up in my room. Phil is in his dorm room. A couple of days ago he turned the computer around and gave me a walking tour of his room that lasted all of twenty-three seconds. Two beds, one neatly made (Phil's), the other a wreck. Two desks, one meticulously organized (Phil's), the other a war zone. Two dressers, one covered with a mountain of dirty laundry and a moldy apple core on top, one with nothing but a single framed picture of Phil's girlfriend, Malinda, who is surprisingly cute.

At five thirty my time, after we've been at it a while, I ask whether there isn't anything he'd rather be doing on a Friday night. I've been feeling guilty about taking up so much of his time.

He clicks his mouse and takes my rook with a pawn. "Pay attention to the game," he says. "And it's me we're talking about. What would I rather do on a Friday night than play chess?" He pauses. "But I need to leave at nine thirty. I'm going over to Malinda's."

"Nine thirty? Isn't that kind of late for a play date?"

Phil hesitates. "It's, um, you know." He clears his throat. "It's a sleepover." The pixilated image of his face on my computer screen tinges cranberry.

My brother, Phil, nerd extraordinaire, is spending the night with a girl. I make a *tsk-tsk* sound and click my digital queen into position. "You should pay attention to the game," I chide him. "Checkmate."

Phil clutches the sides of his desk. "No way!"

Exactly. No way out of the trap I'd set.

"In the words of my friend Ben Franklin," I say, "'You had the best of the game, but something happened to divert your thoughts, and that turned it in my favour.'"

If you want to divert a guy's thoughts? Talk about girls.

I raise my fists over my head in a High V. "I have defeated the fabulous Phil!"

Phil spends the next fifteen minutes dissecting the play to figure out where he went wrong. He looks over his shoulder. "Uh, hang on," he says.

I hear the door open and close. There's an exchange of greetings. Perhaps I get to meet the roommate? Phil's face appears on my monitor. "Hey, tell you what. Since you just beat me, how about instead of another game with me you take on a more worthy opponent?"

"Sure." Leave it to Phil to room with a guy who's a chess geek.

The guy slides into Phil's chair and I nearly fall out of mine. It is not Phil's roommate. Not even close.

"Hi, Nora." He smiles nervously.

"Dad?"

Stop it, stomach! Knock it off, heart!

His eyes search the little Nora face at the bottom of his screen. "My god," he says. "You've gotten all grown up!"

I miss him. I love him. I hate him.

"I hope you don't mind me showing up like this," he goes on, "but when Phil told me you'd been online with him every night I couldn't stand the thought of not getting a little time with you myself. You've been—shall we say—*difficult* to connect with."

He's being generous. The truth is that I have been *impossible* to connect with. I have avoided him like he is a rat infested with fleas infested with the bubonic plague. Phil, who obviously had this whole thing planned, will receive a metric ton of crap the next time we're online. I stare blankly at the little framed image of Dad shifting uncomfortably in his chair. I don't remember his hair being so flecked with gray. And his hairline has made a bold retreat toward the back of his head. But then, I was twelve the last time we were face-to-face—digitally or otherwise.

"I, uh, I understand you have a big chess match tomorrow," Dad says. "I'd love a game with you, if you're up for it."

Phil's face appears alongside Dad's. "She's up for it," he announces with authority. "It's her last chance to practice. So, I'm going to take off and leave you two to your game." He's gone before I can lambast him for setting this up.

It's just me and Dad. I staunchly tuck my emotions away. I know that Phil is right, I should take any practice sessions I can get, and who better to play with than Dad? I speak almost without moving my mouth. "Okay, I'm white."

We play in silence. My move. His move. Fifteen minutes pass. Thirty-five. An hour. I concentrate, calculating several moves into the future before I touch a piece. At each turn, Dad makes a popping sound with his lips as he studies the board anticipating my move. I'd forgotten about that annoying little tick of his and finally it's too much.

"Excuse me." I fumble for the book—the one Dad sent for my birthday. "There's a little something I'd like to share with you from Ben Franklin about chess etiquette." I read to him from "On the Morals of Chess":

You should not sing, nor whistle, nor look at your watch, not take up a book to read, nor make a tapping with your feet on the floor, or with your fingers on the table, nor do anything that may disturb his attention. For all these things displease; and they do not show your skill in playing, but your craftiness or your rudeness.

I continue, "See? So I'm going to hit my mute button if you keep making that noise."

Dad smiles. "I'm glad you like the book."

"Oh. Uh, yeah. Thanks."

"And the chess set?" he asks. "Did you like that, too?"

I shrug. "Not so much at first."

"See?" he says. "If you mute me we can't talk."

"We're not talking," I remind him. "We're playing chess."

He sits back in his chair. He removes his glasses and cleans one, then the other lens with a rag he's grabbed from somewhere off camera. I'm pretty sure it's a pair of Phil's roommate's underwear. He shakes his head. "What do you say we let the chess wait, Nora. I'd really like to catch up with you." He says the next line like he's rehearsed it so many times it's gone stale. "I can't stand the distance that's grown between us."

Snap! The rubber band holding the pieces of my heart in place explodes and I practically spit into the camera. "Distance? You're the one who created the distance when you moved all the way across the country!"

Dad's eyes are fixed with concentration. He examines his freshly cleaned glasses, then puts them back on. "You know what? You're right. I created the distance. But still, for a while there you came out to see me. I thought everything was okay—that we'd worked out a routine. You loved those summer camps at the Museum of Science. Remember? What was that one where you built a little vehicle that knocked over my fish tank?"

I cringe. The fish, named Lumpy, was one of those goldfish that looks like its gelatinous brains are attached to the outside of its head. When my camp creation smacked into the tank, Lumpy splooshed out and flopped on the floor until Phil scooped it into one of Dad's shoes.

"The camp was called Exploring Solar and Fuel-Cell Cars," I say. I can't help smiling at the memory. "And Phil went to the Mini Med School camp—I can still see him trying to give poor Lumpy CPR."

"See?" says Dad, visibly encouraged. "We *can* talk. But not if we don't even try."

Silence. The truth is, I don't like the distance that has grown between us any more than he does. And while he created the physical distance, I know it's me who created the emotional chasm that has gotten so wide that I don't know if there is even a way to cross it. How do you fix something when it's gotten so broken?

"What happened?" he goes on. "I know, your mother and I always agreed that it should be your choice, and Phil's, whether you wanted to spend your summers on the East Coast with me. But suddenly, you refused to come. Whenever I visited during trips to Seattle you'd make plans with friends. You don't answer my calls. Your e-mail replies are thin at best. What changed, Nora?"

More silence. My finger rests heavily on the mouse. With a click I could disconnect our call. But something stops me. I glance down at the book still lying open in my lap. I reread a line I've read before—the one in which Ben Franklin says that, in chess and in life, we should acquire the "habit of hoping for a favourable change, and that of persevering in the search of resources."

Maybe it's time for that change? And maybe Nora Fulbright is the resource that can make it happen? Hanging up would be like sweeping the pieces off the board because your king is in check, when there still may be a move you haven't seen—a chance for a "favourable" change. Maybe it's time to make the move I should have made all those years ago and just tell Dad the truth. It worked with Krista. It worked with Chelsey.

"When you left, it crushed me," I say.

"But—" Dad tries to interject and I stop him.

"See? You always do that. You stop me before I can get my words out."

Dad opens his mouth to speak, then closes it. He steeples his fingers and presses the top of the steeple to his lips.

"You left, and I cried for—seriously—months. Then I would see you in the summer, and when I came back to Seattle I would cry again. No kidding, Dad, for months. It was on the airplane trip back home the summer after I killed Lumpy that Phil dragged out his stupid little magnetic chessboard, and something inside me just flipped. I decided that I was done reliving the whole tragic 'good-bye, Dad' thing over and over again. If I never said hello anymore, then I never had to say good-bye, either. Then, every time you called, every time you wrote, I thought, okay, this is getting crazy. We need to fix this. But I would think again about how much it hurts to say good-bye and I would go back to sort of pretending you didn't exist."

Dad sighs, then sheepishly raises his hand. "May I?"

I turn my face away from the camera and make him wait

while I consider. "Yes, you may."

"Thank you. Since you quoted the venerable Mr. Franklin, I will do the same. 'A man wrapped up in himself makes a very small bundle.'"

He gives me a few seconds to digest his words, then hangs his head. "Nora, I am such an idiot! When I left for Boston I was so damned wrapped up in myself, thinking of the new post at MIT and my career, I didn't stop to think that you were just eight years old. You were always so bright—I treated you like a miniature thirty-year-old. I never stopped to ask how you were feeling, because, honestly, you always seemed fine."

"I never let myself cry in front of you," I say. "I knew it would make you sad." I swallow hard. "I hate you for leaving." I drag my sleeve beneath my nose. "And I wish you'd never left."

Dad's mouth tightens. He reaches toward the screen and I imagine that with the back of his hand, he brushes the cheek of the little digital Nora struggling not to cry at the bottom of the screen. "I'll bet that if we said hello more often, it would take the sting out of the good-byes," he says.

I suspect he's right. And what's done is done. Dad left. But in a funny way, I feel like I just got him back. "I guess life really is a lot like chess," I say. "Once you've made your move, you can't change your mind. What's done is done and you need to just play your game the best you can from that point on."

Dad smiles and it is my own smile looking back at me. The same shape mouth. The same small, square teeth, although his show years of excessive coffee drinking.

"You know, Dad," I say, "I have this friend, and her dentist told her that if you drink your coffee through a straw it'll keep your teeth from getting stained."

He nods. "Duly noted. Now, what do you say, shall we keep this game moving forward?"

We play on. Dad takes his role of coach seriously, and when I ultimately lose, he explains where I went wrong and how I might possibly have recovered. We talk about me. We talk about school. Dad reminisces about his days as Riverbend High's chess champion. "Do they still have that chessboard up on the gym roof?" he asks.

"They do, but the door is locked so no one ever plays."

"That's a shame," says Dad. "There was no better place to spend those rare lunch periods when it wasn't raining. You really should think about college on the East Coast." His eyebrows lift hopefully. "Here, there's this big yellow thing in the sky called the sun. I think you might enjoy it. And I know how much I would enjoy having you here. Just think, we could play chess all the time, me and my little Judit Polgár."

"It's kind of late for that, Dad. I'm never going to be a chess champion."

"You'll always be *my* chess champion," he says.

And when the game is done, we agree to a rematch in a week so that we can say, "See you next week," instead of "Good-bye."

Twenty

IT IS FINALLY THE SATURDAY afternoon I've been working so hard for. After a football game that trudged into triple overtime, the school bus rumbles down the highway as we make our way back to the school. Staring out the window, I alternate between ruminating on last night's game with Dad and catastrophizing about showing up too late to play. I don't even realize the ferocity with which I am chewing the skin rimming my fingernails until Krista gently pulls my hand away from my mouth.

"You'll get an infection," she warns me, and offers me Skittles instead.

I scoop the pile from her hand and toss them onto my tongue—orange, yellow, green—who can be picky at a time like this? Nothing fuels anxiety like sugar. And noise! Not only did the game run late, but our bus broke down and we're forced to ride back to school with the band. At the front of the bus a couple of band guys cheer on Jazmine, who's putting a trombone, and us, through a slow painful death. Nearby them, Chelsey faces backward in her seat. She claps a beat, and shouts an ad-libbed cheer:

Eagles like to eat up fish
Today the fishies got their wish
Cutthroats dragged the eagles down
Held 'em under, made 'em drown

Beside Chelsey, Becca wiggles and uses her hands to make like she has a dorsal fin on her head. With her sucked-in cheeks and puffed-out lips, she looks like a hot teenage trout.

I thrum my fingers on the back of the seat in front of us. "When are we going to get there?"

Krista glances at her phone. "Calm down. The chess thing doesn't start for twenty minutes and we'll be at school in fifteen. You'll get there on time."

"I thought I'd have time to shower and change, and"—it's loud and crazy but still I lower my voice—"Chelsey and I had this talk way back on the first day of school about how chess is for nerds, and I don't know what she would think—"

Krista throws up her hands. "Enough!" She switches to a snarky little voice meant to sound like me. "Krista won't like me because I'm too smart. Adam won't like me because I'm too dumb. Chelsey won't like me because I'm a geek." She changes back to her angry Krista voice. "Get over it, Nora! What would happen if you were just you, Nora Fulbright, who is smart and dumb and geeky all at the same time? Anybody who doesn't like you for who you are is someone you shouldn't waste your time being (*finger quotes*) 'friends' with. If you're genetically predisposed to play chess? Play chess! Stop worrying about what everyone else thinks! Popularity is great—but not if you have to live a lie to get there."

My teeth are clenched so tight my jaw spasms.

"Think about it." Krista moves to the front of the bus and joins Chelsey in another verse of her victory cheer. The tapping of my foot on the bus floor makes a dull *thud-thud-thud* as I watch the trees out the window plod by. Phil is King Nerd, but he's having a great time at school, he's got friends who adore him, not in spite of his nerdishness, but *because* of it. And he has Malinda.

What do I have? Butterfly wings that I still have not quite figured out how to operate.

We arrive at school with four minutes to spare. I squeeze to the front as we pull in so I can be first off the bus.

"Hey, Nora!" Chelsey grabs my elbow. "We're heading over to Life of Pie to celebrate. Want to come?"

I glance from Chelsey to Krista, who is watching me intently. "Actually," I say, "I'm playing in a chess tournament that starts in about three minutes."

Krista nods almost imperceptibly. Chelsey rolls her eyes. "You are one weird girl, Nora." She starts to turn away, then turns back. "But show them that cheerleaders rule, okay?"

I match her smile with one of my own. "I'll do my best."

I find Eric waiting just inside the library doors, wearing a black polo shirt with a small embroidered pawn on the chest.

"Nice shirt," I say. "Very chess appropriate."

He glances dubiously at my pleated skirt, my V-neck top and the extra-large bow clipped just above my ponytail, then says with a smile, "Wish I could say the same for you."

I flinch. "The football game ran really late. I didn't have time to change."

"I thought maybe you'd changed your mind and decided to just show up and cheer on your favorite player," he says, and when my face contorts he adds a quick "just kidding." He gestures to a table with pitchers of juice, cartons of store-bought cookies and, of course, a tub of licorice. "Help yourself to some food. We're about to get started."

With scattered conversations going on everywhere, the library is much noisier than on a typical school day. As I make my way to the food I search the small groups of people standing around. There are chess players, and friends and family of chess players. It's not long before I spot the chess player I'm looking for. Adam is over by literary fiction, talking with a couple of other guys. He's got on the faded blue sweatshirt I spilled sea urchin guts on at biology lab. The tail of a pale yellow shirt hangs halfway down his butt. His sleeves are pushed up his forearms with his hands buried deep in his front pockets, and the right leg of his jeans is still rolled up from having ridden his bike here.

I press my fingertips to a spot above my heart and send it a silent message to calm down. I am nervously gnawing on my second piece of licorice when Eric joins me at the food table. "So I told all the guys that I was abdicating myself for a last-minute entrant, and that I would officiate instead of play," he says.

"And they were okay with that?" I glance at Adam. The guy beside him says something, and Adam laughs out loud, tipping his chin toward the skylights. I want to make Adam laugh like that!

"They weren't thrilled at first," admits Eric. "But I used your line, and reminded them that with me out of the running they all stand a better shot at being school champion."

I pour myself a cup of lemonade. "So who do you think is going to win?"

"Could be Mark. He's the guy in the white shirt talking to Adam. But I think Adam is the guy everyone needs to watch."

Oh, I'll be watching him. In fact, I am having a very hard time keeping my eyes off him. A sudden thought makes my already tattered nerves fray just a bit more. "Please tell me I'm not playing him in the first round!"

Eric tucks a piece of licorice behind his ear for later. "Relax. You're taking my spot, and since Adam and I are officially ranked as the top two players, we're both scheduled to play bottom-ranked players in the first round. You never have the best players face off at the bottom tier."

"But what about the fact that I'm not actually one of the best players?"

Eric grins. "Who knows? Maybe you are."

Maybe I am. And maybe I'm not. What if I mess up and lose the first round? This could prove to be the dumbest swap of all time. The cheerleader who shows up in her uniform to publicly suck at chess.

"Your first match is over there," Eric says, pointing.

The large rectangular tables usually located in the periodicals section of the library have been replaced with smaller ones from the commons. On each table are a chessboard and a game clock. The table he's pointing to has one empty chair, and one that's occupied, by Little Nate.

"It's hard to believe he's a sophomore," I say. "He looks like he was busy playing with Legos when the puberty bus rolled through town."

Eric laughs. "And watch out. He cries when he loses."

I muster a confident smile. "I'm used to reducing the opposition to tears." It'll be like playing the nerdlets all over again. Eric talks to another player, and I stroll over and check out the whiteboard diagramming the tiers of play. Only the bottom tier is filled in with names. Eight games, sixteen names. I locate the box that still says "Eric versus Nathaniel." Adam's name is all the way at the other end of the chart. He's playing Corinna, the only other girl in the tournament. I trace the flow of play with my finger. The way our names are arranged on the board, Adam and I will only play if we each win three games. Then, we would face off in the final match. Could I possibly make it that far?

My stomach clenches and I remind myself that I don't

need to play the final match. I don't need to play against Adam to make the point that I, Nora Fulbright, am worthy of his respect—and more. I could do that by winning just one game, right? All I need is to advance to the second round. I just need to make Nathaniel cry.

Someone taps my shoulder. I spin around to face the Teapot. "Hey! I thought that was you!" She says it so big and loud that everywhere heads turn. I force myself to avoid eye contact with Adam, who has got to be wondering why I'm here—in my cheer uniform, no less.

"I'll be cheering on my little buddy Nate," says the Teapot. "I think I can guess who you'll be shaking your pompoms for."

"Actually, I'm here to play. In fact, I'm playing against Nate in the first round."

She gasps. "Well, butter my buns and call me a biscuit! For real?"

I nod. She looks quizzically from my sneakers to my hair bow and I explain why I'm dressed this way. She does an enthusiastic little victory jiggle at the news that we won the football game.

"Well, now I don't know who to cheer for," she says. Then, in a whisper, "Just so you know, he cries when he loses."

"So I've heard."

The Teapot motions for me to step in closer. "Nate came to my house for a little homecoming shindig—my aunt Jean-Louise was here from out of town and I wanted her to meet some of my fellow thespian. Anyhow, we played a little game of gin rummy. Turns out Auntie Jean-Louise is about the best rummy player in all Louisville. Well, she dusted Little Nate's feathers and let me tell you, that boy cried like a wet baby." She shakes her head ruefully.

I grab her shoulders. "Wait. Your aunt is from Louisville? The *cheer coach* from Louisville?"

The Teapot nods, then rolls her hands, one around the other, her voice rising to a crescendo as she cries, "Go-o-o-o-o, Louisville!" She finishes with a fist punch over the head.

I drape my arm over the Teapot's shoulder and lead her away. "Sarah, I wonder if I could interest you in a little swap."

"All right, everyone, let's get things started." Eric moves to the whiteboard and I slide into the seat across from Little Nate. Adam is at the table farthest from me. The parents and friends who have come to watch find seats set up in rows near the reference desk, though I suspect that once we get under way they'll move around and watch the games up close. Suddenly the library doors fly open and Krista races in.

"Woohoo! Go, Nora!" Krista blows me a kiss and rattles her pom-poms.

She's not alone.

"Win that match!" says Becca.

"Rook that guy's pawn right to the moon!" shouts Chelsey, punctuating her cheer with a straddle jump.

I manage a pained smile as everyone in the room looks from the cheer squad to the lone cheerleader sitting in front of a chessboard. Adam looks confused, but amused, as my personal cheer squad settles noisily into the spectator section.

"Quiet down, quiet down," orders Eric. "We need to get started, but first let's go through a few rules."

Becca reaches over and draws a little imaginary zipper across Chelsey's lips with her index finger and thumb.

Eric turns to the players. He gives a brief lecture about sportsmanship. He explains that all eight games will start at the same time, and that clocks will be set for forty minutes. Players who finish their games in under that time are free to watch other games. "We'll start the second round of games five minutes after the last players in round one finish," he says. "Wish your opponents 'good luck,' and white players, begin your games."

We've been randomly assigned white or black, and in my game against Nathaniel, I make the first move. The library becomes strangely quiet. The only sounds are the slap of chess players hitting the buttons on their clocks, the creak of chairs as people cross or uncross their legs and the tap of chess pieces being put into position. We're only twenty-six minutes in when Corinna walks by and watches us play.

"Did you win?" Nate whispers to her.

"Not a chance," she says.

She heads out to the hall and I become acutely aware that we are still being watched. I slowly turn my head to find Adam right behind me, smiling, his hands clasped behind his back. I turn back to the game as Little Nate slides a knight into position. My heart thumps in my ears. Distracted, acting too fast, I respond by moving my bishop, and instantly lose him to a pawn. Crap! Behind me, Adam releases a breath like he's been punched. We play on, and twelve minutes later I say, as calmly as I can manage, "Checkmate." I've done it! I've made it to the second round. I turn to see the look on Adam's face. Surprised? Impressed? Awestruck? But he's nowhere in sight.

From the seats over by the reference desk a rustling noise breaks the stillness as Krista, Becca and Chelsey shake their pom-poms and mouth a silent cheer. I give them a thumbs-up and hurry to the restroom before it's time for the next match.

I come out of the bathroom and find Adam at the water fountain. He's with Corinna, discussing what she could have done differently in their game. When he sees me, he excuses himself and comes over to me. I have successfully avoided any semblance of a conversation with him since the dance, and now, maybe, just maybe, I have redeemed myself.

"I didn't know you played chess," he says.

I give him my most nonchalant shrug.

Eric steps into the hallway. "Second round is about to start," he says, before ducking back inside.

"Look, I'm playing Marty the next round," says Adam. "It'll be a good game if you want to stick around and watch it."

It takes me a moment to process his words. Wait. What? The only way I could watch his round two match is if I'd just lost to Little Nate. He assumes I lost my match! Would he think differently if I'd had time to change out of my cheer uniform before I got here? I struggle for a clever reply, but before I find it, Little Nate arrives on the scene. He may not be a very good chess player, and he may be a crybaby, but he's a crybaby with flawless timing. He brushes past us, weeping loudly, and disappears into the boys' room. The Teapot is right behind him. She bangs on the boys' room door. "Nate, honey? Come on out of there and let's have a little chitty-chat. It's only a game, remember?"

Corinna, who has been hovering, congratulates me.

"Wow. Yeah. Congratulations," says Adam. "I thought—" He hesitates. We both know what he thought—that I lost.

I politely thank them both. The Teapot, waiting patiently for Nate to emerge, glances from Adam to me. "I just don't know who I'll root for if y'all face off in the final round."

Adam regains his composure. He sizes me up. "That could be an interesting game."

"Very interesting," I say.

My skirt flares as I turn on my toes and head back to the library. I'll show him that I'm not just a chess player—I'm a chess champion.

I win round two in thirty-one minutes. Round three takes twenty-nine. It has gotten desperately warm in the library. Instead of getting more pumped with each successive victory my cheer section seems to be running out of steam. Adam has peeled off his sweatshirt. The Teapot fans herself with a copy of *Hot Rod* magazine. And me? It could be snowing in here and I would still be on fire!

Eric announces that it will be Adam versus me in the final round amid groans of disapproval from some of the other players. It was bad enough that Eric gave me his spot. I am an interloper. They don't want me to take down one of their own.

We have a ten-minute break before the last game and someone brings out a platter of sandwiches. The chess players swarm the food. My cheering section takes advantage of the break in action to put on an impromptu halftime show. Krista invites me to join them but I need a few minutes away from the action to get ready for my final match. I grab my gear bag and head to the girls' room.

The large glitter star that encircled my left eye has smeared so I wash the whole thing off. I let down my hair, brush it, and put it back into a ponytail. I consider changing out of my uniform into the outfit I'd planned to wear all along, but no. It's okay for me to be dressed like a cheerleader—that's who I am.

I brush some fresh color onto my face. Give my lips a quick coat of gloss. I'm zipping up my bag when I spot the reading I'd brought along in case the bus trip got boring. There are Phil's chess notes. A book on openings from the library. And, of course, there's the chess book from Dad with the pages by Ben Franklin that I have read so many times.

With great hope I reread Ben's closing paragraph; what to do if you find yourself obliterating your opponent:

> Snatch not eagerly at every advantage offered by his unskillfulness or inattention . . . you may, indeed, happen to lose the game to your opponent; but you will win what is better, his esteem, his respect, and his affection

Adam has shut down each of his opponents in under twenty minutes—I don't stand a chance of winning, let alone beating him badly. But how I want Adam's esteem! I want his respect. And more than anything, I want his affection.

I join Adam at the table and he sweeps an open hand toward the empty chair. I sit and fold my hands onto my lap. The spectator section empties as the chess club guys crowd around us to watch the final game up close. Eric makes them move back to give us breathing room, then clears his throat. "Shake hands, and white player make your first move."

Adam reaches out for my hand, and I am reminded of that first day out on our front lawn. His hand folds around mine and, *zap!* A pulse travels up my arm and whacks me in my prefrontal cortex.

"Good luck," he says. He studies me. Reads me. "I must admit, I'm kind of surprised to find myself sitting here with you."

His smile disarms me. Dimples should not be allowed at a chess match.

"Good luck to you," I say. "You're going to need it."

Adam, who is playing white, cocks his head and stares

at me. I now know how it feels to be a bug in Joshie's tank. His eyes drift to the board and narrow as he contemplates an opening. Finally, he slides a pawn to e4 and presses the button on his clock.

Game on. Suddenly, it's like when I cheer, or when I did floor exercise routines at gymnastics meets. It's the same feeling I've had these past weeks playing with Phil, and I suspect it's what made me play all the time back when I was a little kid. *Snap!* I am totally here, and I am here to win. All my focus is on the board, deciphering, considering. His opening play was pretty standard, moving toward controlling the center and freeing up his queen and his bishop.

I play an equally standard response and mirror his move. I slap the button on my clock. Adam's next move will clue me in more about his opening strategy. Is he playing Ruy Lopez? Giuoco Piano? King's Gambit?

Adam's hand hovers over the board. He moves his bishop to c4.

I hesitate. Seriously? Could he really think he's going to do me in with Scholar's Mate? It's only the lamest opening ever, used to put away some blowhard chess poser by annihilating him and going to checkmate in four moves.

What would Ben Franklin do? Foresight: I'll let him think he's got me. It'll rattle him all the more when I pull out of it at the last minute, and by looking a few moves ahead I see exactly how I'll do that. I mirror him again and move my bishop to c5. I press the button on my clock with self-assurance and look up at him. He's got a total poker face going, and as I suspected he would, he slides his queen to h5, putting pressure on the f7 square—the weakest square on the board.

Circumspection: I consider all my options and what he'll

do in response. He's expecting me to move a knight, attacking his queen. Then he'll shut me down, take the f7 square and put me into checkmate.

Caution: I need to be sure that whatever piece I move, I place myself in the strongest position possible.

I let my hand drift toward the pawn. Before touching anything, I look at Adam. His teeth rest on his lower lip. His eyes focus on my hand. He thinks he's got me. I wiggle my fingers, then settle them onto my queen instead, and slide her to f6. Adam's eyes narrow as I deliberately press the button on my clock. I give him my wryest smile. "Did you really think you could take me with Scholar's Mate?"

The look in Adam's eyes is mischievous. "I had to make sure your first three games weren't just beginner's luck."

After that little exchange we are both heads-down-nothing-but-chess. We play a slow, cautious game. There's too much at stake to risk making a single ill-planned move. As we take turns sliding our pieces around the board, the clock seems to quicken its pace. By the time we're each down to about twelve minutes remaining, surprisingly few pieces have left the board. The worst would be if I ran out of time before he did and he won simply because it took me longer to make each move. Still, if there was anything Phil cautioned me about these past few weeks, it was to not freak out about the ticking clock. Take time to look ahead, he said. Consider what the ramifications of each move. Proceed with caution.

But it's time to throw caution to the wind. I speed up my moves, and so does Adam.

It's his turn. He grinds his teeth as he considers the board. Sweat blooms on his forehead. Over by the reference desk Chelsey has fallen asleep with her head on Becca's shoulder. Krista, thumbs flying, is busily texting. Time ticks on.

There are stifled groans from the chess club when I make a clever play, and unstifled clapping whenever Adam shines. No guesswork about who the favorite is here.

Usually by this time in a game I have a really clear sense of who is going to win and how they're going to get there. With this game, I am at a loss as to how it will end. It's my move. I narrow my eyes and focus on the lay of the board.

Tick-tick-tick. Bishop? Rook? I slide my knight one square forward and two to the right.

Adam catches me completely off guard when he leans in, and ever so slightly whispers, "You know, I can't figure you out." He makes a move.

"You're trying to distract me," I whisper back.

"I'm not. It's just that I really don't get what you're about. Ever since I met you, you've had me totally baffled." With the rest of the chess club hovering, he speaks so I can barely hear him.

It has worked. I'm distracted. Not just by what he's said, but by the fact that this is the closest we've come to having an actual conversation since the dance. Full sentences with nouns, verbs, adjectives. But the silence these past few weeks has been totally my fault, not his. Every time he has approached me or tried to start a conversation, I've panicked, still mortified by how ridiculous I must seem to him.

I glance again at the clock and my throat tightens. I need to respond to his move. But more than that? I need to respond to what he's just said.

"Is it really that hard to figure out?" I say. "I wanted to get to know you better."

I push my bishop four squares down the diagonal and—No! I see my mistake instantly. But there are no take-backs in this game. If Adam's ploy was to distract me, it worked.

Foresight. He could take me in three moves. I avoid his gaze. Surely he has seen it, too.

"Maybe I wanted the same thing you did." He barely glances at the board before shifting his rook, not taking advantage of my last suicidal move, and instead making himself completely vulnerable!

My eyebrows meet in the middle. What is he up to? Is it a trap?

The chess club guys close in. They murmur. They shuffle. They breathe.

I study the board. I study Adam's face. He doesn't have the look I've seen in Phil's computer-screen eyes when all he wants is to win. Instead, he looks at me to read my reaction, to his words and to his move.

Was that Adam's plan? To say something utterly unbelievable so that I would lose my train of thought and let the clock run down? I tug hard on my ponytail. Focus, Nora. Focus! Foresight. Circumspection. Caution. Do I do the obvious and capitalize on his mistake when he didn't capitalize on mine? Ben Franklin pops into my head. I consider what he said about not taking advantage of your opponent's poor move:

You may, indeed, happen to lose the game to your opponent; but you will win what is better, his esteem, his respect, and his affection.

Oh my god! Could it be? Is Adam trying to let me win? Is he trying to win my esteem? Or respect? My breath quickens. My affection?

I could make a move that will wind up two moves from now with him in checkmate. But what if his last move was a total blunder? Do I look for a completely different option that will let him off the hook? Is that what he was doing for me earlier? I wanted so badly to beat him—and now that I can, why am I hesitating? Isn't beating him the perfect way to end this?

And then I see something I had not noticed just a moment before, and a thought, a beautiful little thought, occurs to me. There is another option. If neither of us wins—then neither of us loses. I move my rook. The murmuring stops. Adam cocks his head. If he doesn't move his king, he'll be in checkmate. Even the kids at Chess Kings know that if you are in check and there is a way out of it, you have to take it. I have left him with no choice. He steps his king one square to the right and avoids checkmate. I move my rook again, and Adam shifts his king to the left. I move. He moves. Back and forth. We could go on like this forever with no one winning. Adam's mouth breaks into a slow, sure grin. His eyes meet mine. "Repetitive check. Game over."

It takes Eric a moment to peel his eyes away from the board and announce the outcome of the game. "Nora has placed Adam in repetitive check. The match ends in a tie. Ladies and gentlemen, I present to you the Riverbend High Chess Cochampions." He lifts Adam's left hand and my right over heads and the crowd claps. Becca nudges Chelsey awake and the cheer squad hoots and shakes their pom-poms.

When the clapping dies down, Eric presents us with an envelope. "The cochampions will need to figure out how to divvy up the prize." It's a twenty-five-dollar gift certificate—to Molly Moon's! The volume rises as Mark and some of the other chess guys chide Adam for not taking me when he had a chance. He claims to have not seen it.

Krista slips in beside me. "Nicely done."

I lean into her. "Thanks for being here. How'd you get everyone else to come with you?"

She gives me a squeeze. "It was Chelsey's idea. Hey, Dex is on his way to pick me up. A bunch of us are getting together at Jake's house to watch a video of today's game. Want to come?"

Adam leans across the table, inserting himself into our conversation. "I believe the champions have a prize to collect."

I smile. "I believe you're right. Shall we?"

Adam climbs from his chair, comes around the table and with affected formality he pulls out my chair out. "We shall."

And we do.

Twenty-One

ADAM AND I KICK THROUGH leaves littering the courtyard outside the school's front doors. The air at dusk has cooled down considerably since I leapt off the bus and raced to the school library over four hours ago. Thankfully, ever since Krista crowned me Queen of the Nipple Kingdom, I always keep a cardigan in my gear bag.

"What do you think?" Adam says. "Too cold for ice cream?"

I respond with a look of utter disbelief. "It's never too cold for ice cream."

We pass by the bike rack. His is the only bike still there. "I'd offer you a ride—" he says kiddingly. "How are you at balancing on handlebars?"

I regard my skirt. "I'm not wearing my most appropriate handlebar attire. How about the bus?"

Adam looks at me with surprise. "Really? I sort of figured we'd take your car."

The muscles in the back of my neck tense. "The car, yeah. It's not exactly an option right now."

As we walk to the bus stop, Adam doesn't ask about the car and I don't tell. Someday, perhaps, I'll reveal why I should never have driven with him back on the first day of school and why, at this very moment, my car is out on a romantic date with Stuart Shangrove and his girlfriend. Instead, he brings up the chess match. "So how'd you like my opening?"

I groan. "You had to know I wouldn't fall for that."

He laughs, and does this adorable sideways gallop thing as we make our way down the sidewalk. "I was just messing with you," he says. "I caught a little bit of your third-round match and it was pretty clear you knew what you were doing. You caught poor Mark totally off guard."

I did. It took him three licorice sticks to get that the game was really over.

Adam presses the button at the crosswalk. I rub my upper arms as the cool air bites through my sweater.

"Oh, hey, put this on." Adam slips off his fleece coat and drapes if over my shoulders. His hand brushes the back of my neck sending a shiver down to my toes.

"Are you sure you'll be warm enough?" I croak.

"Yeah, no problem. I've still got this." He tugs at his sweatshirt.

We walk on and I wrap myself in his jacket. In Adam's jacket. In Adam Hood's soft blue jacket that is warm and fuzzy under my chin and totally smells like boy body. If I were a cat, my purring would drown out the noise of the approaching bus.

"So, who do you usually play chess with?" Adam asks as the bus doors open. He steps back, allowing me to board first.

"It's kind of a long story."

Adam follows me up the steps, into the bus. "We've got plenty of time."

We find two seats together. All around us people mess with their phones or talk in muted voices while I tell Adam about my early days as the next Judit Polgár. About Dad leaving. About me quitting. I blame the recent reigniting of my chess fuse on Joshie and Phil. I pull out my phone and fire up the chess app, which displays the game Phil and I are currently in the middle of. It's Phil's move.

The bus jerks to a stop. A few people clamber off and Adam notices that a woman has left gloves on her seat. He chases after her to return them, and I remind myself that he's not just nice to me, he's nice to everyone. He'd give any girl his coat. He'd let any girl climb onto the bus ahead of him. He is no longer Tallulah's but that does not, by default, make him mine.

The bus makes a sharp turn and suddenly my body and Adam's are pressed together. I try to catch myself and my hand slaps onto the back of his hand, where it rests beside his thigh. His skin beneath mine is cool and smooth. If only the bus could continue this way for the rest of the ride.

"I'm sorry!" I say, repositioning myself in my seat, pulling my hand back into my lap.

"It's all good," he says. And I couldn't agree more. We chat about biology. History. The bus lurches to a stop, and Adam stands, grabbing on to the stainless steel bar that runs over our heads. I am still in my seat and he towers over me, which is nothing new. Even when I'm standing beside him in history or in biology he towers over me, and I love the bigness of him. I love the fact that the sleeves of his coat extend a good six inches beyond the tips of my fingers.

We hop off the bus. "Molly Moon's," Adam announces as we arrive at the ice cream shop. He opens the door and follows me inside. There's no one waiting to place their order, and I beeline to the counter. "Two scoops of Theo's Coconut Kiss in a cup, please."

"Wow, remind me to never get between you and a dish of ice cream," Adam says, laughing, as he catches up to me.

"Hey, I take my ice cream very seriously."

He's still smiling as he studies the chalkboard on the wall behind the counter and I try not to be too obvious about studying him. I find myself wondering what he looked like when he was Joshie's age—cute. Very cute.

"Earl Grey in a cone," he finally says to the girl waiting to take his order.

"I would have pegged you as a Cherry Chunk guy," I tell him.

Adam smiles. "I'm full of surprises."

I am eager to be surprised. I head to the counter by the window and sit on one of the tall wooden stools. Adam grabs a paper cup of water and meets me there. As he sits, a drip of ice cream slides from his cone onto his sweatshirt.

"Would you mind?" He offers his cone and I hold it as he wipes at the errant drip. A wave of hair spills over his face obstructing my view of his nose, his cheekbones, his eyes. What if I reached up and tucked his hair behind his ear? I picture him pulling my hand away and tenderly pressing his lips to the tips of my fingers. I imagine us, right here and now, admitting our passion for each other. To honor the moment, years from now, our wedding cake will be made of ice cream: bottom tier—Coconut Kiss; middle tier—Earl Grey; top tier—Salted Caramel and Vivace Coffee with sprinkles, for my maid of honor.

Crap! Don't go there. I remind myself again, this is not a "date"! We are here to collect our prize. He's nice to everyone.

Adam finally sits. "I love this place," he says, looking around. "We came here the first day we moved to town. I even got a T-shirt."

"I know," I say, instantly regretting it as he looks as me wondering how I know intimate details of his wardrobe.

"You, uh, you were wearing it the first day I met you."

He smiles and takes a lick of his Earl Grey ice cream. "Wow, good memory!"

I resist the urge to tell him the other things I recall from that day. The way the pale hairs on his forearms stood out against his toasted marshmallow skin. How the muscles in his hand flexed as he gripped my apple between his middle finger and thumb. That even his toes were tanned.

Don't obsess, Nora. Don't obsess! I close my eyes and savor a spoonful of Coconut Kiss instead. Taste bud elation. When I open my eyes, Adam is watching me, and the intensity of his gaze makes me look away for fear I will misinterpret it. Instead, I allow myself to seem interested in life outside Molly Moon's plate-glass window, where a couple of college-age girls stroll past holding hands. A guy whizzes past on a skateboard. A car pulls into an empty parking space.

Ice cream catches in my throat. No way. No possible way! What are the chances that of all the cars in the greater Seattle area, mine would be the one sliding into a parking space right in front of Molly Moon's? Two scoops of crap in a sugar cone! Stuart Shangrove climbs out, then opens the door for his girlfriend.

"Look, a car just like yours," Adam says.

"Um, that actually *is* my car. I sort of loaned it to a Stuart and his girlfriend."

Adam licks a renegade drip off his cone. "That was nice of you."

I nod dully.

When Stuart and his girlfriend come in, I wish them a happy anniversary and mentally will them to get their ice cream and get the hell out of here, and at first it seems to have worked. But no such luck. They wander over, licking their cones.

"Excellent ride," says Stuart, his arm wrapped around his girlfriend's shoulder. "Thanks for setting up the whole switcheroo."

"Yeah, the car is great," says his girlfriend. "And it'll be really nice to sit together at a football game for once." She rises up on her toes and plants a kiss on his cheek.

"See you at the game!" says Stuart as they leave.

"Go, team," I say, like I'm the cheerleader at a funeral.

With my plastic spoon, I flip over the lumps of ice cream in my cup and so I can scrape off the softer ice cream around the edges. And so I can avoid Adam's gaze.

"'Switcheroo'?" says Adam.

A gust of cold air blows in as Stuart and his girlfriend leave.

For the first time in my life, I lose my appetite for ice cream. "I kind of arranged a little trade. Stuart gets my car, and in exchange, the guy who's usually the mascot is going to announce a game in Stuart's place."

"And Stuart is going to be the mascot? He doesn't seem like a fish suit kind of guy."

I glance at the ceiling for help, but get none. "No. Actually, Eric is going to be the mascot."

Adam chokes on his ice cream and gulps some water to stave off a full-on coughing fit. "Eric?" he finally manages to say. "Chess Club Eric?"

I nod and watch as a flicker of understanding lights up in Adam's eyes. "And Eric gave you his spot in the chess match. Kind of like how you traded that guy at the dance a date in exchange for my schedule?"

I feel so incredibly small. Small and lost and dumb. I moan and hide behind my open hand. "I am so embarrassed."

Adam

hand away ~.   ~~~ ~~~~ gives my fingers a tender little
squeeze before letting go. He looks at me with such incredible warmth that I almost feel worse. "You shouldn't be embarrassed," he says. "I was flattered about the whole schedule
thing." There they go—his earlobes tinge pink.

A cavalry of butterflies beat their wings silly inside my
stomach. I finally meet his gaze. "Really?"

He doesn't quite smile, but he nods, and the corners of
his mouth curve up just enough to tell me that he means it.

"When Mitch had that tantrum at the dance I wanted to
run away," I say.

Adam looks at me skeptically. "Which, as I recall, is exactly what you did. Can I ask you a question?"

"Do I have to answer it?"

He smiles. Dimple! "Yes, you do. Why? Why did you want
my schedule?"

I am full-frontal cringing. I choose my words carefully.
"After you showed up at my house that day in your Molly
Moon's shirt, I knew you were someone I could be—friends
with. I mean, we *are* practically neighbors, right? Joshie had
fun with you. The dog liked you—and Copernicus is a great
judge of character."

Adam, never taking his eyes off of me, rests his elbow on
the counter and his head against his hand. Hair spills out between his fingers. He looks at me as if to say, "Go on."

I glance at the ice cream melting in my cup. "I didn't
stand a chance of getting to know you if we weren't in some
classes together, and Mitch wouldn't show me your schedule
unless I agreed to a date."

Adam's forehead creases in thought. He looks like he is
trying to solve a problem with way too many variables. "And

suddenly you were at my lab table in biology, and my partner in the history project? More 'switcheroos'?"

"Well, there was no point being in your classes if I'd never get a chance to talk to you, right?"

He looks into the distance and nods. "Yeah, I guess that makes sense. But if all of this was about getting to talk to me, and becoming friends, why have you been totally avoiding me?"

I wince. "Seriously? After the dance I figured you thought I was a crazy stalker. I mean, I already knew that you'd written me off as a half wit, you know, a dumb cheerleader—"

He bolts upright. "What?!"

I am left momentarily speechless by the look of absolute incredulity on his face.

"Come on!" I say. "Every time you saw me in my cheer uniform, or with other cheerleaders, you got all Icicle Boy on me, like I wasn't good enough for you." I quickly backpedal. "I mean, not smart enough. You know. To be friends with you."

"Wait. Wait wait wait. Wait!" Adam says, waving his arms in front of him to get me to stop talking. "Me getting all 'Icicle Boy' had nothing to do with you being a cheerleader. Or with the fact that you're always surrounded by other cheerleaders. There are plenty of brilliant cheerleaders in the world, and I would never judge someone like that. But as you may recall, at least up until the dance, you were also always surrounded by a certain enormous football player, and I didn't want you or Jake to get the impression that I was making a play for you. The guy is huge, Nora! His biceps are the size of my thighs! And back at my old high school, guys like Jake made life miserable for anyone that even talked to their girlfriend."

I stare at him, feeling like the dumbest cheerleader ever. Not a half wit, more like a quarter wit, or an eighth wit, perhaps. "But I was never his girlfriend."

He looks unconvinced. "Come on, he popped up everywhere, or other people brought his name up. Jesus, Nora, you had a giant heart with his name and yours drawn inside your locker door!"

"Krista wrote that! She thought it would be funny. Really, I was never going out with him."

He lets this sink in. "Well, it wasn't until the dance that I found out Jake was going out with Fuzzy, not you."

"Fluffy."

"Whatever. So, after the dance I figured it was safe to talk to you in public, but whenever I tried, you ran away. I couldn't figure out what was going on. You'd done the whole crazy swap with Mitch and gotten into my classes. You managed to sit near me. And now I find out that you cleverly got yourself a spot in the chess tournament—where you just about kicked my ass, by the way." He shakes his head.

"But I'm not running away from you right now," I say meekly.

He shakes his head. "I'm glad you're not running away. Although this *is* an ice cream shop, so I don't know whether it's me or the ice cream that's keeping you here." He relaxes into a smile. I smile back, and there it is again, the feeling that he is a planet and I am an intergalactic butterfly being pulled into his gravity. In a shaky orbit, I flutter around and around and around him. But I am tired of spinning. I am tired of fluttering out of control, wondering whether he could ever be mine.

"Nora Fulbright," he says. "You confuse the hell out of me. What is it that you really want?"

I press my lips together to keep the first word that comes to mind from leaping out. You. That's what I want to say. I really want *you*. But I know there's more to it than that. More that needs to be said. I take a deep breath. "What I really want, first of all, is to apologize for confusing you. I confused myself, too. And a lot of other people along the way. Next, what I really want is for you to know that all those crazy swaps were about this." I point to myself, then Adam, then my melted ice cream. "They were about me and you hanging out, without it mattering who is smart and who is dumb and who is a cheerleader and who is a chess geek—"

"Chess geek?" Adam jerks back, feigning a look of horror.

I laugh. Okay, actually, I giggle, and it is silly and lame, but it is a giggle that starts in my heart and ends in Adam's ears and causes him to tip his head and gazes into my eyes like they contain the world's deepest, most profound secrets. "So it was all about wanting to hang out with me? Like, as friends?" he says.

He holds out his hands. I reach for them, my eyes never leaving his, and he pulls me close.

"Friends. As in boyfriend and girlfriend," I say.

Time stops. The air that fills the space between us grows sweet and warm. I am a butterfly with taste buds on the bottom of my feet, standing on the sweetest flower under the bluest sky. Not a Monarch. Not a Cabbage White. I am a whole new taxonomic anomaly—the wing-flapping, pom-pom-shaking, chess-playing creature called the Nothing but Nora. Adam leans forward. My eyes drift closed, and when our lips touch I understand why *kiss* rhymes with *bliss*. And for the first time in a long time I don't try to talk my crazy heart off the ledge. I leap, and it is luscious.

Adam presses his lips to my earlobe and whispers,

"'Boyfriend and girlfriend.' I like the sound of that."

He kisses me on my cheek, my chin, on the bridge of my nose.

"That's what I want. It's what all the swaps were about."

This time I initiate the kiss, pressing my lips hard against his, wondering what would happen if I allowed them to part ever so slightly, and when they do, I discover that Theo's Coconut Kiss and Earl Grey are two flavors that were meant for each other.

Oh my god. We are kissing! We are kissing at Molly Moon's! As we pull apart Adam asks me a question. "The swaps," he says. "Were they worth it?" He places a tender hand on my cheek and looks into my eyes.

I close my eyes and press my cheek into his hand. "They were worth it. They were so very, very worth it."

"And now they're done," he says. "Right? No more swaps?"

I pull away, still holding his hands and smile up at him. "One more to go."

My final move.

Twenty-Two

TODAY, THE DAY OF THE FINAL football game, I wait for Adam by the bike rack. Despite the grayness of the morning and the cold, misty air, I glow inside as he pedals up to greet me. He lets his bike clatter to the ground and folds me into an urgent kiss that makes me want to pull him down onto the sidewalk right then and there.

"I brought you a present," he says. "Close your eyes."

I close my eyes and hold out my hands. He places one foil-wrapped chocolate kiss into each hand; one for each week since our first kisses at Molly Moon's. Someday, I will need a wheelbarrow to hold them all.

"Did you miss me?" he asks.

"Terribly," I say, kissing him again. It has been exactly twelve hours, thirty-three minutes and fourteen seconds since Mom demanded that we break up last night's chess game, which could have gone on for hours. Sitting side by side on the sofa, each of us hyperconscious of the warmth where his thigh and mine press together, our chess games move at a glacial pace. Neither of us is ever in a rush to be done.

Adam sighs as we pull away from our kiss. His arms, those awesome arms, are wrapped around my waist. I gaze up at him, my hands clasped at the back of his neck, and cannot believe I am allowed to do this!

"Sarah texted me about thirty times this morning," he says, grinning. "She is so excited!"

"Vanessa is, too," I say.

"Looks like your final swap is working out according to plan."

"They always do."

It is really hard to laugh and kiss at the same time.

I arrive at the locker room to find Chelsey putting the finishing touches on the glitter star that surrounds the Teapot's left eye.

"Y'all, is this just the best day ever, or what?" the Teapot drawls.

Chelsey had been skeptical at first about the Teapot cheering in Vanessa's place at the final game. But at practice on the Monday following the chess tournament, the Teapot proved beyond a doubt that she knew her stuff. And the fact that Mrs. Teapot is taping the game to send it to Aunt Jean-Louise over at Louisville made it an offer Chelsey couldn't refuse.

My phone vibrates in my pocket. "Look at this." I show the incoming text to the Teapot and Chelsey.

Good luck at game. Conference AWESOME. Tell Sarah thanks for trading places with me. And break a leg!

In the attached picture, Vanessa and her mom smile outside the convention center where Vanessa is overjoyed to be attending the US Intellectual History Conference. Her mom is hardly recognizable without the ancient cheer sweater.

Outside, the band warms up, and music drifts in through the open locker room windows. Jazmine jumps onto a bench and dances. Becca marches in place. With a hairbrush, Gillian bangs out the beat on a locker. The Teapot grabs a megaphone and belts out the tune "There's No Business Like Show Business."

"Did I ever thank you for talking me into doing cheer?" Krista asks.

"I don't think so. Did I ever thank you for agreeing to do it?"

She holds out her hand. I shake it. "Thanks," we say at the same time. During those awful weeks following the homecoming game, I couldn't wait for football to be over. I dreaded the fact that we'd be cheering all winter at basketball games. I wondered if it was too late to switch to gymnastics. Now, I can't imagine doing anything but this. It's not that I'll wind up like Vanessa's mom, wearing my skirt and hair bow at the old folk's home. But for now? I know I made the right choice.

"Okay, girls, last game of the season. Are you ready to give it all you've got?" Chelsey, who has climbed onto the counter over by the sinks, holds out her arms like she's hugging the world. We shriek and hoot, and with our pom-poms on our hips, we leave the locker room and jog out to the football field one last time.

"Okay, let's start with some stretches." We spread out in front of the bleachers and warm up, stretching and jumping. I do a couple of tumbling passes on the damp ground. The band has taken their seats in the bleachers, and the stands fill with parents who file into the parent section and students who practically knock one another over as the pour into the student section.

I can't believe it's really our last game of the season.

"Nora!" I look up to see Joshie jumping up and down in the second row. Beside him Bill waves, Mom blows me a kiss and points with her thumb to the person standing beside her.

I catch my breath. "No way!" I run up the steps, scramble into the bleachers and hurl myself at my brother Phil. "I can't believe you're here!"

"Believe," he says.

"It has been killing me to keep this a secret," says Mom, who is wearing the sweatshirt I gave her last week, which says CHEERLEADERS ARE SUPREME! and features a picture of Ruth Bader Ginsburg, former cheerleader and Supreme Court justice. There *is* a place for cheerleaders on the feminist agenda!

"I came out early for Thanksgiving," Phil explains, "so I could catch a game. And kick your butt in chess."

"I don't know about that," I tell him. "I've got a new regular partner so I'm pretty on my game these days."

Krista calls from down on the sidelines. "Nora! Chelsey says to get back in line."

I kiss Phil's cheek and turn to leave.

"Wait," he says. "Before I forget. Dad wanted me to deliver this." Phil removes a chain he's been wearing under his shirt. A brass key dangles from the end of the chain. He drapes it around my neck. I examine the key.

"What is this for?"

Phil shrugs. "I have no idea. Dad said you'd figure it out. Or if you can beat him in an online game of chess, he'll tell you."

"Nora!" Krista calls again.

"Gotta go." I gallop down the steps and have just joined the rest of the squad when I hear my name called from a different direction.

"Nora!" Adam waves from the steps where he is standing with Eric and Mark. He runs down to the track, wraps his arms around me and lifts me off the ground, spinning in a circle as we kiss. He tilts his head to the clouds and exclaims, "I can't believe I'm dating a cheerleader!"

"A chess champion," I correct him.

"Cochampion," he corrects me back, and kisses me again.

"Oh, for crying out loud. Is this is a football game or a love feast?" barks Chelsey.

"Fest," says Becca.

Adam grips my shoulders. "See you after the game?"

I smile. "If I'm lucky."

We line up and grab our pom-poms, ready to get the crowd chanting as they continue to pile into the bleachers.

"Come on, y'all, let me see those pearly whites!" A woman who could only be the Teapot's mother stands between us and the bleachers. She is large and round and dressed all in purple—and in front of her, she's got a digital movie camera fixed on a tripod. "Go on, give up a cheer for Aunt Jean!"

We do a cheer. The Teapot and Chelsey break into a dance as the band blasts out a boppy jazz number. The band stops, and Geoff's voice echoes through the stadium, "Ladies and Gentlemen-*men-men*, please welcome your Cutthroats-*oat-oats*!" He waves to me from the announcer's booth. I wave back, then search the bleachers for familiar faces. I spot Stuart Shangrove beaming beside his girlfriend. A few rows below them a large-breasted girl in a tight sweater jumps up and down and in the aisle closest to her, Mitch captures the moment on film. Over in the parent section Krista's mom and dad are dwarfed by Dex, who is planted between his future in-laws with an ear-to-ear grin.

The crowd leaps to their feet, clapping and stomping as the football team bursts onto the field from behind the bleachers. Leading them is Eric, who is truly a gifted trout. He blows kisses, gesturing with his flippers from his big spongy fish lips out to the crowd, and totally hams it up as he dances out onto the field. Who would have guessed that it's possible to turn cartwheels with caudal fins?

By the time the game is over we have cheered our hearts out. The football team has won in an astonishing comeback victory, and Chelsey is on the sidelines doing an up-close-and-personal cheer for the camera. Look out, Louisville, here she comes! The football players surprise us by running out onto the field with Jake in the lead. They do one of our standard dance formations with deeply exaggerated butt waggles. Then, Eric starts a conga line, and before long a massive trail of football players, cheerleaders and even some fans snake our way around the football field. My hands rest on Krista's shoulders. Behind me, the Teapot's hands are on my hips.

"Chelsey asked me to stay on cheer through basketball season." The Teapot shouts to be heard over the din.

"Did you say yes?" I shout back.

"No, ma'am. I said '*HELL YES*'!"

The band winds down. The crowd thins out. The football players head off to the showers. My family comes down to the field to say good-bye, and Mom asks me to invite Adam over for dinner.

Adam Hood at a Fulbright family meal? If anyone can handle the pressure, he can.

We're putting our gear back into our bags, and I shriek when Adam appears out of nowhere and hugs me from behind. "I didn't mean to scare you! Eric and Mark are taking off," he says. "I told them I thought I might have alternate plans." He brushes a stray piece of hair off my cheek, then kisses it. My cheek. Not the hair.

"Guess what!" I gush. "My brother Phil is here! You need to come to my house for dinner so you can meet him."

"Will I really be required to answer math problems?"

"Only if you ask Bill to pass the salt."

He pulls me into a hug and kisses me long and hard. So

much for the theory that Adam Hood is PDA averse. "Shall we go?" he asks.

I wince. "Remember? I need to stick around and clean the stadium."

I've told Adam about the *Hamlet* paper and the paper I gave Highlights. He knows the truth about the ill-fated ride to school and that it will be months before I can legally have him in the car. And he still likes me! "I'm dating a convict," he says, grinning. "And, no big deal about cleaning up. I'll do it with you. I mean, I'm kind of part of the problem, right?"

Is he awesome or what?

With large plastic garbage bags in tow, Chelsey and her boyfriend take the parent side of the bleachers. Adam and I take the student side. Krista and Dex have offered to stick around and tidy up the band section. Dex, it turns out, thinks Adam is awesome because not only can Adam talk basketball like a pro, he has two cousins who plays basketball for the University of Colorado Buffaloes. Our double date with Dex and Krista at the prom is going to be amazing!

With all of us pitching in, we're done cleaning up in almost no time.

"Whew! That was a lot of work," Chelsey says, draining her water bottle. The guys carry the loaded garbage bags to the Dumpster. Chelsey stares up into the bleachers. "I wonder how messy the stadium gets in Louisville?"

"I suspect you'll find out," Krista says.

Chelsey gives me her off-the-charts-PQ smile. "Hey. Thanks, Nora. For the whole video thing with Sarah's aunt Jean." She claps excitedly. "Check this out." She straightens her skirt and launches into a cheer:

Look out, Louisville

Here I come
Chelsey's gonna take you to Number One!
Boys love race cars!
Girls love horses!
Gonna get As in all my courses
Go-o-o-o-o-o, Louisville!

The guys, back from dropping off the garbage, clap.

"Isn't she something else?" says Chelsey's boyfriend.

She is. She really is.

We all head off the field, but Adam takes my hand and stops walking. "Oh. I forgot something up in the bleachers," he says. "We'll catch you guys later?"

The rest of the garbage crew leave. I look at Adam. He looks at the sky, and we run, hand in hand to the top of the bleachers.

"What did you forget?" I ask, slightly out of breath, looking around for a scarf or some gloves.

He drops onto the uppermost bench, pats it, and when I sit beside him he turns to face me. "What I forgot is that I've always wanted to make out with a cheerleader in the bleachers."

Make and *out*. Two words that are okay alone, but put them together and, *zing!*

We eventually come up for air and my face is freshly sanded by Adam's sparse stubble. He drapes an arm over my shoulder and pulls me close. "Look at that." He points to the gymnasium roof, where the sun glints off a metal vent beside the faded chessboard. "It would be fun to go up there with you and play sometime."

"Mmm. I'd like that."

"Eric and I tried to get up there once," he says. "But they

keep the door to the roof locked."

I smile and touch the outline of the key that hangs from a chain around my neck. "You know, I have a feeling we'll figure something out."

Dad knows how to give just the right gift.

Adam breathes out a contented sigh. "They say that chess is a lot like life," he says. "And I would definitely say that as chess games go? This one is better than anything I could have hoped for." He leans in and kisses my hair.

I breathe in the cool fall air and nestle into Adam's arms. There is nowhere in the whole wide world that I would rather be. "I know exactly what you mean," I tell him. "I wouldn't swap it for anything."

Acknowledgments I am humbly grateful to all the family and friends who have supported me while I whiled away hours with Nora, Adam and the rest of the gang. There are a few amazing people who cheered me on in over-the-top ways:

A huge Herkie jump for the creative geniuses on Penguin's publishing team who initially came up with the concept for *How (Not) to Find a Boyfriend,* especially Julia Johnson and Jill Santopolo, the head cheerleaders who helped shape Nora's world. Gooooooo TEAM!

A touchdown stance for the faculty and students at Vermont School of Fine Arts. A pike jump for my ever enthusiastic friends at the Western Washington Chapter of the Society of Children's Book Writers and Illustrators.

A high V for my writing (and reading) friends who looked at early drafts and were proud of me anyway: Lily Garfield, Diana and Elsa Bonyhadi, Holly and Renee Chaffin, Heather Singh, Kathy Douglass, Linda Valentine, teen readers Mallory Fortier, Julia Cochran and Christina Paoletti, and my critique group buds (in order of height) Lori Heniff, Madeleine Wilde, Molly Hall, Cora Grubb, Tom Brenner, Elizabeth Koenig and Joni Sensel.

A fervent pom-pom shake for Mark Pfister, ever generous with his chess brain and his humor, and cheers for Martin Caspe, who churned out game scenarios for the final chess scene.

A clap and a stomp for the Issaquah Coffee Company for serving up goodies and solitude and the Kuan Yin Tea Company for understanding that writers, when put together in quantity at one table, are not as quiet as one might expect.

A punch stance for Julie Wood, therapist extraordinaire, because every storyteller needs a compassionate listener.

A thunderous round of applause for the students and faculty at Issaquah High, especially counselor Melanie Bonanno, biology teachers Elaine Armstrong and Lena Jones, cheer coach Laura Couty and her fabulously talented cheer squad.

Finally, a roundoff into about thirty back handsprings for Ari and Eli, who always kept it real and appropriately taunted me about scenes too ridiculous to show even my critique group (I still maintain that you *could* get an infection from a wound inflicted by a plastic knife covered with cake frosting), and Evan, the sweetest husband in the world, who always believed it was just a matter of time.

For Evan, the boyfriend I was incredibly lucky to find.

PHILOMEL BOOKS
An imprint of Penguin Young Readers Group. Published by The Penguin Group.
Penguin Group (USA) Inc., 375 Hudson Street, New York, NY 10014, USA.
Penguin Group (Canada), 90 Eglinton Avenue East, Suite 700, Toronto, Ontario
M4P 2Y3, Canada (a division of Pearson Penguin Canada Inc.).
Penguin Books Ltd, 80 Strand, London WC2R 0RL, England.
Penguin Ireland, 25 St. Stephen's Green, Dublin 2, Ireland
(a division of Penguin Books Ltd).
Penguin Group (Australia), 707 Collins Street, Melbourne, Victoria 3008, Australia
(a division of Pearson Australia Group Pty Ltd).
Penguin Books India Pvt Ltd, 11 Community Centre, Panchsheel Park,
New Delhi–110 017, India.
Penguin Group (NZ), 67 Apollo Drive, Rosedale, Auckland 0632, New Zealand
(a division of Pearson New Zealand Ltd).
Penguin Books South Africa, Rosebank Office Park, 181 Jan Smuts Avenue,
Parktown North 2193, South Africa.
Penguin China, B7 Jiaming Center, 27 East Third Ring Road North,
Chaoyang District, Beijing 100020, China.
Penguin Books Ltd, Registered Offices: 80 Strand, London WC2R 0RL, England.

Published simultaneously in Canada.   Printed in the United States of America.
Edited by Julia Johnson.   Design by Semadar Megged.
Text set in 11-points ITC Galliard Std.
Library of Congress Cataloging-in-Publication Data
Schrier, Allyson Valentine.   How (not) to find a boyfriend / Allyson Valentine.
p. cm.   Summary: When varsity cheerleader Nora falls for brilliant new student Adam,
she struggles to maintain her popularity while proving to Adam that she is actually a
genius in disguise. [1. Popularity—Fiction. 2. Cheerleading—Fiction. 3. Genius—
Fiction. 4. Dating (Social customs)—Fiction. 5. High schools—Fiction. 6. Schools—
Fiction.] I. Title. PZ7.S379353Ho 2013 [Fic]—dc23 2012019316
ISBN 978-0-399-25771-1
1 3 5 7 9 10 8 6 4 2